ACCLAIM FOR MELISSA FERGUSON

"Melissa delivered a book that is filled with both humor and heart!"

—Debbie Macomber, #1 *New York Times* bestselling author, on *The Cul-de-Sac War*

"Melissa Ferguson delights with a grand sense of humor and a captivating story to boot! With vivid detail that brings the story roaring to life, *The Cul-de-Sac War* brings us closer to the truth of love, family, and home. Bree's and Chip's pranks and adventures turn into something they never expected as Melissa Ferguson delivers another heartwarming, hilarious, and deeply felt story."

—Patti Callahan, *New York Times* bestselling author of *Becoming Mrs. Lewis*

"Melissa Ferguson's *The Cul-de-Sac War* is sweet, zany, and surprisingly tender. Bree and Chip will have you laughing and rooting for them until the very end."

—Denise Hunter, bestselling author of *Carolina Breeze*

"With her sophomore novel, Melissa Ferguson delivers hilarity and heart in equal measure. *The Cul-de-Sac War*'s Bree Leake and Chip McBride prove that sometimes it isn't the first impression you have to worry about—it's the second one that gets you. What follows is a delightful deluge of pranks, sabotage, and witty repartee tied together by heartstrings that connect to turn a house into a home worth fighting for. I was thoroughly charmed from beginning to end."

—Bethany Turner, award-winning author of *The Secret Life of Sarah Hollenbeck*

"Witty, wise and with just the right amount of wacky, Melissa's second novel is as charming as her debut. Competition and chemistry battle to win the day in this hilarious rom-com about two people who can't stand to be near each other—or too far apart."

—Betsy St. Amant, author of *The Key to Love*, on *The Cul-de-Sac War*

"Ferguson's delightful debut follows a first date that turns quickly into a childcare quagmire . . . Ferguson's humorous and chaotic tale will please rom-com fans."

—*Publishers Weekly* on *The Dating Charade*

"*The Dating Charade* will keep you smiling the entire read. Ferguson not only delights us with new love, with all its attendant mishaps and misunderstandings, but she takes us deeper in the hearts and minds of vulnerable children as Cassie and Jett work out their families—then their dating lives. An absolute treat!"

—Katherine Reay, bestselling author of *The Printed Letter Bookshop*

"*The Dating Charade* is hilarious and heartwarming with characters you truly care about, super fun plot twists and turns, snappy prose, and a sweet romance you're rooting for. Anyone who has children in their lives will particularly relate to Ferguson's laugh-out-loud take on the wild ride that is parenting. I thoroughly enjoyed this story!"

—Rachel Linden, bestselling author of *The Enlightenment of Bees*

"A heartwarming charmer."

—Sheila Roberts, *USA TODAY* bestselling author of the Moonlight Harbor series, on *The Dating Charade*

"Melissa Ferguson is a sparkling new voice in contemporary rom-com. Though her novel tackles meaningful struggles—social work, child abandonment, adoption—it's also fresh, flirty, and laugh-out-loud funny. Ferguson is going to win fans with this one!"

—Lauren Denton, bestselling author of *The Hideaway* and *Glory Road*, on *The Dating Charade*

"A jolt of energy featuring one of the most unique romantic hooks I have ever read. Personality and zest shine through Ferguson's evident enjoyment at crafting high jinks and misadventures as two people slowly make way for love in the midst of major life upheaval. A marvelous treatise on unexpected grace and its life-changing chaos, Cassie and Jett find beautiful vulnerability in redefining what it means to live happily ever after."

—Rachel McMillan, author of the *The London Restoration*, on *The Dating Charade*

"Ferguson delivers a stellar debut. *The Dating Charade* is a fun, romantic albeit challenging look at just what it takes to fall in love and be a family. You'll think of these characters long after the final page."

—Rachel Hauck, *New York Times* bestselling author of *The Wedding Dress*

The Cul-de-Sac War

Also by Melissa Ferguson

The Dating Charade

The Cul-de-Sac War

MELISSA FERGUSON

THOMAS NELSON
Since 1798

The Cul-de-Sac War

Published in Nashville, Tennessee, by Thomas Nelson. Thomas Nelson is a registered trademark of HarperCollins Christian Publishing, Inc.

Published in association with Hartline Literary Agency, Pittsburgh, PA 15235.

Thomas Nelson titles may be purchased in bulk for educational, business, fund-raising, or sales promotional use. For information, please email SpecialMarkets@ThomasNelson.com.

Library of Congress Cataloging-in-Publication Data

Names: Ferguson, Melissa (Assistant professor), author.
Title: The cul-de-sac war : a novel / Melissa Ferguson.
Description: Nashville, Tennessee : Thomas Nelson, [2020] | Summary: "Melissa Ferguson's new novel proves that good fences make good neighbors-and that sometimes love and hate share a backyard"-- Provided by publisher.
Identifiers: LCCN 2020024520 (print) | LCCN 2020024521 (ebook) | ISBN 9780785231042 (paperback) | ISBN 9780785231059 (epub) | ISBN 9780785231066 (downloadable audio)
Subjects: GSAFD: Love stories.
Classification: LCC PS3606.E7263 C85 2020 (print) | LCC PS3606.E7263 (ebook) | DDC 813/.6--dc23
LC record available at https://lccn.loc.gov/2020024520
LC ebook record available at https://lccn.loc.gov/2020024521

Printed in the United States of America

20 21 22 23 24 LSC 10 9 8 7 6 5 4 3 2 1

The Cul-de-Sac War

Chapter 1

BREE

They say 95 percent of the time the first impression you have of a person is right.

Well, if anyone in the audience was watching her clutch a plastic fern with one hand and the slumping fabric on her chest with the other, all the while beads from her costume scattered across the shadowy stage with a thousand *ping-ping-pings*, they'd have a fairly accurate picture of the woman formally known as Bree Leake. Or, in this particular moment, Mustardseed, fairy servant of Titania, as vital to *A Midsummer Night's Dream* as the fern in her hand.

"How canst thou thus for shame, Titania . . ."

Glitter floated in the green-tinted spotlight as Bree stood far upstage, where she stayed approximately . . . *always*. She took a step to the right. Then another. And another. Beads dropped with each movement, no matter how she adjusted her hold on the intricate fabric dissolving in her hands. Leave it to her roommate, the Barter's one and only costume designer, to go overkill.

Actually, leave it to her roommate to plan a wardrobe malfunction like this. Evie had probably gone to great lengths, in fact, to attach the shoulder straps with just enough strength to hold up until Bree made one fatal step onto the long tulle train that—now that she thought of it—no other fairies in the cast possessed.

She could just see Evie now, in the dim light of their basement, laughing maniacally over her sewing machine.

So here Bree stood, newest member of the nation's oldest live-performance theatre, trying to shield herself with a plastic plant while smiling a not-too-convincing stage smile as heat crept up her neck. Not that anyone would notice her blushing, given that her face and neck were painted Andes-mint green.

While she understood all of this was very, very important, her immature side couldn't help seeing it as also very, very funny. But laughing was, by all means, the most critical thing to avoid at this moment.

Do. Not. Laugh.

She *mustn't* laugh.

She was a professional artist, and artists were at all times calm, cool, and engaged.

She took a step to the right.

Ping-ping-ping.

Slid her left foot to meet her right.

Ping-ping-ping.

One creeping step to the right.

Another.

With three more swift *ping-ping-ping* steps she slipped offstage and broke into a run between the curtains.

"Evie!" Bree hissed, passing a couple of stagehands waiting beside overhanging set trees.

Bree swept past portable columns and hanging windows and hedged around Titania's set bed laden with roses and vines. Stephen, the stage manager, caught sight of her while talking rapidly into his headset, but before she could propel the manic-driven man into overly manic drive, she let go of her hold on her dress long enough to give him a thumbs-up from across the room.

Nothing to see here. Just your newest actress jumping ship.

She pushed open the doors to the back hall.

Half a dozen doors lined the long hallway, one of them open to the dressing room, whose dozens of vanity bulbs were blinding even from where she stood twenty feet away. She made for the room but only found the ever-disgruntled understudy on her phone.

Bree halted beside her chair. "Have you seen Evie?"

Celia looked up. Blinked. "She just left to get coffee."

"She went all the way to Zazzy'Z?" Bree said, her tone inching higher.

She shook her head and tilted her chin toward the door. "No, Styrofoam coffee. To the front. The gift shop."

"Oh. Okay. Thanks." Bree reemerged into the hall. She had to get back onstage for one line—*one.* True, it may not be an important line, but it was *her* line.

And by golly she'd be there to give it.

It was going to take ages to throw open the back door, dash down the metal stairway, and fly around parked cars and pedestrians to reach the front of the theatre while hanging on to her dragging dress and slumping top. But she could kiss her job good-bye if she took either door leading into the shadowy aisles of the theatre's auditorium.

She would just have to run.

She picked up speed as she moved down the empty hall in her leather slippers. As fluorescent lights shone overhead, beads fell like breadcrumbs behind her. The *Exit* sign loomed and she shoved the doors open with her fern.

As she pushed her way through, her fairy wings knocked against the doorframe, fighting against her as if crying out, "This is the exit door! Get back onstage, woman!" But with a final wrench of her drooping costume and an explosion of beads, the wings gave way and she took two stumbling steps onto the metal platform in the bright midday air.

Bree grabbed for the railing with her right hand but felt the impact of something against her knee before she could reach it.

Her foot slammed into the unidentified object. Before she could stop herself, she found herself flying forward.

"Whooooa—"

The world was suddenly upside down.

Pavement and steps now above her, racing toward her head.

But just as the tip of her braid whacked the steps, she felt something grab her by the waist.

Her body tilted like a carnival ride. Only the ride was a man who had reached around her waist and was pulling her backward. A man who had been sitting on the top step of the metal stairway leading to the back parking lot. A man who, after her knee had knocked him in the back of the head, had stood, grabbed her flying body out of thin air, heaved her backward by the force of his might, and landed her back on the metal platform.

Where she now stood. Frozen.

Clinging to her potted fern.

She blinked. Looked down at the fern. Then up at him.

"I'm . . . sorry. Thanks."

"Sorry—thanks," the man repeated, stooping down for his phone, which had toppled three steps down. "Well, I'm sort of the reason you tripped, but I'll take it."

A smile ghosted his lips, his sharp jawline softened by a five-o'clock shadow. His brown eyes—crinkly at the temples, as though he dispensed of smiles easily—were just a few inches below hers. Which was incredible, given he was now standing two steps below her.

And she was six feet even.

The fabric at her chest started to droop, and she adjusted her grip. Only then, it seemed, did he look down. "Oh. I see you've still got that problem there."

Bree felt her green face flush. "Ah. So you saw."

He let out a breathy laugh. "Saw you inch your way offstage like some sort of plant-loving alien backup in a music video who wasn't supposed to be there?"

Bree's eyes narrowed.

He coughed. "Because that is *definitely* not what I saw. That is *definitely* not what made me start taking a video and get kicked out by a ninety-year-old usher for violating Barter rules." He paused, grinned. "I'm Chip. And believe me, you were the highlight of my evening."

He put out a hand.

"Bree." Bree's smile twitched as she looked to his outstretched hand, her own hands still occupied by her dress and plant. "And now you're taunting me."

His smile was as good as a wink. "Just a little."

Her eyes lingered on his before a shout came from onstage.

Her mission. Right.

She edged around him, hiked up her dress a few inches, and took a couple of steps down the stairs.

"I need to find my costume designer," she said. "And I have about, oh, two minutes to get back onstage."

"So, tons o' time."

"Loads," she said, her eyes flashing back at his with a smile.

"Well," he said, resting his arms on the railing as he scanned the empty parking lot. "I'd venture a guess she isn't out here. But if you're looking for a quick fix, I have something in my truck that might do the trick. It's across the street, but I could be back in forty-five seconds."

She paused, her foot hovering over the third step down.

Glanced down the brick wall leading to the front of the theatre, which was growing farther away by the second.

Turned back to him.

He gave her another smile. The kind of companionable smile that said, *Hey, let's go on an adventure.* The kind the first kid gave the other kids when he convinced them to jump off a bridge, and they did.

Her gaze followed his across the street, past the sixteen-foot bronze *A Midsummer Night's Dream* fountain, up the stairs, to the unseen truck in the other parking lot a football-field length away. She pressed her lips together.

The clock was ticking. She knew Evie may or may not still be at the gift shop. Even if she was, how long would it take for her to work her magic?

She looked back to Chip. "You really think you can fix it?"

He shrugged. "Fix a dress with zero seamstress skills in forty-five seconds? Sure. Who couldn't?"

Bree raised her brow at his confidence. Part of her knew it would be better to push on toward Evie, but a bigger part of her wanted to see him try. "Make it forty?"

A spark lit in his eyes, as though she didn't realize exactly who she had just challenged.

And that was how thirty-six seconds later, the mysterious man in a fine gray suit was racing across traffic while Bree stood at the top of the metal platform, shouting numbers across Main Street.

"Thirty-seven!" Bree cried, and two shoppers turned to see who was making the commotion.

The man's tie flapped over his shoulder as he reached the bottom of the stairs, grabbed both sides of the railing, and heaved himself up three at a time.

"Thirty-eight!" Bree's voice rose higher.

Chip leaped up four stairs. His toe clung to the edge of a step, and he wobbled. He balanced and jumped another three.

"Thirty-nine!" Bree called, bouncing on her leather slippers as she watched him now halfway up the staircase.

She hesitated, just a hundredth of a millisecond, before opening her mouth for the last number.

As Bree drew a breath to call out, the man reared back and lobbed the camo-green duct tape in the air.

"Forty!" Bree cried as the duct tape bounced, rolled, and landed on her slipper.

The man collapsed onto the steps five feet below her, sprawled out, his chest heaving.

She laughed, several beads pinging on the platform as if in

amusement. The two shoppers smiled slightly at the two bizarre strangers and moved along.

She nudged the duct tape onto its side and hooked it with her toe.

"You know, I didn't think you had a chance against that minivan."

"Never underestimate a competitive person." His head popped up, and before she knew it, he was standing on the step below her, eyes shining. He picked up the duct tape. "Especially a bored competitive person."

"Oh, I'm sorry. I should've made myself clear." Bree pressed the fern firmly against her chest with one hand and put out the other. "I'm Bree Leake, extremely competitive person, turns explosive when bored."

He took her hand with an easy grin, held it for a moment longer than expected. The crinkles along his smiling temples grew deeper, then he blinked and they were gone. "So," he said, letting go and holding up the duct tape. "Shall I?"

Bree's brows shot up. "Oh, right. Yes. Thank you."

She turned to face the door, feeling her cheeks warm as he stood behind her.

She heard a ripping sound as he tore off half an arm's length of duct tape. She looked over her shoulder and saw him kneeling on the platform, folding the strip of duct tape inside itself. He reached into his back pocket, unsnapped a pocketknife, and looked up. "Now, how much do you care about this costume?"

She was alone, on a back-lot staircase, with a stranger wielding a knife. She didn't want the moment to end. Her survival instincts were nonexistent.

Sixty-two seconds later, Bree held still in her camo duct tape–strapped dress as the man stood behind her, close enough that she could smell the aftershave on his neck. But something else was there too. More natural, more subtle. Authentic scents of cool pine, of the Appalachian Mountains in the distance.

She felt his breath release on her shoulder as he slipped his pocketknife into his back pocket and stepped around to face her on the small platform.

"All done," he said with a satisfied grin.

She smiled back. Her voice was not her own as she heard herself say, "Thank you."

Titania's lines echoed down the hall.

"Well, I've gotta—" Her words faltered. She tipped her chin toward the stage. Half of her body wanted to stay. The bizarre suggestion swept in and out of her thoughts. *I don't need this job that much. What if we just left it all and went for ice cream? A high-school track? An equally insignificant and isolated stairwell?*

She wasn't sure, but she sensed he felt it too. Their scene closing. The time for their bizarre meeting, their sudden moment, to come to an end.

And the reluctance. At least for her. She dared a quick, deeper glance to his eyes, searching for some clue.

"Good luck." He smiled. Then set the duct tape in her hand. "In case you need some backup."

She held it up. The moment had passed. It was time to move on.

She put on an overbright smile as she pulled the door open. "Thanks."

Twenty seconds later, she floated onstage to deliver her important line.

She stopped beside Birdie—in this moment, Cobweb—fellow fairy and closest friend in the six months since she'd moved to Abingdon, Virginia.

She dipped her head toward Titania.

Met her gaze.

Opened her mouth.

Sensed the hushed auditorium.

Took a breath.

"And I."

Done.

She stepped back, the brave line given its due in the spotlight.

While the scene continued, Bree couldn't help scanning the shadowy audience for one certain gentleman, even though he'd said he'd been kicked out by one of the ushers. Even though she'd left him standing on the metal platform. Even though—

Her roving stopped.

Because sure enough she found him, three rows back. Right.

Their eyes locked.

He gave her that smile. A knowing smile. A private smile. A smile that couldn't look more delighted for her if she had just recited a flawless ten-minute monologue.

Despite the hard-and-fast rule in the first chapter of every acting book on the planet, she smiled back.

Just as her eyes fell upon the woman beside him looping her arm through his.

♡♡♡

Four scenes and sixty minutes later, Bree dodged the cast relaxing backstage to get to the dressing room. She changed so fast she was tempted to brag to Stephen about it. After all, no one but actors talked competitively over dinner about the record speed with which they could change into and out of clothes. But because she was about to attempt the impossible feat of driving home, pulling together something edible, and bringing it back for the Barter's 30th Annual Spring Gala in less than twenty minutes, she had to forgo the opportunity to brag to her supervisor—or for that matter, sneak into the front of the house just to "run into" the duct-tape man who'd saved her night.

Not that she really wanted to spot Chip arm in arm with a woman who was a physical manifestation of the word *pearly*. Silky smooth blond hair, flawless cream skin, two rows of perfectly white teeth. Not that Bree had noticed while she sat stuck on her mossy log prop for the rest of the play. At all.

And yet . . .

She slipped her phone out of her pocket as she exited the front of the theatre and skipped down the steps two at a time. Sure, maybe the actors typically used the back doors to escape to their cars. Maybe she had only eighteen minutes to get home and back with something edible. Maybe Stephen had expressly forbidden the cast from exiting through the front doors in slouchy sweaters and holey jeans while the patrons filed out in diamonds and silk ties.

But what was life without mixing it up, eh?

She pressed on Cassie's name in her list of contacts and held the phone up to her ear.

Bree appreciated the view from beneath the illuminated awning overlooking Abingdon's Main Street. The air was crisp and cool as it nipped at the hem of the dress she had borrowed from her roommate, one of the dozens of ostentatious outfits poking out of Evie's closet. It was a solid three inches too short, but then, beggars couldn't be choosers. Though the Barter paid a decent share, Bree wasn't about to splurge on a two-hundred-dollar dress she'd only wear once in a while.

The matinee audience had spilled out of the theatre and now milled about the area, some walking along the sidewalks, some moving across the crosswalk. Waiting cars hummed on both sides of the road.

Yes, Bree thought, turning slowly in a circle, this was a delightful view.

Inspirational.

She was glad to take a beat and experience the Barter world from this angle, with no ulterior motive whatsoever—

"What are you doing?"

The sound of Cassie's voice in her ear jumpstarted her.

"What do you mean, what am I doing?" Bree turned and started, a little wobbly, down the sidewalk.

"I answered the phone two minutes ago. You've been doing that thing with your teeth."

"I don't know what you're talking about."

But of course Bree did know what her best friend of twenty-six years was talking about, and of course Cassie knew that Bree knew exactly what Cassie was talking about.

Leave it to her best friend to answer the phone and sit there listening to her nervous tick like a creeper.

In the background of Cassie's line, screaming erupted.

"Hold on a sec." Cassie's voice was brisk and husky, which really was the appropriate term for the woman who in the past year had gone from single chum and adventure pal, to single chum in custody of three kids, to, as of precisely thirteen months ago, married chum loaded down with six kids—four of them under five.

After some prodding, then vague threats, the screaming died down to a reasonable level.

"So, what's going on down there?" Cassie asked. "Why the beat-box session?"

"Nothing. Absolutely nothing." But Bree's feet slowed as her eyes fell upon him. Chip. Her right foot floated six inches off the ground.

Keep moving! she commanded it, but her foot was as stubborn as her. She felt like she was pulling it through quicksand, but she managed to push one heel to the ground and move on to the next step.

Bree's eyes stayed on him. He was across the street, standing on the curb beside a gleaming pearl-colored SUV, with the pearl-dressed woman in his arms. She with her pearly cheek pressed against his chest. He looking down at her with that same smile he had bestowed upon Bree on the metal stairway.

Honestly, what did she expect would happen? She had come out of her way to see this little picture of the cozy couple. All they needed were a few butterflies and songbirds and the scene would be complete.

Did she really expect him to be incapable of thinking of anyone but her for the rest of the play? To be unable to tear his eyes away from her while she lounged upstage in her mossy surroundings?

To be standing beside that gleaming SUV right now, breaking that shiny girl's heart by explaining he had just experienced an ethereal moment with the green girl holding a potted plant, and by golly, he just had to find her? Right there? Right then?

Yep. That sounded about right.

Instead, there he was, hands in both of his jacket pockets while he waited for the woman to slip inside her SUV, grinning in that same charming, crinkly-templed way.

The engine turned, and he headed toward the parking lot where his truck was parked.

Bree faced forward and resumed her pace.

No, no. She'd made a fool of herself enough tonight, thank you. No need to add *Staring at Stranger from a Distance Like Vengeful Imaginary Ex-Girlfriend* to her list.

She would just forget him. Put everything about him behind her.

In fact, good for shiny blond girl. Way to find a good one.

Bree hopped off the curb.

Focus, Bree. Task at hand.

"So, Cass, tell me," Bree said, unlocking her car. "What makes a better impression at a party: a bowl of pistachios or two cut-up bananas and a splash of watermelon?"

"How much watermelon are we talking?"

"One, maybe two cubes."

"How nice is the bowl?"

"Lime-green plastic. But dishwasher-level clean." Bree slipped the keys into the ignition. "And quiche! I can steal three, maybe three and a half, pieces of Evie's quiche."

"Didn't she start locking her food up in those plastic containers?"

"*Please*. These are desperate times. I can pick a lock if needed."

Bree cranked the car, then reached for the five-hour-old coffee in her cup holder. She took a cool sip while Cassie's voice went fuzzy.

"Hand it to me. *Give. It. Now. Drew* . . . No, I'm not doing the mean voice . . . Well, if you weren't trying to poke his eye out with it—" Cassie's voice switched over at lightning speed. "Are we talking about a fancy party here?"

Bree turned the wheel with her pinky and ring finger while

gripping the coffee cup with the rest. "A high-profile gala where my boss can judge me by my sad food contribution while sorting out the cast placements for the summer season."

"Ah. So nothing special or important in any way."

"Precisely."

She turned onto Church Street to avoid the steady post-play traffic on Main. She eased to a stop at the Plumb Alley crossing, and her eyes ticked up to the rearview mirror while she waited for a pair of joggers to cross.

She frowned.

Behind her, monster truck tires vibrated beneath a block of rattling red metal—although the owner of the ancient Ford F250 resting his fender two inches from her bumper would've no doubt called the color "the blood of the latest buck I shot with my Ruger American Magnum." From her vantage point, which was nearly beneath the massive vehicle, she saw oil dripping from the chassis.

"So, your mom was asking me the other day . . . ," Cassie started, hesitation deep in her voice.

"You're going to have to talk louder. I have an earthquake squatting behind me," Bree shouted.

Cassie raised her voice. "Are you going to make it back next weekend for Anna's birthday party?"

Bree's lips pursed, that same involuntary wave rolling through her body whenever she heard her eight-year-old niece's name. Anna.

Bree had seen a lot in the six months since she'd left her home of twenty-six years and made her way to Abingdon to live with Nana and try her hand onstage. No one had any clue that Nana would pass away that morning four months ago—especially not Bree, who'd found her. Who'd shaken her. Who, in a state of panic, had made a shabby attempt at CPR until the medics came and finally pulled her away. None of them knew how much that moment had tipped Bree over the edge.

She knew her family had their suspicions that losing Nana was harder for Bree than she let on. The fact was, they didn't know how hard. How deep she had sunk. How dark everything had become in recent months.

Unlike everyone else in the family, Bree couldn't keep herself together when she saw Anna. Ironic as it was, she—the only one getting paid to pretend—was the only one in the family who couldn't slap on a happy face and keep conversation light in Anna's presence. Her niece, just a child, was dying, and one day someone would wake up and find her the way Bree had found Nana. She tried to muster courage two months ago, at a family supper, and panicked. Ended up in a bathroom stall heaving.

Bree pushed everything about Anna away—her name, her image—looking instead to the fuming grill that edged closer to her bumper with each second.

"Chill out, you old rattletrap," Bree said aloud, waving with her old coffee cup toward a couple pushing a stroller across. "You think I don't have somewhere to go, too, buddy?"

For a moment she considered darting around them, and her toes lifted off the brake. But then a curly-headed boy on a bike jumped in front of her, pedaling fast toward his parents.

One more agonizing moment of watching the boy cross the road, and she hit the pedal.

"Sorry, Cass. What were you saying?"

"I was asking about next weekend."

"We have shows all day," Bree said, stopping at the stop sign and looking left, then right, then back at the truck who hit the gas at an alarming speed.

She turned onto Valley Street and, to her chagrin, the truck lurched in her direction with so much vim she jerked her wheel. Drops of the cold black coffee splattered the skirt of her borrowed dress.

"Shoot." Bree rammed her cup into the cup holder and began swiping at the spill.

The engine behind her roared.

"I'm going to kill this guy behind me."

Deidre's muffled voice came from far off in the background.

"No, honey," Cassie said. "Bree isn't going to kill anyone. She didn't really mean that—"

"Yes, I did," Bree said.

"Ha-ha!" Cassie replied in an overbright tone. "No, of course she didn't."

Bree bit her lip. "Did."

There was a pause. Muffled words in the background.

"*Of course* she won't go to jail," Cassie said.

More muffled words.

"Yes, well, even if she does go to jail, she'll still send you Christmas presents . . ."

She turned on Court Street and blinked as the truck jerked left as well.

"You've got to be kidding me," Bree hissed.

Was he following her on purpose? Who was this guy?

Bree maneuvered with sleek precision around a car parked along the slim street. She did a full swivel-head twist at the truck riding so close to her Subaru anyone would have assumed it was hitched to the back.

"Bree."

Perhaps it was some eccentric art critic who didn't appreciate her costume fiasco. Her disruption in the play was entirely out of line, and in order to save the world from terrible actors, he was hunting her down.

"Bree?"

The Deranged Art Critic Serial Killer. He'd be known in the newspapers simply as The Critic. He would ride her bumper until she hit the lip of a small road, right next to a cliff, and ease her right on over . . .

Cassie's thoughts must have been on par with her own, because the next thing Bree knew, Cassie's voice was off speaker and booming in her ear. *"Bree."*

Bree winced and pulled the phone away. "What?"

"Don't do anything stupid. Just let the guy pass."

A chant of "stupid, stupid" began in the background.

Bree squinted in the mirror. It was time for a dose of his own medicine. "Oh, I'm letting him pass."

"No, you sound like you're forming an evil plan. Use a normal voice. A nonmalicious voice. Let's try it now. *I am letting him pass.*"

"I'm letting him pass." The words held all the unyielding weight of Thor's hammer.

"See? That's exactly what I just told you *not* to sound like."

With a quick, one-handed swerve, Bree stole between two parked cars in front of a two-story Colonial. The roar of the truck's rusted-out exhaust pipe shook her car as it passed. She gripped the worn leather of the steering wheel, her hawk eyes now as focused on the truck as if it were her last meal.

"Don't forget you have a dinner to get to," Cassie said, snatching for a distraction.

Too late.

"Unbelievable." Bree's preying eyes locked on his bumper—or what she could see of it. As if tailing innocent vehicles and contributing to noise and earth pollution weren't enough, the bumper was covered in outlandish, chauvinistic stickers. The kind that should've been illegal. The kind that made a person speed up to see what sort of woman could *possibly* sit in the passenger seat beside such a moron.

Bree's blood pressure rose as her eyes moved from *Then Satan said, "Let women drive"* to *Looking for your cat? Try under my tires.*

Surely the police wouldn't charge her if she rammed him. Surely they'd give her an underhanded fist bump and wish her on her merry way.

The truck began to ascend the hill.

"Bree, where are you now? What are you doing?" Cassie said.

Bree's tires answered for her, squealing as she gunned it after his trailing black smoke.

The nice thing about her 1998 chipped green Subaru was exactly that—it was a 1998 chipped green Subaru. Car insurance? They practically paid her. The road took on new meaning in such vehicles, one being the overwhelming impression that life was just one big game of bumper cars.

"*Please,*" Cassie said on the other end of the line, "please tell me you aren't silently doing your villainous monologue about the world being a game of bumper cars. Please."

The old Ford diesel flew up the road toward her neighborhood. With her foot pressing the pedal to the floor, the Subaru bravely held on, huffing as it chugged up the hill. She tightened her grip, leaning forward until her nose nearly touched the wheel.

There? How does it feel? She eased back to make the turn into her neighborhood.

But just as her car broke off to give him space and make the turn, the truck turned onto her street.

Her street.

She jerked her car after him.

Standing along the sidewalk beside a hedge, her neighbor Mrs. Lewis tugged her dog leash close to her heart and watched the pair speed down the road. Bree gave a sheepish wave and ducked her head but kept on.

What was there to apologize for, anyway? She wasn't the criminal here but the hero, chasing the man out of her neighborhood, seizing him by the collar and giving him the boot. Showing the inconsiderate hooligan exactly what it feels like to get pushed around.

They covered the length of the street quickly, rushing toward the cul-de-sac and its abrupt end. The truck flew by each house, the options for where it was going dropping by the second. There were only six, five, four houses left before it'd have to turn around—

The beast of a truck pulled into a driveway.

Bree barely managed to swerve in time.

At the same moment Bree hit the brake, her head whipped around to stare as she passed the parked truck. The world was moving in slow motion. Her mouth popping open and dangling like a codfish at the shock of being above water.

Ten feet into the cul-de-sac, her car came to a stop.

She put her car in reverse.

Pulled back.

Turned her wheel.

Drove into her own petite, graveled driveway.

The engine of the truck beside her cut off.

She cut hers and climbed out of the vehicle.

His door popped open.

Out of the heinous truck, with nothing but a tiny patch of grass between them, hopped Chip. Duct-tape man. With the bright, innocent face of a cherubim.

He shut the door, oblivious to her while he pressed a phone to his ear. "Well, then just upgrade service to 200 amp. But hey, I gotta go. I'll call you when I get to Rodefer." He kicked a chunk of gravel at his feet. "Sounds good."

He slipped his phone into his pocket, and she watched as he put his hands on his hips and looked up at the run-down two-story brick house before him—from the limp *Sold* sign in the meager front yard to the crisp, white-capped Blue Ridge Mountains in the distance. A smile played on his face as he surveyed it all, as though he was now lord of the Biltmore. When he spotted her, his smile widened.

"It's you."

"Bree?" Bree nearly jumped at Cassie's voice in her ear. "What's happening?"

She lowered the phone to her side and stood motionless, her eyes moving from the sign and back to him. To the sign again.

What was happening?

Oh, nothing.

Nothing except the fact that she was standing in her driveway staring into the face of the man who'd owned the range of her emotions for the past two hours, who just so happened to be her new neighbor.

They say that 95 percent of the time the first impression you have of a person is right.

And in this case, she had been dead, *dead* wrong.

Chapter 2

CHIP

Sixteen hundred square feet of 1906 red oak flooring ready to be restored to all its herringbone-bordered perfection. Twenty-two windows—three of which were cracked—ready to be torn out and replaced with double-pane, energy-efficient, crystal-clear glass. One tired but nonetheless chugging along oil furnace. Two Pepto Bismol–pink tubs. Fourteen hideous green cabinets begging to be thrown into the dumpster that was making its way up Main Street this very moment.

One incredible, panoramic view of the frosted peaks of the Blue Ridge Mountains.

And one mysterious fairy he'd had the surprising pleasure of meeting on a nondescript staircase, now staring at him.

Granted, this stare wasn't entirely of the positive kind. She was frowning. And still caked from forehead to throat in pea soup–green makeup, matched by a stunning green dress (also the object of a recent coffee spill, it seemed) that enhanced her striking emerald eyes.

A discreet cough in the back of his mind brought him back into line.

Right.

He had a girlfriend. A terrific, wonderful girlfriend.

Yes, this woman had striking green eyes, but he could've noticed that about anyone. It was a perfectly harmless, meaningless observation.

Just like he'd noticed how nice that green dress looked on her, so very appropriately her color. Good for her. It was hard to find such color-complementary clothing these days.

Well, whatever the cause of the frown directed his way, he felt himself rising to the challenge to turn her frown around. And he *could* do that. In fact, he *had* done that, just two hours before. His behavior was perfectly appropriate, with or without Ashleigh—his wonderful, steady, and also very color-coordinated girlfriend.

He could start by bringing up the happy coincidence that they were now neighbors. Mention how coincidental it was that they had both left the theatre and followed one another here.

Maybe the topic of his driving skills wasn't the best to bring up in a moment like this. Fact was, he could hardly see her little green Subaru from the cab of the lifted work truck he'd bought off Craigslist this morning. It had over three hundred thousand miles, oil and antifreeze leaks, burned-out turn signals, no air, and so many unsavory bumper stickers even the Marion jailhouse citizens would be scandalized. And the way the gas and brake pedal jolted him every time his boot so much as graced the pedal . . . well, it wasn't his best look.

He'd do better, much better, to opt for a general statement.

About her green makeup, which she clearly had no qualms about wearing in public.

About the house.

The neighborhood.

The surprising moment they'd shared behind the theatre.

The way he'd stood there alone on the platform after they'd said their good-byes, then how he found himself racing to the front to get back inside. The way he'd managed to soft-soap the elderly usher with a few sweet words to get back into his seat before she delivered her line. The absolutely *epic* two-word line. Then how their eyes met, as he felt himself hoping so much they would. And then—

No. The neighborhood. He'd stick with a nice, safe topic.

The neighborhood.

He opened his mouth as a rumble down the street drew his attention away.

And there was his opener.

"That'll be my dumpster," Chip said, grinning. "Funny to see you again. Becca?"

Whatever level her frown had been at before, it was now a ten. "Bree."

"Right. Bree."

At a honk, Chip turned his attention to the roll-off truck now in view and his friend Andy behind the wheel.

Bree. It was important to remember his neighbors' names. Bree.

He began striding toward the road, arms waving above his head.

Andy was a man of labor, a man like him. Except he lived on a houseboat on Holston River, and his main Saturday-night entertainment was sharing Cheetos with the fish.

His forehead carried the permanent ripple of four waves stacked upon one another, racing toward the shore of his receding hairline. And when he was disgruntled, the one closest to his eyebrows grew like a tsunami threatening to spill onto his heavy, brooding lashes. As the truck approached, he could see Andy had miraculously managed to grow a fifth wave across his forehead.

The truck squealed, shuddered, and gave a huff as the air brakes released in front of his house. Andy threw the door open. All five-feet-two of the man slid onto the pavement. What Andy lacked in height, he compensated for with the size of other objects. His phone, for example, was as big as a laptop. Sleeveless shirts were always six inches on the long side. And trucks, company or otherwise, were of the type to take over a four-lane road.

This one was no different.

Out of the corner of his eye, Chip noticed Bree checking the time on her phone.

"Ain't no way we can drop this here, Chip." Andy slung his head up and down the street. "Ain't no way. This road's too narrow—"

"I'll admit it's a bit on the slim side," Chip replied.

"All these parked cars everywhere—"

"There are a few cars."

"Power lines are hanging down like they never recovered from the 2011 tornado."

"I only see that one line hanging by about five feet—"

"The front yard's too muddy," Andy forged on. "We're going to tear the yard up . . ."

Bree started toward her house.

Chip waited while Andy laid out a string of doomsday possibilities. But when he started to worry about disrupting chickens' egg-laying production, Chip stepped in.

"Now, come on, Andy. It's not going to be all that bad. Do you see any chickens around here?" Chip waved his hand around the neighborhood. "I don't think you'll have to worry about hitting a coop and having a mass breakout."

"I'll be darned if I don't see one," Andy replied, nodding over Chip's shoulder. Sure enough, a weather-beaten, mint-green coop stood in Bree's front yard beside a couple of overgrown bushes. Red shutters, a weathervane with a rusted rooster tipping his nose east in the breeze, and a large chicken-wire run. Several beady eyes flashed his way with unblinking eeriness, as though the brood smelled the Chick-fil-A wrapper in his truck.

Bree stood watching from the porch of the two-story, white-vinyl Craftsman in need of a good pressure washing. The front steps were lined with pots of a variety of shapes and sizes, all void of life in the March frost. In the yard a bright yellow box held the cursive words hand painted down the side: *Our Little Free Library*. Two cats cat-walked along the balcony of the front porch, tails flicked high.

Right. So roughly the opposite taste, in every possible way, of Ashleigh.

Wind chimes tinkled from Bree's porch, and she opened her screen door and stepped inside.

He turned back to Andy and resisted putting a hand on his shoulder. "I'm not asking you to turn the corner on the driveway. Just drop the dumpster on the front yard. I'll need it emptied in two days anyway."

"Front yard?" Andy said. Chip rubbed the spittle off his neck. "What front yard? You got less space than a median here, Chip." He shook his head. "I don't think we can do it. I know I said I'd help you out here, but this just isn't possible. You're just going to have to use your truck—"

"This'll work," Chip cut in. "C'mon."

No need to mention to Andy that his other work truck, which until that morning had been his *only* work truck, was currently at the Deadmore Street job. Or that as of this moment, his business's bank account was about three hundred dollars from going in the red. "I gotta start demo right away, Andy. This is my new residence. As in, my home. Right *now.*"

The waves on Andy's forehead rose. His short, fat finger shot toward the house. "You're living in that? Now?"

Incredible. It was the first time in thirty years Andy's bushy brows rose enough to reveal he had baby-blue eyes.

Chip swung his body back to face his new palace. "It's not so bad."

As if on cue, an owl shot out of the chimney—or rather, the tarp currently covering a hole in the roof that would one day become the chimney.

"It's going to need some work, I admit—" Chip began.

A gust of wind blew and the drooping roof over his front porch let out a weary creak.

"But I only need a few weeks to whip her into shape."

A second later the one nail holding up the shutter on the left-hand window gave and the whole thing clattered to the ground. God and His angels were conspiring against him. Chip shut his mouth to prevent the house from collapsing.

"Does your father—" Andy began.

Chip raised his brow.

Andy shut his mouth too.

There were three disadvantages to growing up in a town where everyone knew you. First, they also knew your father. Second, they could still recall you as a fifth grader, which killed any authoritative tone you might try to pull off as an adult. Third, they felt the right to pause on occasion to give you detailed instructions on how to run your life.

"C'mon," Chip repeated, only a whisper of pleading in his voice. "Let's do this."

Andy sighed, glanced up and down the road again, and gave a short nod. A second later, he disappeared into his truck.

Chip turned at the sound of a screen door slamming and saw the fairy woman back on her porch, locking her front door.

Andy began rolling toward him, his truck's massive tires overtaking the small road. He crawled past a parked Suburban, sparing inches between the truck and the sleek body of the huge vehicle. Stopping ten yards before the house, exhaust running, Andy waited for Chip's signal.

Chip beckoned Andy on.

The ground began to rumble as the brake lights turned off and the truck, with dumpster attached, moved backward.

"Watch the car." Chip signaled to move around the Suburban and Andy corrected, pulling forward into Bree's front yard.

Bree stiffened, watching the front of the large vehicle roll onto her grass.

"He's just gotta get the truck aligned," Chip called out to her. "Should take just a moment."

Andy rolled the window down and strained his neck out to look up and back. Chip could already see he was going to have to move farther into her yard to overcorrect the steering wheel, avoid the power line drooping like low-hanging fruit, and dodge the two parked cars and mailboxes.

Chip feigned a smile in her direction.

Turned his head back to Andy as he waved him on.

Flicked his eyes toward the tires, now farther into Bree's yard.

Felt his stomach tighten with each inch of grass flattened underneath Andy's massive tires.

Hurry up, Andy, Chip thought. *Get in and get out.*

Much longer and this was going to get worse. Much longer and—

Chip's jaw flexed as he watched the front tire sink like a horse losing its step midcanter. It was but an inch, maybe two, but he saw the distinctive dip.

Oh no.

No. No. No.

Andy hung his head out the window and spotted the damage, then let loose a round of curses. The mother across the street covered her toddlers' ears as she rushed them inside.

Chip winced. "Andy. Andy!" he called, striding forward as the grass around the tire started to fill with water.

Andy's hand slapped the side of the door. "It's that *bleepity bleep* car in my way. If they could've just *bleep bleepity bleep* parked like a normal person . . . And I told you I couldn't do it, Chip. If you had just listened to me!"

Andy fiddled with his jacket pocket in search of a cigarette and waved another hand toward everything from the power line to "all those *bleepity* blue jays" as he began defending his superb driving skills. Meanwhile, Chip inspected the damage. He guessed this little mistake would cost upwards of fifteen hundred dollars to fix.

"I know it's not your fault, Andy. Nobody here's blaming you."

Andy took a deep drag from his cigarette.

Chip took advantage of the momentary silence and launched into what he hoped would be a soothing monologue. "It's going to be okay—"

Andy's mouth moved around his cigarette as he spoke. "Like *bleep* it is. I don't have money to throw at this. And *you definitely* don't have this kind of money."

As Chip was about to interject, a firm and painful tap on the shoulder cut him short.

He turned.

The green-faced nymph was inches away from his face as she had been just hours before. Only instead of a potted fern, she now gripped what appeared to be a bowlful of nuts.

Something was different about her eyes right then. Perhaps it was the fire dancing in them, but they flashed so green they reminded him of the cool, frosted pines he'd biked past on the mountains that morning. She was like one branch in particular, which had slapped him unexpectedly around mile seven. He could still feel the sting on his cheek.

"I need you to move your truck."

"I, uh, sure. Absolutely." Chip slapped the back of the dumpster and called up, "You go on, Andy. I'll handle things from here."

Andy escaped only too readily, the truck rumbling down the hill in such haste Chip feared he would break something else along the way.

Chip turned around. "I'm so sorry about this—"

But his words faltered.

She was nowhere in sight.

The ignition of the Subaru sounded and he turned in time to catch the flash of the woman's red braid whipping around her as she looked back over her shoulder.

Her car bounced as it avoided the mailbox and reversed onto the road before she pushed the gearshift into drive. She paused in front of him. Rolled down the window.

He inhaled and took a step toward her. Ready to explain. Ready to apologize. Ready to listen.

"Don't drown the chickens."

Before he could reply, her Subaru sputtered off down the road.

Don't drown the chickens.

Don't. Drown. The chickens.

He straightened. Well, at the very least he could avoid that.

His oxfords—his one and only pair of oxfords—dragged with each soggy step as he went to his truck and reached over the side of the bed for his channel locks, then made his way toward her meter box. His mind raced, but oddly enough, his thoughts didn't linger on the cash he'd need to cover the cost of this mess. His mind rested on her.

On those intriguing eyes.

He wondered which version of the woman he'd just met—the carefree fairy in the stairway or the tense, distant neighbor—would be the one to whom he'd have to say, "I'm sorry, but you're going to be without water for several days."

Chapter 3

BREE

"Our precious home is flooding, dear."

Bree slipped the words into Evie's ears as she picked up a flute of champagne and moved around a group of small-talkers. She maneuvered through a sea of sequins and tuxedo shoulders jutting out at every turn. As crowded as the room was, nothing but space existed between the tip of her head and the glass globes and antique chandeliers of the vaulted ceiling high above. The Barter would stand for nothing less than holding their Annual Spring Gala at the Martha Washington Inn.

Holding the bowl of nuts like a football, she squeezed around another couple and snaked through the narrow labyrinth toward the food table. People of all sorts were at the Barter galas, and from one sniff, Bree could tell which side of the fence they played on. Elizabeth Taylor's Passion, Chanel No. 5, Soir de Paris, Guerlain's L'Heure Bleue—these were the scents of the standard patrons, the ones who enthusiastically supported the nation's oldest live-performance theatre.

Her side, the actors' side, smelled like either Bath & Body Works Tropical Passionfruit body spray or essential oil of a gumbo tree. Like Cinderella, the actors slipped into a pumpkin-turned-carriage for several Barter-sponsored events per year and mingled with sponsors who talked about vacation homes in Tuscany. Actors responded shrilly with, "Well, who doesn't?" and laughed at the patrons' jokes, ever mindful of how many crab cakes were left on the tray.

The patrons smiled indulgently at their prized actors' eccentricities. The actors smiled back at their patrons who were rich enough to get away with eccentric behaviors of their own.

These fundraising events were sprinkled throughout the year, but the Barter's Spring Gala was the biggest of all. And this was Bree's first.

Bree slid her bowl of nuts between a platter of smoked salmon and what appeared to be some sort of edible intestine. As she did so, the unmistakably overpowering scent of tea tree oil came from behind her.

Ah. Evie.

"My house is *what* now?" With cat liner up to her temples, Evie stood with both hands on her hips—or rather on her skirt, which as of yesterday had been the patchwork quilt draped across their sofa.

Right.

Bree had lived in the house with Evie for six months, had equal ownership in the house inherited from *Bree's* grandmother, and yet her grandmother's former caretaker couldn't once admit the house was theirs equally. Not once.

Honestly, just because Evie lived in the house for five years with Nana she thought she owned the place.

Bree scanned the food options and picked up a cherry tomato with cheese on a toothpick. "Well, I'm no professional, but I'd say a truck broke the water line. Do you think this is swiss?"

Evie clutched the quilt skirt at her thighs and, with some effort, moved herself closer. "Did they fix it?"

"No idea."

"Is the water stopped?"

"Not a clue."

"Who was there looking at it?"

"Some man." Bree would not say his name. She would not admit out loud that she had remembered his name when he had so flippantly looked her in the eye with that quizzical *do-I-know-you?* expression and said that horrible word, "Becca?"

Evie took a step toward her. "What kind of man?"

"Well, after a surprising turn of events, I'd say a terrible-human-being kind of man."

Her eyes narrowed. "Are you helpful in any way *at all*?"

Bree pointed her toothpick toward the ceiling. "I told him not to drown your chickens."

Evie's eyes dropped to Bree's dress. "And what happened to *my dress*?"

Bree glanced down to her skirt, where the coffee stains had most definitely dried. Oops. "Oh. I'll, uh, throw this in the wash the second I get home."

Evie glared.

Bree lifted a finger, trying to remember Evie's previous lectures. "But only after putting dish soap on to spot-clean—"

"*Vinegar.* And you'll do no such thing. When you get home, hand it over to me."

Evie huffed with Scarlett O'Hara indignity before lifting her piles of skirt and turning. With some difficulty and a rigid jab, she pushed the side door open. "Spot-clean with dish soap," she muttered. "Leave it to me to sort *everything* out . . ."

"Bye, honey!" Bree called, watching Evie and the perma-stormy cloud above her head disappear. "I'll miss you too!"

"Sort out what?" Stephen, the stage manager, slid up to the cheese tray, his gaze focused on the lobster toasts.

Bree picked up another toothpick of cheese and tomato. "Oh, just a little hiccup at the house. You know, town water supply streaming in. Gallons of water flooding the yard. Same old, same old."

"Well, good for you two," Stephen said, shoveling a fifth lobster toast onto his plate. "I admire the dedication you have to making your living situation work."

And by *living situation* he meant the fact that after her step-grandmother's funeral, the family discovered Nana's beloved live-in caretaker was to inherit 30 percent of Nana's home. Another 30 percent went to Bree, and the remaining 40 percent (plus most of the furnishings) went to Bree's stepfather. At the writing of the will, Bree and her parents lived three hours away in Gatlinburg. Nana had clearly assumed the three would either sell the home and split the profit or let Evie buy them out. Most shocking of all was that Nana had imagined Bree could *ever* let Nana's place—her special place—go. The second the will was read to Bree, she stood up and declared, "I'll take it."

Almost as quickly, Evie said the same thing.

So here they were, four months later.

At a stalemate.

"Now as for your act tonight," Stephen said, shifting to face Bree. The thin, bald man settled into his sternest frown and dropped his voice an octave. "If I catch you breaking character to make googly eyes with someone in the audience again, you're out. You understand? This isn't some high-school musical production here. If you can't act like a professional, you won't stand up there."

Bree swallowed. She wanted to defend herself against his accusation. She wanted to say, *Hey now, I do more than just "stand up there." I lounge too.*

Then again, he did hold the key to her salary.

"Yes, sir."

"Good." Stephen turned his attention to the deviled eggs. He dropped a couple onto his plate. "And lose the makeup. There's a time to be in character, and there's a time not to be in character. This time's the latter."

In character.

In character?

In . . .

She dropped her toothpick on the bone china plate and touched her cheek. Her fingers came back mossy green. *Character.*

Well then. She was in a room full of influential people, wearing a coffee-stained dress three inches too short and a Shakespearean fairy's makeup, getting chewed out by her boss, and offering up a bowl of nuts, half an hour late. She couldn't have set herself up for a better evening.

"Terrific," she muttered as Stephen moved off.

A voice behind her spoke. "What's terrific?"

Bree recognized the voice and, for a wild moment, considered running out the door Evie had just exited. But it wasn't as though Theodore hadn't seen her like this a dozen times.

Slowly, she turned.

A rueful smiled formed on her lips. "Oh, nothing. Care for a cubed cheesecake?"

The man's onyx eyes matched the tuxedo tailored around his broad shoulders.

His jaw dropped slightly before he recovered. "Actually, I prefer my cheesecake cut into other shapes, but thank you. Have you tried the crab?"

"Shellfish allergy." She shrugged. "Besides, I'm more of a pickle-chip girl."

He paused for a moment. "So, are you headed back to the theatre tonight?"

She peeled off one of her magnetic lashes, and he took a startled step back. She laughed. "To answer your actual question, I forgot to take this makeup off."

To her credit, she spent hours every day layering on the avocado-colored foundation, brightening her cheeks with a heavy rouge, and installing magnetic lashes around her thick eyeliner. At some point she lost all awareness of the makeup that once so bothered her.

And here she had been smirking over Evie's heavy-handed cat eye. She could only imagine how she looked right now.

She caught a glimpse of herself in a gilded mirror on the wall.

Scratch that. She *wished* she could only imagine how she looked right now.

Her long red braid fell to her waist, and the short green satin gown hugged her figure. Her avocado-cream face stared back at her. Basically, she was Mrs. Shrek.

Well, at least that settled what she was going to be for Halloween this year.

Theodore followed Bree as she moved over to the row of coats and dug inside the pockets of her beaten parka. She pulled out a crumpled package of makeup-remover wipes and yanked a few out. Oh, the price of the career; she was ever finding a bit of green behind the ear.

"So," she said, rubbing from the cheek inward, "any word on the fall lineup? What's the inside scoop?"

Theodore Watkins III, financial adviser to the Barter's chief administrator, well-known supporter of the arts, and heir to the town's beloved Christmas tree farm, set down his flute of champagne. His amiable brow creased. "I don't know what the 'inside scoop' is, but I do believe Mr. and Mrs. Richardson were just discussing the next show with some interested parties." He tipped his chin up and over, where sure enough the reclusive Mr. Richardson and his wife were standing among a small party, all furs and feathers.

While caking her wipe in green foundation, Bree kept her eyes on the renowned chief administrator, his wife, and the "interested parties" who circled the couple. With large and intense eyes, they resembled chickens awaiting their after-dinner scraps.

There was interested, and there was *interested*.

And now Bree, too, was *interested*.

"Do you mind?" Bree heard Theodore say, and she forced her eyes back his way. He inched closer, tugging one of the wipes free from her palm.

He smiled tentatively as he held it up.

"Oh. Oh yes. Sure." Bree lowered her wipe to let him sub in. She sucked in her breath as he stepped closer and entered her bubble.

He had never entered the bubble before. And yet every chance encounter since their first six weeks ago seemed to present another opportunity for them to draw closer. Greetings lengthened. Greetings disappeared altogether as the two slid directly into conversation, as though the days between their last meeting had been but a pause. Their smiles widened when they saw each other. And as of last week, for the first time, they didn't even pretend not to look for the other after the Friday show.

He rubbed the wipe against the tip of her green nose.

He moved to her cheek.

Each brow.

The business of the room slowed.

"There now," Theodore said at last, pushing the wipe into his pants pocket as if it was one of his many monogrammed silk handkerchiefs. He took a step back and the room returned to a breezy 72 degrees. "Much better."

"So . . ." Bree released a breath. Where was she? Her eyes ticked back to Mrs. Richardson. Oh yes. "Let's get a little closer, shall we?"

"You mean you want to spy on your employers from an auspicious distance instead of walking into the group and joining the conversation."

She smiled. "Exactly."

Bree led the way and together they danced around clusters of people, sidestepping platters of shrimp and the stray arm flinging out in dramatic story. Theodore followed her lead as they melted into the regal drapery, twenty feet of royal blue cascading from an empire valance. The perfect vantage point for eavesdropping.

Mr. Richardson glanced toward his wife. "And yet as much as I'd love to put our actors to work, I can only imagine how they'd handle a paint bucket and a brush. Things have changed just a bit since Porterfield's time."

"Nonsense!" replied Mr. Thieves, owner of no fewer than four restaurants in town and never spotted in any of them. He set his quiche cup on his plate. "If the casts of old days could earn their keep collecting props and running the cafeteria, they certainly could be useful to you now with some hammers and caulk. After all, besides their little acts, what else must they do during the day? Might be good to keep them busy." He leaned in conspiratorially and tapped his nose. "Might even get the crime down."

Theodore raised his brow to Bree with a tilted smile. In this town, with a verifiable crime rate of nil, the cast's weekend trips to the farmer's market were positively barbarous.

"Yes, well," replied Mr. Richardson, less enthusiastically, "thankfully we don't have to do a lot of things we had to during the Great Depression anymore. I for one can't remember the last time we boarded a rabid dog or criminal beneath the stage."

The group laughed politely, everyone well aware of the Barter's fascinating history. The area beneath the stage at one time had served as a jailhouse, and at another, a pen for suspected rabid dogs. The theatre itself had garnered its name from the fact that actors worked for vegetables, dairy, livestock—even snakes and underwear—during the Depression years.

When Bree heard all the bizarre facts of the Barter's past, she didn't take Evie's word for it. One quick internet search verified it was true—everything down to the fact the actors had to shout to make themselves heard over the pigs and chickens during the plays.

Now that would've been a heck of a time to be an actress.

"No, I'm afraid a few buckets of paint would not solve this theatre's problems," Richardson said. "The Barter needs more than a freshening up. It's time to take it down to the studs and give it something that will last another hundred years. The Barter needs a facelift."

The women touched their foreheads and cheeks, the very word clearly reminding them of distant—and in the case of Mrs. Thieves, not so distant—procedures.

The group was silent for a moment.

"I can't agree more," Mrs. Richardson replied, removing her hand from her slender jawline. She picked up her glass of champagne from a side table with a smile. "To new youth!"

The huddle scurried to raise their glasses.

"To new youth!" they replied, lifting the glasses to their lips.

"When are you going to do it?" Mr. Henderson asked, drawing Mr. Richardson's attention.

"It'll have to be in between seasons."

"Who's going to do it?" Mr. Henderson inquired. "You know, Turner just completed the entire renovation of the administration offices at the hospital—"

"Maybe Turner was fine for you, Gerry, but I don't want just anyone coming in to slap tile on the floors and ceiling and call it a day. We're talking about the Barter here. We're talking about *art*. If the man can't brushstroke an oil painting just as well as he can build a skyscraper, I don't want him so much as driving a nail."

Mr. Henderson, the hospital's top donor, tightened his smile and his grip on his glass. He held a long pause. "Yes. Well, I'm sure that'll be difficult to find in this area. I wish you luck."

As the conversation turned to someone's latest trip to Sicily, Theodore and Bree slipped away.

"Well now," Theodore said quietly as he led the way through the crowd. "Was that everything you dreamed it would be?"

Bree trailed him, blinded by his broad shoulders. "The Barter getting a renovation? Riveting. Someone alert the papers."

"By next week they'll all know." He pushed open a door.

And suddenly they were standing outside, overlooking the elegant curved driveway. The parking valets stood in the distance, bouncing on toes as they shivered in the cold. Theodore slipped one hand into the pocket of his tux. "Sorry. It was getting a bit stuffy."

"No, this is a good idea," Bree said. She crossed her bare arms across her chest.

Theodore shifted to look over Main Street, then turned back to face her.

"It is a nice evening out. Would you"—Theodore paused—"care to . . . stroll?"

The sky was clear. The bright yellow moon hovered over the Barter just across the street, its maroon-and-yellow flags flicking in the light breeze.

Her eyes fell on the road between the Barter and the Martha, where Chip had raced across in his fancy suit, his tie flapping as he grinned like a golden retriever with a Frisbee.

The man with a girlfriend.

The man who drove like a maniac, whose bumper stickers alone had proven him to be the type of man she'd *never* be interested in.

The man who had thought so little of their interaction he couldn't even remember her name.

And she had stood there like a fool and smiled at him onstage.

"A stroll would be perfect," Bree said, her words swift and sure as she reached backward for the door. "Let me just get my coat."

Chapter 4

CHIP

Chip tried really, really hard to keep a smile from playing on his lips as Bree stomped out of the sleet and onto his concrete porch in black galoshes. She pushed her damp, dripping hair out of her eyes and swung the five-gallon paint bucket off her hip onto the ground between them.

To top off the moment, she pulled a half-eaten Slim Jim out of the back pocket of her jeans and ripped off a chunk. "I need water," she said through her mouthful. "Fill 'er up."

This time he couldn't help it. He grabbed the smile and pulled it down with his hand. The two-day-old stubble on his chin bristled against his calloused palm. The smile started to creep up again.

She smiled in return, but only, it appeared, to show off her teeth.

"I'm sorry," he said for the fifteenth time in five days. "Had I known your roommate would take to the, uh"—he shifted his gaze to their porch where Evie, head flipped over, with a smile a mile wide, was dunking her hair in a bucket—"to the *natural lifestyle,* I would've put you girls up in a hotel."

In truth, he didn't have the funds to set the girls up in a hotel. Even so, it was a nice sentiment.

For almost a week now, trucks had been pouring into Stonewall Heights, bringing in heavy equipment and throwing dirt around Evie and Bree's yard like confetti. The girls hadn't been prioritized in the way they deserved, as Chip couldn't justify hiring a twenty-four-hour plumber for twice the cost when his own company, Redpoint Construction, could do the job. That meant he had to shuffle three jobs—a fact two of his clients weren't happy about. It would cost him relationally, if not financially, but at the moment he had no choice. He was nearly broke.

Which explained why he had broken off a job site yesterday to meet his plumber and why he himself had just hauled back three bales of wheat straw and seed to smooth over the girls' yard tomorrow morning. He was paying for his mistake. In every way. Heavily.

It just turned out that they were too.

Correction.

Bree was too.

Evie was having the time of her life.

After going without water for five days, Evie apparently had experienced some sort of lifestyle revelation. Judging by the way she dunked her head in the bucket now, the already eccentric costume designer from the Barter had found her calling just short of going entirely off grid.

"Or you two could stay at my place." Chip gestured toward the living room behind him. "The invitation still stands."

She squinted through the Sheetrock dust cloud permeating the unfurnished room. "I think I'll pass." She enunciated each word. "Now if you'll please give me some water . . ."

Chip took the bucket, observing a sort of nest developing in the bun on top of her head. In fact, if he tilted his head a few degrees, he could imagine a bird in there.

Bree's frown turned to a scowl, and he watched as she ripped off another chunk of meat. Her eyes dropped to the object in her hand.

"Dinner." She raised a brow. "I was going to make spaghetti, but you can imagine how silly I felt when I tried to turn on the faucet." She waved the Slim Jim and the long meat stick wobbled. "About that water . . . ?"

He snapped his attention into place. "Right. Sure thing. Be right back." He pushed the door open behind him. He paused, then added with a significant smile, "Bree."

Using customers' names whenever possible was a thing he did to bond. He was doing it with his new neighbors—everyone from Jerry, the man who wore a bathrobe to the mailbox, to Mrs. Lewis, the kind elderly woman with the dog across the street. But Bree? He must've said her name fifty times in the past five days.

Maybe it was because she was trudging over to his house for water five times a day. Maybe it was because he felt like he'd spent more time at her place than his these past few days, sorting out this water problem. Maybe it was because their cars sat a foot from each other in their pocket-sized driveways, and it happened to be impossible to walk outside without seeing her.

But it mattered to him that she knew he knew her name. Not just because they were neighbors, or even because right now he needed to get on her good side. It mattered.

And yet, since the moment he first stepped foot on his driveway five days ago, she acted as though they'd never met.

This bothered him in a way he couldn't explain.

He stepped over the paint buckets and around several tubes of caulk on his way to the kitchen. As he turned the faucet on, he glanced up to the window above the sink. It had become a habit. The sky was a blanket of rolling gray clouds; the humble mountains spiked like the heart rhythm of an EKG from corner to corner.

The mountains within the Pacific Crest Trail were wild, untamed. The Rockies were sharp and dramatic and figuratively—and, if you were hiking, sometimes literally—took your breath away. The quiet, unassuming Blue Ridge Mountains were home.

He may not have heat. He may not have furniture. But the view was worth every penny.

He turned his head back in the direction of his neighbor, who watched the chickens as she ripped off another piece of jerky.

Russell must've heard the water filling the bucket, because the jingle of his collar sounded upstairs, and a moment later his nails tapped the stripped wood as the 230-pound English mastiff trotted down. Chip moved to the back door and picked up Russell's empty water bowl. Back at the sink, he pushed the faucet to the left side. The bowl began to fill.

Then he heard it: a warble of words at the front door, a string of yelps and incomplete sentences from Russell *and* Bree. He dropped the bowl and it clattered in the sink, water splashing as he rushed toward the door.

"Russell! Down!" Chip yelled, trying to assess the damage.

All he could see when he reached the living room, however, was Russell's enormous backside and the soles of Bree's galoshes.

Chip mustered up his deepest voice. "Russell. Down. *Now.*"

The dog lay down on Bree, sniffing her face, neck, and arms. She grunted.

Russell was a well-mannered dog. He could sit. He could shake. He could stay by Chip's side, racing obediently through a ride in the mountains.

But Slim Jims? Slim Jims were another matter.

"Russell," Chip said, his teeth grinding as he grabbed the collar buried deep within the rolls of the dog's thick neck. Russell licked the length of Bree's face.

Bree squeezed her eyes shut and gave a muted shriek. Her arms, pinned to the porch by Russell's haunches, strained to be free.

Chip yanked the dog, but it had the same effect as trying to move a bank vault by the handle.

Bree grunted as she attempted to shove him off before getting slapped, quite unfortunately, in the face with a stray bit of drool while Russell shook his feverish head.

"Uuuugh," she groaned. She turned her face away from the dog as she cried out between her pressed lips, "Get. It. Off!"

"Impressive tone," Chip replied, while giving another yank. "Now if only you could just redirect your frightening command from me to my dog—"

"It's *your* dog," Bree practically shouted. "Get *your* dog off me—"

But her mid-yelling spiel turned into a yelp as her eyes widened. Her whole face seemed to condense into her neck, like a turtle seeking shelter in its shell. Only, of course, her face had no shell to seek refuge in.

"Ohhh, that's a doozy," Chip said, seeing the cause. "Okay then."

In spite of Russell's terrific traits—true companionship, perfect manners—he did have one teeny, tiny flaw. Russell seemed to produce his weight in saliva every thirty minutes, and with nowhere to go, it pooled in his slack, sweet-natured jowls. In today's case, the drool was lowering from his jaw by centimeters every second, inching closer and closer to landing squarely on her face.

It was time to take action.

Chip straddled Russel, dug his face into the dog's neck, reached around his ribcage, and pressed as hard as he could to one side.

They tipped over, and Chip landed hard. His head pounded the concrete, and his back cracked under the weight of man's best friend.

Russell rolled off like it was a circus act and ended up back on all fours.

Bree pulled herself up to sitting, wiping her face with the cuffs of her sweater.

After a moment's shake, Russell jerked his head toward Bree with steely determination in his eyes.

"Give it—to him." Chip wheezed his words while clutching his ribs. "Throw the—Slim Jim."

Bree whipped her head toward Chip, her eyes widening when she saw the dog preparing for another round.

She started ransacking her oversized sweater for her pockets. "I don't—" She shook her pockets out frantically, then pulled out a bit of plastic. "It's just a wrapper!"

"Now," Chip wheezed, making a limp reach for Russell's collar as the dog jumped. *"Throw it now!"*

She flung the Slim Jim wrapper at the dog like a wallet toward thieves in a dark alley. For a moment Russell appeared ready to pummel her, but his massive paws skidded to a stop inches away from her upraised hands shielding her head.

He dropped his face from her to the wrapper, sniffed, then snatched it up.

Lifting his tail high in the air, he trotted inside.

The porch went quiet.

Chip had curled into a fetal position, rocking like a football player with a torn ACL as he tried to gain back his breath. Bree stared into his house as if waiting for any sign of the dog's return.

A moment later, the spell broke.

She jumped up in her oversized boots. Rubbed the saliva off her face with the crook of one elbow, then the next.

Peered down at him.

With one painful motion, he turned to lie flat on his back. He looked up to those bright green eyes half hidden behind a mass of tangled hair.

Holding his ribcage with one hand, Chip lifted the other like the wounded traveler waiting for the Good Samaritan to reach down and save his life.

She tilted her head. Frowned.

Then, with one giant step over his body, Bree moved across the porch and marched down the porch steps.

Chapter 5

BREE

"I know, *hate* is a such a strong word. But honestly, Cass. I think I'm starting to hate him."

Bree's bare arms shivered as she paced on the grass outside the Barter's rehearsal building. She felt the damp earth soaking through the thin cloth of her handmade fairy slippers.

Given how things were going of late, she could predict the consequences: back at the house, Evie would yell at her for twenty minutes about ruining theatre property, and Bree would casually pick up Evie's new book, *Minimalist Secrets to a Peaceful Life*, and begin flipping through. Evie would see it. Pause. Do some sort of closed-eye meditation while her mouth parted like a surfaced trout. Then, looking like she was making a great sacrifice, Evie would silently put out her hand and Bree would surrender the slippers.

Right now, Bree didn't care. All she wanted was a fifteen-minute chat with her busy best friend. When the best friend had six kids, you didn't complain about poor timing when the phone rang. You just picked it up. Always. And you wore your fairy slippers outside if it was the only place you could find some peace and quiet.

Beyond the small row of cars along the gravel entrance was an aged fence and a slew of Hereford cows dotting a field. One stood close to the parking lot, sniffing the March air with its pearly white nose as though smelling the storm coming in. It was a fiercely cold day, temperatures in digits so low the schools had been shut down. Everybody was out stockpiling goods at the only Kroger in town, hoarding all the milk, eggs, bread, sweet tea, and tobacco they could get. Everyone but Bree and the cows.

"Angela, quit pulling on your tights," Stephen shouted inside the warehouse.

"But they're riding up," a voice retorted.

"Then let them ride!" Stephen said. "'Cause you're sure not going to fix them in the middle of Theseus's wedding. Where's Mustardseed?"

At the sound of her cast name, Bree moved past a trailer hitched to the Barter van, toward the single, nondescript door of the 7200-square-foot warehouse. Surely no one would spot her there.

"So this guy tailed your car and ran over your water pipe, and his dog knocked you over for a Slim Jim, and he may or may not have accidentally turned your housemate into a hippie." Bree could hear Cassie's knife chopping in the background, could practically see her standing over the row of potatoes, slicing them in perfect half-inch blocks. "Forgive me if I'm wrong, but I believe you ran across more terrorizing eight-year-olds every day during your last job at the aquarium. I don't know if I'd start shooting off the *H* word yet."

The *H* word. Hate. Cassie was *such* a mom.

"No, no," Bree said, pausing midstep. "That's just what he wants you to think. That it was all done in innocence. That he's just this nice, handsome—"

"Handsome?"

"—guy who can waltz into your life and screw up everything about it. He knows we're inconvenienced, but I *know* he's enjoying it. I see the smile in his eyes when he looks at my greasy hair. And the way he laughed when Evie mentioned how much energy we'd save by doing without a hot-water heater. He thinks it's all *so* amusing. Like I just shouldn't take it so seriously."

There was a pause.

"Bree, you act that way too. With everyone. Every day. Of your life."

"Do you know how long I've gone without water?" Bree raked a hand through her hair, feeling the grease coat her fingers. "A week. A week, Cass."

"You backpacked the Appalachian Trail for three months. I'm not understanding the problem here."

Bree clenched her fist. "I chose to, yes. But right now I'm going through three cans of hair spray a week and tubs of green foundation for this role. Do you know how hard it is to get hair spray and foundation off without water? Do you know how hard it is to get dog drool off without water?" She was starting to pinch her words. Was she on the verge of losing her mind? "That dog's started following me. He waits for me by the front door. Every day. Like a serial killer."

"Can we go back to the part where you called this guy handsome?"

Bree kicked at the gravel. "You know who he's like? Jesse. You remember Jesse."

Cassie's sigh was audible above the chopping. "Jesse Hicks? From elementary school?"

"You remember him in music class. The one with all the recorders. And the way he walked around, humblebragging to everyone when he was voted Chief Justice of the Supreme Court." Bree started to kick at the gravel again but turned at the sound of tires crunching. A Lincoln Town Car was pulling into the lot, and Bree quickened her steps toward the warehouse door.

"In our mock vote during history class?" Cassie continued.

Bree could practically hear Cassie setting the knife down with the delicate touch of a psychiatrist about to explain things to her patient. "Unfortunately, Bree, I don't recall the fifth grader taunting you with recorders and imaginary careers from twenty years ago. You'll have to remind me."

"Don't you dare pretend you don't remember," Bree whispered, quietly slipping through the door. "Okay, Cass. Gotta go."

She slipped the phone into the hip of her fairy costume as she entered the dark warehouse, her eyes adjusting to the dim lighting. The only brightness came from the makeshift stage in the center of the open floor, where the restless cast fidgeted. Pole-mounted lighting and curtains hanging from portable rods surrounded the stage, making it seem small in the vast space. The warehouse ceiling was at least forty feet high, covered in the kind of material even cell phone signals had trouble penetrating. Though the ceiling was high and vast, the floor was covered. Abandoned props and old sets lay in shadowed corners: racks of armor and medieval frocks, bedazzled flapper dresses, the drooping form of a human-size candlestick. Dozens of costumes lay around one entire section of the building, tulle and lace and polyester strewn about.

In the middle of it all, Evie held pins between pursed lips as she tucked and fitted a glittering skirt around one of the fairies. Evie was a short woman, but her hair alone was a foot tall—a style somewhere between a 1950s twist and an owl's natural habitat. Her horn-rimmed glasses (without prescription lenses) tipped the picture more toward the owl side of the scale.

Bree paused for a moment to enjoy the view.

"And what are we looking at now?" came a whisper at her side.

She grinned at Theo's presence but didn't move.

"Oh, I'm just enjoying watching my roommate turn into a tree," Bree replied, keeping her position with crossed arms.

He crossed his arms too, a cuff link glinting beneath the low lights.

Together they watched as Evie rose on the tiptoes of her tan ballet flats, in her tan tights, to pin together the extra fabric on the fairy's shoulder.

Theodore nodded toward the set. "Aren't you in this scene?"

Bree shrugged. "I'd rather wait for the owl to pop out of her hair."

For several more seconds they watched.

Disappointed when no nocturnal birds materialized, Bree turned to face him. "What are you doing here anyway? Don't you have a job to get to?"

By the stage, Stephen tapped on his clipboard with his pen. "Come on, someone work with me. Has anyone seen Mustardseed? I don't want to move on from this scene until it's *ab-so-lute-ly* perfect."

Theodore's brows rose with a challenging twinkle in his eye. "Don't *you*? Mustardseed?"

Bree met his challenge with a smile, but after several seconds, the pressure became too much. She waved a hand in the air. "Fine.

Fine. I don't see how they could *possibly* go on without me, but fine."

She moved around a rack of Elvis and Johnny Cash costumes, popped into Stephen's view, and hopped onstage. Bree nudged Birdie a few inches over and slipped into her lounging position by a mossy tree.

There was silence for a few moments.

Stephen stared at her. Appeared to be contemplating a lecture. Then flung his hands in the air like an orchestra conductor as he settled into the director's chair. "Right. From the beginning."

Bree's eyes flicked over to Theodore's with the silent words, *See? Look how critical I was. I'm upstage left, hidden behind six actors and Titania's bed.*

As much as she noticed, and enjoyed, the way Theodore's gaze kept turning to her through the scene, other pieces of a puzzle caught her attention.

Like how Theodore was not alone.

It wasn't easy to miss Mr. Richardson—the theatre's chief administrator—standing behind Stephen's chair. Just as it wasn't easy to miss that his rare presence meant something important.

Stephen grew more and more irritable at the cast's distracted missteps and bungled directions until finally, following Birdie's gaze, he looked back over his shoulder. Up.

The sight of Mr. Richardson and Theodore less than three feet away startled him like a kid caught in the candy jar.

"Mr. Richardson, I didn't know to expect you," he said, tripping over the director's chair to shake his hand. "So sorry I didn't see you."

"That's quite all right." Mr. Richardson gave an uncertain glance around Stephen. "Is Don here?"

"Uh, no." Stephen scratched the back of his head. "No, I believe he's out."

And by "out" he meant absent for the past five years.

Don was a brilliant director, or so Bree had heard. But he'd lost enthusiasm for the long and erratic hours of theatre life after decades in showbusiness. He showed up for performances but left the actual work in the competent hands of the stage manager. For Stephen, the compulsive man who followed the "If you want something done right, you have to do it yourself" mantra to the point that it was a plaque on the wall of his closet-sized office, this arrangement worked well. The director took it easy and got credit, and the stage manager got to see the shows done precisely how he believed they should be.

Either Mr. Richardson wasn't aware of this, or he was the good administrator they all claimed and feigned ignorance.

"You'll see to telling him the news then, I'm sure," Mr. Richardson said, doffing his black Stetson Chatham and taking a step toward the stage.

"Telling him what, sir?" Stephen said, trailing after Mr. Richardson as he took a few steps toward the group.

The cast gathered around.

Mr. Richardson played with the brim of his hat before raising his voice. "We've had a bit of a . . . a snag regarding next season's *Much Ado About Nothing.* Seems somebody purchased the wrong license."

He sent a furtive glance to Stephen, who started meticulously straightening the pencil attached to his clipboard.

"But despite that *grave* mistake"—again, sly glance—"this problem can be amended." There was silence, and Mr. Richardson managed a smile. "With a little sacrifice."

Invested despite herself, Bree leaned in with the rest of the actors.

Whereas those around her had been here for years, sometimes decades, she was nothing in this company, after all. A jobbed-in actor, not even qualified enough to get temp housing in the Barter Inn, their exclusive cast dorms. Played nothing but the backdrop fairy in *A Midsummer Night's Dream*. She'd been casted for Ursula, yet another stand-by-the-main-character-nodding-and-bowing-for-three-hours personality in *Much Ado About Nothing*. Really, how could her part possibly get any more dull than Ursula?

"The production for the March to May lineup at Stage One will now be a musical," Mr. Richardson continued, turning the Stetson in his hands. "And, by happy coincidence, one of my favorite musicals." He paused momentously. "*Singin' in the Rain*."

Bree smiled as his words started to register.

No more Ursula.

No more silent, bored lady in waiting.

Now, she'd seen *Singin' in the Rain* on-screen before. She just had to think.

Who were some characters in that? Some nice characters who stood beside the planters, watching Don Lockwood and Kathy Selden tap-dance into the night and applauding on cue? Oh, she'd *love* those costumes. Something bright and floral, the 1950s at their finest. No more sixteenth-century Renaissance clothing. No more green face paint.

"Now, what that does mean for you all, unfortunately, is a smaller cast. I'd say a loss by"—he paused, lifting his eyes to the rafters as though calculating—"Forty percent."

Bree blinked.

Wait.

What?

Eric spoke up. "But we've already been cast for our slots in *Much Ado.*" He scratched a spot under his heavy goat's-head wig. "What'll happen to those who get cut? It's too late to get in on anything at Stage Two, isn't it?"

Mr. Richardson paused, knowing just as well as they did the plays located in the adjacent building—the lesser-known plays, and those aimed for kids—were already taken by the second strings.

"Yes. Well, it seems those at Stage Two have already signed their contracts."

"And so have we," Eric retorted. "We signed them . . . well, we were *going* to sign them . . ." His words stalled out. He practically choked out the whispered words. "Next week."

Mr. Richardson nodded, grim-faced. "Those in Barter Two have signed their yearlong contract. But for everyone else, everyone here . . ."

The silence in the room finished his sentence.

"So, as such, Don"—Mr. Richardson hesitated, then turned to give Stephen a slap on the back—"or if by some circumstance Don is unavailable, *Stephen* will be doing auditions as soon as possible. Those who fill those slots, fill them. As for the rest . . . I'm sorry. We'll just have to welcome you back for our fall lineup."

"But that's *months* without work!" someone whispered furiously.

Murmuring began around the room, hushed tones turning frenetic. Birdie glanced to Bree, her eyes wide.

"What'll we do?" she whispered. "There's no way we can compete." Her eyes were on the leads, now huddled together like they were District 1 in the Hunger Games.

Birdie began muttering to herself, phrases like "forty percent" and "Daddy is going to kill me" and "should've married Billy."

As the hum of the group's murmuring grew to the point of sniffles and tears—Bree knew for a fact at least two cast members were trying to expand their résumé skill set with cry-on-cue talent—Bree's attention turned to Theodore, who was walking her way.

Behind him, Bree saw Mr. Richardson turn to Stephen. His words were muffled, but she read his lips all the same. "I want this sorted out by the end of April. And see what you can do about reaching out to the other playhouses about temp work that may line up. This town's too small for a bunch of actors cooling their heels for three months."

And with that he rested the fedora back on his head.

Theodore stopped beside her. He leaned in, whispered low in her ear, "Wipe that look off your face, fair fairy. If anyone's a shoo-in for the next show, it'll be you."

Bree leaned back, looking into his eyes with the question in hers. The question, however, got no answer.

"Off to lunch then, Theo?" Mr. Richardson called. "The salmon's not going to eat itself."

Bree felt a quick, subtle squeeze of her hand before he left her to fall into step beside Mr. Richardson.

There were so many things Bree wanted to say as she watched them walk out into the gravel parking lot. But the tingle on the tips of her fingers as his hand left hers, the settling realization of the new situation at hand, the sudden Hunger Games stares as the remaining cast members warily watched each other—it was all a bit much for a witty retort.

Because there was a most unfortunate thing that Theodore did not know about her.

After a lifetime of jumping from hobby to hobby, job to job, Bree had learned a great many skills. Ask her to scuba dive with sharks, whip up a four-tiered cake, or hand dip a colonial-times wax candle, and she was your gal. But there was one activity that had never crossed her path.

One thing she most *certainly* couldn't learn to do within five weeks.

Tap dancing.

Chapter 6

CHIP

Chip couldn't go over and help.

He didn't have time.

If anyone needed help, it was *him*. Right now he had no working toilet and a damaged subfloor in the bathroom. Right now, any time nature called, Chip found himself driving down the street to a gas station—even at midnight.

He had problems of his own. The priority here was clear.

Chip stood under the light of his own porch in the crisp, mid-March air, determined not to look at the elderly woman across the street hobbling from her parked car toward her door. Everything about her small brick ranch was lightless. Every one of her four visible windows, the shadowy line of her slanted sidewalk, the petite stoop. Two grocery bags swung from her arm as she shakily grabbed the railing and began to ascend.

He looked down at the circular saw in his hand and the

plywood between the sawhorses at his feet, then back toward the woman across the street. Why wouldn't her porch light come on? Why, in a week and a half, had it never come on?

Was the bulb burned out?

Did she not flick the switch up before leaving?

The woman stopped at the screen door and began digging in her purse.

He'd watched her do this the other night too. It took a painstaking five minutes to find her keys, and when she finally did, it felt like she spent half an hour trying to find the lock and turn the knob.

He dropped his gaze to the measured line on his board. He considered pulling the trigger and starting the saw. He glanced up again.

Still rooting in her purse.

He glanced at the board again. Set the saw down.

"Mrs. Lewis!" he called, stepping off his porch and then jogging across the street.

She looked up at the sound of her name and watched him until he reached the bottom of her steps.

"I can't help noticing." He pointed up above her head. "Is something wrong with your light?"

Mrs. Lewis, still holding the key, blinked a few times. Apparently she wasn't used to men approaching her in the twilight of eight thirty.

"My light?" She turned back to the door. Craned her head upward. "Oh, yes, I've had trouble with that light for a few months now."

"Would you . . . care if I take a look?" He gave her an easy smile. "I do know my way around a light switch."

She flapped her hand dismissively. "Oh, honey, I see you out there working. I know you do." If he didn't know better, he'd say he heard a bit of teasing in her voice. She turned toward the door. "Just let me . . . get us inside here . . . and—"

"Here." Chip slipped his phone out of his pocket and turned on the flashlight.

With the knob illuminated, it took but a moment to get the lock turned and them both inside the tiny foyer. Mrs. Lewis turned the living-room lights on and began walking toward the kitchen with her bags.

Chip turned toward the row of switches by the door.

"It's the far left one. Can I get you something?" Mrs. Lewis's voice carried from the kitchen. He heard a refrigerator opening. "Tea?"

Chip flicked the switch three or four times. Nothing.

"No thanks," he called back, then stepped outside to get a closer look. "Have you tried a new bulb?"

"A neighbor tried a few weeks ago," she called back. "No luck."

He frowned. "I'm going to grab some tools from my truck. Can you direct me toward your basement?"

When his attempts at a quick fix tripped the breaker twice, Chip knew he'd be spending the rest of the evening working in Mrs. Lewis's house, running a new circuit from the panel to the light fixture.

Well. Who needed indoor plumbing anyway?

After three more polite refusals of tea, coffee, and crumb cake, he was in the basement, halfway into removing the existing wire from the 20-amp breaker.

He heard the front door creak on its hinges and muffled voices upstairs.

Mrs. Lewis said, "I don't care how much trouble the sequined body suits are giving you, Evie. It's our spades night. If you want to work on costumes, you should address it on the fridge calendar. Honestly, it's like you don't respect the schedule at all."

Chip paused in unscrewing the panel.

The hardwood floor above squeaked. "Mrs. Lewis, tell Evie she can't sneak off to her basement to work." He knew that muffled voice. He'd know it in his sleep.

Mrs. Lewis spoke. "She's right, my dear Evie. Work your fingers to the nub, and you won't have any fingers left to be my partner. Not that it makes a difference, as we'll lose either way."

Evie grunted.

He knew it was Evie, because the first time he heard that grunt he'd thought it came from a wild animal. But no, it was just Evie, sulking and grunting as Bree dragged her into the passenger seat of her car for work most mornings.

Bree and Evie were quite the odd couple. Fascinating. But odd.

A new voice spoke up, just as the rhythmic *thud-thud, thud-thud-thud* of a tapping foot came from above the joist a few feet to the left. "Forget spades. Can we talk a minute about how I'm going to *lose my job*?"

"C'mon, guys! Listen to you all!" Bree interjected with all the spirit of a football coach down at half. "It's game night! Where's your spirit? Where's your pinazz?"

"It's at the Barter," the woman with the tapping foot replied, "where I also left my hope for a living wage and a bright future."

"Birdie," Bree said, "you've got the face of an angel and the toes of Ginger Rogers. You've been tapping for three days straight, though, so if you don't sit down and rest your feet this instant, *I will pin you down and sit on you*. Evie, I brought you General Tso's chicken. If you want it, you will have to do what normal people do and *have conversations.* With other human beings. Away from the basement. And Mrs. Lewis, you're the most positive person in the group right now, so if I lose you, too, I'll lose everyone. Tell ya what, tonight we'll take nil off the table."

"Nil!" Birdie protested. Her tapping foot stopped. "But that's my only skill! You know how badly I overbid otherwise."

"Just give in now and cut the deck, Birdie," Mrs. Lewis said. "I've known Bree since she was a little girl, and I've never seen her lose her argument when she put her mind to it. She once convinced her grandmother, God rest her soul, to take her out to the flea market, and they came back with a pet flying squirrel."

"Nana loved Puddles," he heard Bree say defensively.

"Of course, dear. And Puddles—aptly named for all those puddles it left around her poor house, if I remember correctly—running off through that open window the week you left for school was entirely coincidental."

The conversation continued as Chip gave the screw one more turn and the wire slipped out from the panel.

A moment later, Birdie spoke and his ears perked.

"I just can't imagine why Mr. Richardson would think about remodeling the Barter," she said. "It's absolutely perfect as is. Maybe expand the dressing rooms—convert that empty room into a second dressing room so we won't be so cramped—but the auditorium itself? It's gorgeous."

"Well," Mrs. Lewis said, "Clarence has always been a peculiar fellow. Has been since I taught him back in grade school. He must've had a new lunch box every other week for the whole year, always declaring whatever new color or cartoon figure it had on it was his real favorite. Not that his parents couldn't afford for the boy to have thirty-seven lunchboxes."

"If that's the case, I'm surprised he didn't decide to remodel the place earlier," Bree said.

"He's not going to shut it down to do it, is he?" Birdie said, her tone pitched high. "Surely he would've said so when he told us about changing to *Singin' in the Rain—*"

"He's not going to shut the place down, Birdie," Bree said. "Theo said it would be done during the break between seasons. But I'm sure we'll know everything we can when it hits the paper next week. Let's eat before it all gets cold."

Chip reached down for the wire cutters as the conversation was buried under the clatter of flatware being pulled from a drawer and dishes being placed on the table. So. The Barter was getting a facelift. He could feel the wheels in his brain starting to turn.

Some minutes later, Mrs. Lewis said, "Oh, I forgot about my young man."

There was a pause.

"Your young man . . . ," Bree said, "whom you keep in the basement?"

"Where else would I keep him?" Mrs. Lewis retorted. "You know everything keeps better in a cool, dark place."

Chip smiled to himself as he continued cutting out the wire.

"You doing okay down there?" Mrs. Lewis called from the open door at the top of the stairs.

"Doing just fine," Chip called back, reaching up to snip around the stapled wire.

"Is that—?" Bree's voice lowered to inaudible murmurs.

"Yes, he's come to work on my porch light."

"But . . . he's in the basement."

"Yes, because the problem seems to be a short in the circuit."

Another pause. A rather long pause.

"Should we . . ." Bree dropped her voice again.

The rhythmic *thud-thud-thud* began again. "How can you be sitting here, Bree, talking about food and spades and men in basements? I honestly haven't slept in three days."

"It's all very simple, Birdie. I can't tap-dance. I have accepted the fact that I can't tap-dance. So I'm going to find another job."

Even through thick layers of hardwood, subfloor, and floor joists, he heard the gasp. "Find another job?" Birdie exclaimed. "You can't *leave* and *find another job.*"

"Sure I can. My half of the bills are cheap—right, dearie?"

Evie gave her patented grunt. The crinkling of bags, along with the sound of several chairs scraping against the floor, told him they had all sat down with their food.

"But who will sit with me at dress rehearsals?" Birdie sounded desperate. "Who will whisper stories to me when we're stuck sitting on logs for hours listening to Titania drone on about 'thee amiable flower beds' and 'thy coy cheeks,' and I'm falling asleep *onstage*? Who will make sure I don't fall off my log and *get fired*?"

"Hey, guys?" Evie spoke up. "Where's my General Tso's?"

After the crinkling of more bags, Bree replied, "Shoot. They've forgotten the spring rolls too."

"I'll go—" Evie began.

"Oh no you won't. There will be no sneaking out of this house, missy. You'll never come back and then we can't play at all."

"Then I can—" Birdie began.

"Shh," Bree said. "And I won't have you sneaking away to go practice. Everybody stay here. Mrs. Lewis, use whatever force necessary to keep them here. By golly, ladies, we are going to *have fun* tonight if it's the last thing I do."

Chip listened as the creaks of Bree's footsteps followed her out the door.

So, the Barter sprite was about to be out a job, Chip thought, snipping around a second staple. What kind of job would a girl like that go for next? The town of Abingdon was Hallmark-Christmas-movie-town small, after all. Only so many places would even have openings.

Unless, perhaps, she wasn't opposed to moving? Going elsewhere?

Despite himself, he found his brain scrolling through his contacts in town for any mention of employment opportunities. His mother had said something about needing a new house cleaner, hadn't she? And that someone from the board was frantic because their manager quit and left a restaurant on Main Street to run itself into the ground. Which restaurant was that?

Of course, it didn't matter to him where the woman who'd made his life more difficult lived.

He hadn't started thinking of her as difficult until the issue of the Invisible Fence came up. When Russell began knocking Bree over at her own front door, she had demanded Chip pull out the dough for yet another painfully expensive, unplanned project. And after the money it had cost him to get the water line sorted out, coughing up cash for a buried electrical fence was not an easy thing to do.

But yesterday, two days after he put the line in, Bree started complaining that the fence was on her side of the property line. That she couldn't park and get out of her car without Russell attacking her. That the dog lay in wait for her all day in the tiny grass median between their driveways (that part was true). That she had taken to crawling through her passenger door every time she got in or out of the car (also true, but funny).

At this point he had taken to dodging her when he left in the mornings and sneaking from his truck to his house—once with an actual dive behind the bushes—at night. To any bystanders it would seem he was either a burglar robbing his own home or out of his mind, but it was worth it. He didn't have the money, or the time, to make himself a more neighborly neighbor. Even if, technically, partially, he was to blame.

Wasn't his sister-in-law's bank looking for a teller?

Ten minutes later Chip stood on Mrs. Lewis's porch—phone flashlight nestled between chin and chest as he faced the wall sconce. He was just disconnecting the wire from the wire nuts as the headlights of Bree's car turned into her parking spot. His eyes drifted as he watched her brake lights turn off. Beneath the pale yellow of the streetlight, he watched her long lean leg reach for the pavement as the driver's door cracked open.

My, but she *was* beautiful.

She was wearing black leggings and ratty house shoes that had seen better days. In one of her arms she gripped the take-out bag no doubt containing the missing Chinese food.

What if he was eating Chinese tonight? The thought, the desire, flicked in his thoughts in a heartbeat. An image of him sitting on the back stairs of the Barter with a box in his lap, watching her sit cross-legged on that top step holding chopsticks, that long, burnished red braid of hers carelessly draped over one shoulder. Laughing. Daring.

A dog barked.

He blinked.

Russell swung out of nowhere, his legs racing around her open driver-side door.

Where had he come from?

Bree screamed and threw herself back into the driver's seat, slamming the door just as the dog pounced.

For a moment or two Russell just stood there, propped against Bree's door like a six-foot Frankenstein monster with his paws pressed to the top of her window. Finally he dropped down.

And sat.

He watched Russell's pouty face as the dog stared at her, his nose pressed against the window, his tail wagging ferociously.

Russell licked the window and left one long, steady saliva stream behind.

Chip laughed.

He leaned his forearms against the stoop's rail and watched Bree climb over the gearshift to the passenger seat. With one arm she pushed the passenger door open. Only after one rather unladylike spill onto the safety of her own yard did he openly chuckle at her again.

Bree's head whipped toward him as she scrambled to standing, the takeout swinging wildly on her wrist. She pulled a leaf from her sweater. Then her hair.

"Your dog is a *menace*," she said, stalking toward him.

"Come now," Chip said, putting his hand on his heart. "Don't say that in front of him. You'll hurt his feelings."

"And that collar *doesn't* work."

"Nonsense. I've checked it every time you've asked me. Every. Single. Time. Which makes, like, fifteen."

She frowned as she stalked up the stairs and stopped on the front porch beside him.

He felt the smile of his eyes crinkling more as he watched her fiery ones. And boy were they fiery. Another dead leaf stuck out from the top of her braid.

Tentatively, he pulled it out.

Bree stiffened.

The world around them went quiet.

His voice was soft. "C'mon. You act as though you've never had a fan before."

Bree's brow furrowed slightly, and he tipped his chin toward Russell.

"He just likes you."

She pressed her lips together but didn't put up much of a fight. "He wants to eat me alive."

"He wants to smother you with kisses. Is that the worst thing in the world?"

There was another pause.

His eyes flickered to her lips, and he snapped them up when he realized what he'd done.

Heat climbed up his neck as he stepped back.

Chip cleared his throat.

He felt something hit the top of his shoes and glanced down. "Um, you may want to do something about that."

Bree blinked, then saw the sauce dripping out the bottom of her bag. "Shoot." Cupping her hand beneath it, she stepped back. Sauce dripped onto her palm as she pushed the door open. "Chicken emergency, coming through!" she called, dashing through the living room, past the group of sitting women, and into the kitchen.

For a wild moment he felt the urge to follow her but then stopped. Looked down at the tops of his sauce-laden shoes. Pulled the door shut.

He didn't belong in there. With her.

He *shouldn't* want to belong in there. With her.

At the very least, he didn't *want* to want to belong in there.

In fact . . .

He tapped a text to Ashleigh before settling his phone back in his pocket: What do you think about lunch tomorrow?

He smiled when her positive response came back two minutes later.

For the next two hours, though, he couldn't help turning an ear toward the raucous laughter and shrill cries as the women's spades game turned into what appeared to be the competition of the century. As he walked along the basement concrete, following the path of the old wire, filling in the space with new, he listened to Birdie's complaints and Bree's consolations. As he used the push rod to get the wire from the basement up into the stud cavity, he grinned at how hard Bree worked to draw Evie into the conversation. As he shut the panel, he noticed the volume of Mrs. Lewis's laughter at Bree's jokes. Bree was the glue of that group. Whether they realized it or not, she had single-handedly brought them all a little magic that night.

Upstairs, he flicked on the light and shut the front door softly. "Not too shabby, Green Fairy," he murmured. The new porch light radiated but for a small smudge on the glass. He leaned in, rubbed it off with the cuff of his jacket, settled back again.

He picked up his tool bag and stuck one hand in his pocket as he jogged down the stairs.

At another burst of laughter inside the house, an idea popped into his head. He pivoted from his path to his front steps to his truck.

He stopped at the rear. Pulled down the tailgate. Hopped into the bed of the truck and dug around.

Pulled out a Frisbee.

Grabbed a Sharpie from his bag and scribbled a hasty note on the disc.

He set the Frisbee on the hood of Bree's car before turning to go inside.

♡♡♡

Funny thing about women. When you take them out on a first date, the conversation bounces along nicely from topic to topic like a stick bouncing off the slats of a fence as you drag it along, or a playing card flicking against the spokes of a bicycle wheel as it spins.

How many siblings do you have? Terrific! I have three sisters too!

You hate sushi? Me too.

No, I've never been to Europe, but it's always been a dream of mine, ever since . . .

But for Chip, the questions soon turned to the subject of his work, which for the past fifteen years had always been the same. Construction. Really, for a McBride boy, there was no other option. Every Abingdon girl he'd taken on a date knew the facts of his family background well in advance. Any riveted expression just showed him how well his potential future girlfriend could lie.

Folding her hands softly together and resting them under her delicate chin?

Lying.

Leaning forward with fluttering mascara-laden lashes as though what he just told her was positively *fascinating*?

Lying.

And some of the words that came out of their mouths as they tried to relate . . . frankly, it was comical.

"You are joking!" one had said with a tinkling laugh. "You

know, just the other day I was breaking out my tile saw for a little she-shed project I was doing on the bathroom—"

"I'm not entirely sure what a she-shed is," Chip had interjected, setting down his wine.

She had shrugged. "Oh, you know, just a little shed for gals. Like to hold all your little crafting and sewing projects."

He remembered how distinctly his brow rose. "You sew?"

"Ha-ha-ha!" She laughed as though he had said something completely outrageous. "No. Anyways, I was on my way up the stairs—"

"I don't think sheds typically have bathrooms. Or second floors."

"And I tripped on the new hardwood floors—"

He had put up his hand. "I'm not entirely sure we have the same definition of a shed here. We might need to back up—"

"And realized those steps were entirely too narrow!" Her eyes had twinkled at his, like she had just shared an inside joke between handymen. "So now I'm having to go back and do it all over again, but it's going to take me ages to find the right repurposed barn wood. Maybe if we happened to go together . . ."

This was Ashleigh. As it turned out, Ashleigh had no idea what to do with a tile saw. And after a revealing conversation he had with her sister weeks later, Chip discovered Ashleigh had shipped the saw to her house fourteen hours before their first date.

Just so they could have a conversation piece.

Ashleigh really did have a "she-shed" (with a full kitchen and two bedrooms) in the backyard of her "little bungalow" (with five bedrooms and three baths). He would have called them something else, but who was he to quibble over definitions with his girlfriend?

College students occasionally knocked on her door asking to rent out that she-shed.

His beautiful, elegant, family-friendly girlfriend carried enough charm in this town for the both of them. At the moment, his girlfriend also happened to be standing with her cream-colored heels firmly on the threshold, her eyes scanning his gutted living room as though expecting the floor to collapse at any moment.

Chip set down the pry bar he was using to peel the baseboards away from the wall.

"Ashleigh, are you sure you don't want to come inside?"

"I am inside," she answered, her arms crossed over her chest. She looked pointedly down to her shoes, and he did too.

"Yes, well, would you like to come more than one inch inside? I could turn on the space heater."

"Oh, I'm not cold," she replied in an upbeat tone, though her shoulders visibly tensed at the sound of a creak upstairs. "I like the fresh air."

"It's thirty degrees."

"I'm warm-blooded."

"You're shivering."

She looked down at her slim forearms, lined with goose bumps, as though they weren't hers. She began rubbing them furiously.

He sighed and reached for a towel. It was only 5:00 p.m. He had planned on getting in roughly three hours of work before their dinner reservation—hoped to, with a little luck, have the wall down.

"How about we just head over to 128 Pecan now? I could do with a meal anyways." He cast a glance back to the inoperable oven and the cellophane-wrapped stainless-steel range beside it. It'd been days since he'd had a hot meal.

"Don't be silly," she replied with a smile. "I'm fine, Chip. Really. I said I wanted to see your work-in-progress and I meant it." She bit her lip. "And I would be all for helping with that"—she paused, looking at his pry bar—"plier, too, if I had remembered to change out of these clothes." She looked down at her creamy pencil skirt like it was an obstinate toddler and shrugged. "But I am loving what you are doing with the place," she added, and ventured to unlock her arms to prove her point. She put her hands on her hips, then thought twice and put one on the doorframe, then decided it was better not to touch anything and leaned with her shoulder.

"I wouldn't," Chip said quickly. "That frame is still a bit unsteady."

She jumped back into her pencil-straight formation.

While he moved to the kitchen, she spoke louder. "I can see you've gotten a lot done already. What with the new windows and cabinets and"—there was a pause—"this clean floor in here. So spotless. I can hardly see any dirt."

He glanced back to see her squinting at several dust particles highlighted by the setting sun. Her arms stiffened at her sides as she resisted shooing them off.

Either Ashleigh really loved him or she was one of those girls who really, *really* wanted to get married. He hadn't figured out which.

Honestly, both ideas were a bit too scary to examine.

He flicked on the faucet and the icy water nearly froze his hands.

One nice thing about Ashleigh was that she did try. This construction stuff was about as far out of her wheelhouse as Kate Spade was from his, and yet she made the effort to visit him, to compliment him. To pick up terms here and there so she could use them to say things like, "That tankless water heater was a great choice for Jim and Tara's home, Chip. And the way you got it to work with that flex hose . . ."

He had to give her credit; if there was one thing a man loved, it was getting a little self-esteem boost from a woman who took his work seriously.

Two days ago, when Chip had told Ashleigh the news that the Barter was about to open bids for a major renovation, she was nothing but supportive, overwhelmed with excitement. They'd spent the whole evening talking strategy. It didn't matter to her that his father—king of Abingdon construction—was going to be his competition. Or that the eccentric Mr. Richardson was the illogical sort of fellow who had once bought up and renovated an entire row of dilapidated houses simply because they made his wife sad when she drove by.

Chip could almost feel like these facts didn't matter to him either. Almost.

Yes, he was coming to realize a supportive woman was one of the best things a man could have in life.

Enthusiasm.

Kindness.

Respect—

"You've gotta *move* that fence."

Chip swiveled around to see all six feet of his neighbor standing in the doorway beside Ashleigh and shaking a pointed finger at him. Bree's hair was in more of a strangled bun than usual, and she wore a gigantic deep-blue alpine parka with what appeared to be muddy bear-claw marks down the length of the coat. Ashleigh was clutching her chest and leaning into the rickety doorframe as though the deranged woman was the greater danger.

Which, to be fair, was probably true.

Bree—or possibly just Bree's humongous coat—pushed Ashleigh aside as she marched toward him.

"You move that fence. Or I'm going to move *your house*."

It was hard at the moment to decide what to do. Part of him wanted to laugh hysterically, and part of him felt the smile slipping off his face. He turned off the water.

"How exactly do you plan to move my house?"

"And can we talk about the Frisbee for a second?" Bree said, breezing past his question. "Because, honestly"—she whipped the disc up next to her crazy eyes—"giving your neighbor a Frisbee with the instructions to 'roll down your window and throw it as far as you can before you step out of your car' is not a real solution to my problem here. And for the record, it also *doesn't work*." She motioned to her muddied coat, enunciating each word. "As. You. Can. See."

His smile wilted.

He had meant the offering to be a playful joke, even hoped it might represent a clean slate. Honestly, he figured Russell's overenthusiastic greetings toward Bree would have calmed down by now. The dog wasn't trying to maul her. He just *loved* her. Like, really, *really* loved her. If she could just understand, pet the dog a little, Russell would calm down . . .

"Do you know he's watching me all night now?" Bree's eyes narrowed. "All. Night?"

Chip laughed. "No, he's not. He sleeps in my room—"

"At the foot of your bed," she continued. "Sitting on that blue sleeping bag of yours. Staring at me through the window. Every time I open my eyes, he's watching."

He watched her for a few moments. Waiting for her to blink.

She didn't.

"Um." Chip swallowed. One glance to Ashleigh confirmed he would be getting curtains from her in the next hour. "Ashleigh, I want you to meet my next-door neighbor. Bree. Bree. Ashleigh."

Bree's eyes stayed on Chip as she nodded. "Hello."

"Hello," Ashleigh replied.

Chip put up a finger. "Shall we not overlook the fact that this means *you* look into *my* room all night? 'Staring'?"

It was disconcerting. A little bit intriguing. But also disconcerting.

She threw her hands in the air. "It's different! You know what I mean!"

On the second floor, Russell began scratching against the hardwood. Then came the sound of a tornado blowing down the stairs.

Bree ran toward Chip, grabbed him by the shoulders, and threw herself behind him.

From under the hood she had pulled over her head, her muffled voice cried out, "See! See! The murder dog wants me!"

Ignoring Ashleigh, Russell hit the bottom stairs and skidded across the floor toward Bree like a kid in ice skates. Even from a distance, Chip could see the foot-long drool on both sides of his slackened jaw. Chip squatted, and when Russell was just hitting the kitchen, he pounced.

He struggled mightily with Russell's collar as he moved toward the door to the back porch. "That's it, boy. Time for a nice run, huh? A nice"—Chip struggled to push the door open—"long"—the door opened, and he used every muscle in his body to push the dog outside. He slammed the door and turned. Chip put his hands on his hips, smiling at his success. "Run."

Russell's huge body lunged against the door. It quaked.

Chip turned the lock.

He heaved a sigh and turned back around. "There. Now. Where were we?"

What he saw when he turned around, however, was not a woman. It was a ball, a giant blue ball on the floor beside the unfinished cabinets, a jumble of downy, deep-blue quilting.

He stepped closer.

The ball didn't move.

He squatted next to it.

"Um . . . Bree?"

Nothing.

"Hey. Bree."

He reached out with tentative fingers and touched the ball's surface.

Bree exploded out of her defensive crouch. Her eyes were as fiery as he'd ever seen them. "I want that fence moved. You put it on my side and I *need that fence moved.*"

Her voice had taken a desperate turn.

He sighed. Rubbed the stubble of his chin.

It was time to get real.

"Do you know what you're asking? It took me a full day to get the fence installed." He motioned to the rooms around him, all empty but for the bare essentials. "And look around. Does it look to you like I have the time or money to dig up the driveway, *again*, to move it a couple of feet?" He stepped over to the light switch and flipped it up and down. Of course, it did nothing. "What's more important here: running electricity or having a fence moved twelve inches?"

"The fence moved twelve inches," she answered.

He paused, seeing the lack of sympathy in her eyes.

Ashleigh still stood in the doorway, holding out her phone. She pointed to it as if to say, *Just give the nod. I can have the police here in five.*

He glanced back to Bree. As with all things regarding his new neighbor these past weeks, he was going to have to do this the hard way.

He tried once more to pull a little understanding from her. "Honestly, Bree. It's just a dog."

"Just a dog who is trying to kill me."

"Look," Chip began. "I know it may not be convenient"—her brows rose and he forged on—"but technically, that fence *is* within the bounds of my property. And he needs that space. As you are well aware, my lot doesn't grant much yard as it is. What am I supposed to do, move it over so he can have five feet to roam in? He's practically five feet long himself!"

"I'm well aware of his size," she said, pointing to the dried mud marks on the shoulders of her parka. "But if you're so keen on him having some space, you should find him another house to live in."

Russell barked.

They both jolted as the door shook.

"Give me twenty-four hours, Chip." Bree leveled her gaze. "I'll find him a place to roam."

Ashleigh was starting to whimper, her fingers hovering over the phone's screen.

Chip looked from Ashleigh to Bree, to the porch door, and back again. There would be no winning here. The Invisible Fence was hard enough to put in, what with pulling up the yard, and avoiding a dead phone line straight from the sixties . . .

A phone line. A dead little phone line, straight from the sixties.

And she, little Barter actress with no construction knowledge, wanted so desperately to have the fence moved.

The Barter.

"You want the line moved so bad?" He straightened, a smile forming as he put out his hand to shake. "Fine. Let's make a deal."

Chapter 7
BREE

If Chip thought he was going to get anything out of Bree, he was in for a rude awakening.

That being said, it brought her unspeakable joy to sit cross-legged on her inflated donut on the gravel supervising as he broke into the dirt with his shovel.

"So, give me everything you got on Mr. Richardson," Chip said, pulling his shovel back with a load. "Everything. Where he likes to eat, what his hobbies are. What he gave the cast for Christmas presents. Everything."

Bree crossed her ankles and plastered on the patented sweet, innocent grin that had landed her every one of her jobs. She tried not to look at Russell, who lay at the edge of the line on the other side of the car, panting and staring at her.

"Oh, what can I say? There's just so much." She pressed her finger to her chin and tapped it twice in thoughtful musing.

In exchange for his moving the fence line, she had agreed to give him inside information about the Barter heading for a complete renovation. That would've been all well and good, but for the fact her backside was still so sore from the dog's latest tackle that she had to carry around one of those pillows for people recovering from tailbone surgery. She *wanted* to be helpful, but Evie had been so fond of her new wannabe-minimalist lifestyle that she had "forgotten" to pay the water bill the same day a truck delivered twelve empty barrels for their "new rainwater harvesting system." This was followed by Evie's enthusiastic lecture on how they could "forgo drinking recycled pharmaceutical pills and sewage and instead live on the crystal clean water from the sky."

There had been a pamphlet.

There were also red circles on their fridge calendar, dates when Evie was planning to cut things out of her life she had owned or paid for since before Bree moved in: the television, the dishwasher, the rugs, all plastic Tupperware . . .

So, forgive her, but Bree just couldn't summon up the energy to be "helpful." This was about the insanity this man had so cheerfully brought into her life. The way that he chuckled at her demise. The way he acted as though she just took life too seriously.

Too seriously?

Bree Leake of all people most emphatically did *not* take life too seriously. She was the epitome of easygoing. Her middle *name* was easygoing. Two years ago, when she'd spontaneously hopped on a Greyhound for a round trip to California just to see a West Coast sunrise, every one of the passengers called her Miss Sunshine.

Miss. Easygoing. Sunshine.

She sensed her eyes grow a bit stormy just looking at him. Thunder grumbled in the distance.

To some degree, that's what really irked her in all this. Easygoing was a part of her identity, yet this man riled her up. The whole Leake family crammed inside her parents' house over Christmas, and what did she do while her stepsiblings grumbled about having to share a bedroom with their toddlers? Snagged a blanket and said, "No big deal, guys. I'll just hunker down on the rug." Whenever Stephen forced the cast to stay late just to nail down one scene? "Sure. No prob, Boss," was Bree's response while everyone else onstage moaned.

One day her tenth-grade teacher said the dictionary definition of *easygoing* was simply this: "Bree Leake."

Miss Easygoing.

And here this man waltzed in, pulling out her very identity from beneath her as though she didn't deserve it.

But really, no matter how relaxed a girl was, there came a time when enough was enough. That moment came two mornings ago, at 9:36 a.m., when he reached down a hand to help her up from Russell's latest tackle. She'd wiped the saliva slime out of her eyes and she saw it: those big brown eyes batting back tears of mirth.

That was the moment she snapped.

And now? Now her number-one goal was to get him to fix the fence line while providing him with the least useful information possible.

Bree adjusted the inflated pillow beneath her tailbone. "Well, here is what I do know: Mr. Richardson is fairly bald. And short," Bree said.

Chip paused in his shoveling. "Short."

"Mm-hmm."

"How short?"

"Oh, shorter than the average man. But definitely taller than some others." She paused at his frown. "Think . . . LeBron James."

His brow rose.

"Minus a foot or two."

He set his foot on the shovel. "A foot. *Or two.* Right. Where's he go around here to eat?"

"Why—are you planning to stalk him?"

He grinned. "I've got a business approximately four weeks old, and I'm working out of an empty bedroom. So, yeah, maybe. I'll do whatever it takes."

Bree started to lean forward, then winced and straightened. "And how exactly is that going to work? You're just going to slip your business card in his wineglass?"

"I was thinking butter plate, but something like that."

"Oh good. And I suppose your girlfriend will do the distracting. With her looks she'll make the perfect accomplice."

There was more of an edge in her tone than she'd meant to convey. Bree shut her mouth. Chip opened his but then shut it again.

"So . . . back to Mr. Richardson," he said.

Bree's shoulders eased.

She paused for a moment, then lifted her finger as though stumbling across something of vital importance. "I'll tell you one thing. I've never seen him eating chicken. Or steak."

She also hadn't ever seen him eat anything, but she wasn't about to get tangled in technicalities.

His brow furrowed. "What, like, he's a vegetarian?"

It was sad, really. You could practically see the wheels inside his head churning, flipping through his mental yellow pages for vegetarian restaurants in town.

She pointed at the ground. "Are you digging?"

He raised a brow. "Are you answering?"

"Yes," she replied promptly, and he flung more dirt. "He is definitely a vegetarian . . . unless I'm incorrect . . . which is a tiny, infinitesimal possibility."

"Right." He dug farther down the line, then paused, eyeing her. "So he's a vegetarian, unless he's not."

Bree nodded fervently. "Exactly. You got it."

He waited a moment.

Then two.

Then he pushed the shovel into the sodden ground.

Resting one boot on the blade, he wiped his perfectly clear, sweatless forehead. "Well I'm beat." He clapped his hands together. "Sun's going down. I'd say this is enough for today."

"Wait. What?"

He turned around and whistled. "Russ! Who wants to go for a walk?"

Russell jumped up.

Bree's eyes widened. "No, no. You don't need to—"

Chip reached down for the dog's collar. "Now let's just get this nasty collar off you, buddy. Can't be going on a walk when it's trying to zap you." He gave Russell's side a hearty rub. "How about we try for some of that free-range walking we talked about, too, huh? You don't need an old leash holding you back."

"You keep the leash," Bree said. "Leashes are good."

Chip arched his head back to flash her a smile. "You know, Evie is the one who enlightened me about leashes being a form of animal cruelty. Limiting them in their natural habitat—"

"We live in a cul-de-sac, Chip. In a suburb—"

"Denying his primal right to yield to his desire to roam the land—"

"*I* am his desire. He desires nothing but *me*."

Chip winked. "That must feel good. Doesn't it?"

Bree stiffened.

He wouldn't do it.

She was sitting on a plastic doughnut. Surely he wouldn't do it.

Darn him, his hand actually started to slip the shock collar over Russell's head.

Bree put up a finger. "Now hold on just a minute. Let's not be so hasty," she said, pushing herself up. She jutted her chin toward her front porch, then back to the impatient dog. She'd never make it in time. "I can think of loads more to say about Mr. Richardson while you work."

Chip raised his brow, but the collar kept sliding across the dog's fur. "I don't know. It's been a long day for both of us. You're tired . . . I'm tired . . ."

"No, really! Loads of stuff." Russell pawed the grass while Bree bent to snatch up her cushion. "Like . . ." She tried to think. "Like . . . like how he always wears a fedora."

He lowered his brow. "C'mon, Bree. We both know that's not news."

"And he goes everywhere with his wife."

Russell yelped, then turned his neck as though to yank off the collar himself.

"And . . ." She racked her brain. "And . . ."

And then something surprising happened. Mr. Richardson's face came to mind along with the last words she heard him speak before she retreated from the gala weeks ago.

Huh.

Well. Well. Well.

A smile crept up her lips.

Bingo.

"Actually," she said, her voice rising, "as it just so happens, I do know something about the bid. Something important."

Suddenly Russell knocking her over and officially breaking her tailbone no longer mattered so much. Now, armed with truly valuable information, she felt confident enough to shift her weight to one hip as she crossed her arms without a care in the world.

Chip must've known it too, because he started tugging the collar back down, the wry grin on his face melting at her victorious smirk.

His teasing tone dropped. "What do you know?"

The dog started nudging his knees.

"Oh, you know. *Things.*" Bree turned on her heel.

She walked through the yard and opened the screen door.

"What do you know?" he called after her.

The thrill of knowing she had something, *something*, over that man was worth a dozen dog knockdowns.

"Bree. Please."

She halted. There was something about the way her name came from his lips. It triggered an odd eruption of emotions so tangled she could hardly unravel them. Irritation, defiance, the complete and utter joy of winning, of course, but almost . . . No, she must've misunderstood herself. There was no possible way she had felt . . . a flutter.

She turned with her hand on the handle. Frowned.

And yet there it was again, as she met his brown eyes. The wrinkle across his typically smooth, carefree forehead. The tautness of his shirt against his chest as he inhaled and then paused, holding his breath for her answer.

She could win right now. Walk inside and slam that door shut behind her. *Win.*

Maybe in her older years she would think back on this moment and fondly recall the irrepressible joy as she shut the door and watched his face fall. She would laugh to herself, alone in a rocking chair, while she imagined him somewhere small and seedy, driven mad after years of wondering just what secret she refused to share. A lonely, bitter old man in his own rocking chair somewhere—

She shook her head.

She was really losing it.

"You get this fence moved by midnight, and I'll tell you."

He started to reply and she threw up a hand to stop him.

"Midnight. Not one millisecond past."

And just to prove to herself she still had some guts in her, she slammed the screen door behind her.

She pushed the front door shut and immediately began pacing the length of the eight-by-eleven-foot rug.

Lifting her gaze to the window, she saw Chip shoveling down the median, pulling up the narrow line of soil. His arms worked swiftly now, muscles working with such seamless rhythm the action seemed second nature. As though he'd been shoveling, and hammering, and wearing that slim-fitting, holey long-sleeve shirt all his life.

He looked up and met her eyes through the window.

There it was again. That flutter.

She practically jumped into the kitchen.

Caffeine.

It was definitely time for caffeine.

Bree walked into the small square kitchen overlooking the Appalachian Mountains. Like everything else in the house, it was dated, black-and-white tiles peeking out from the spaces teal area rugs didn't cover. She reached above the stove for her coffee mug sitting on the open cabinetry and set it beside the sugar jar. She set the percolator in the sink and turned on the tap. Water flowed, though for the first time in days she barely registered the relief she had felt at seeing it rush—ice cold or otherwise—so steadily.

She glanced around the kitchen, at all the articles that were not hers. She'd come to this house with a duffel bag. It'd taken her six months to buy a coffee mug.

Nobody at home had said it, but she knew they thought she wouldn't make it a month beyond Nana's passing before turning tail and heading home. They didn't think she had it in her to stay away from Gatlinburg. They also didn't think she had it in her to stick with her job. Why would they? She had never worked long at any one place before. Now, it seemed, the choice to leave the Barter was taken before she had the chance to run.

Bree rubbed her toe against the thick mat in front of the sink still filled with yesterday's dishes. The dishwasher had gone last Thursday, because Bree didn't get a say, because she didn't technically own it, because Evie had oh so conveniently bought it herself after Nana died.

The window of the kitchen door seemed to flash at her, a siren luring her to peek through. Just to see, for a moment, what that bizarre reaction was when she'd looked at him. Just to see if it would happen again.

Because of course, that was all it was. An experiment.

Against the unruly, rude-through-his-charm neighbor. Who had a girlfriend.

She took another step, the fibers soft against her bare feet.

Another.

She reached the window and ever so casually glanced out.

His hedges were directly opposite.

She inched her gaze left.

And the cars.

Left farther.

And the dumb dog.

Left farther.

And there he was, shoveling, half the median overturned. Him and his perfectly unkempt-yet-kempt hair, and that holey shirt of his.

As if sensing her, he started to look up, and she turned on her heel.

The percolator light turned on, and she poured the steaming coffee in her mug. The clock on the stove said it was 7:02 p.m. The sun's last beams filtered through the window, and she watched it melt into the blue hue of the Blue Ridge Mountains. She frowned as the pink clouds started to dim.

Abingdon was still new to her. She had less than a bicycle to her name and was as valuable as a mannequin onstage—and even that was being ripped away. Her housemate was becoming an off-the-grid junkie, a maniacal dog wanted to kill her, and a taunting, handsome-yet-maddening neighbor lived twenty feet away. She should leave now.

She could.

She could leave the house to Evie and get out now.

Her fingers slid across the laminate counter as she watched the sky.

Even now, though, she could hear Nana's words in her ear. Feel the press of her hugs, the smell of oatmeal-raisin cookies wafting from the old stove right where she stood the first time

Nana met her as an eleven-year-old stepgranddaughter. She could smell the incoming rain swirling from those clouds hanging over the Blue Ridge Mountains. See them both slipping on rain boots to splash in the puddles that came. Her eyes drifted to the umbrella stand where the old, frayed polka-dot umbrella of her childhood still stood beside Nana's tattered one.

She didn't want to get rid of it.

She never would get rid of it.

Nana's love still lived in this home. Though Bree had merged with her stepfather's family at the ripe age of eleven, and Nana had a dozen full-blooded grandkids, Bree had never felt like anything besides Nana's own granddaughter. Bree had taken to her more than any of the others. Partly because they were so similar. Partly because, unlike the other grandkids, she never took Nana for granted. And partly, she suspected, because Nana had known what it was like to merge with the unconditional love of another family.

Some kids went to camp in the summer. But Bree? Here was where she went. Even through her teen years, this was where she always went.

How could she ever let this place, these memories, go?

Her throat stung, and she swallowed a sip of coffee to force it away. She gave the old laminate a final tap.

Okay then. New plan.

She just had to figure out a new job. Yes, a new job. If she wanted to stay in Abingdon, in this wonderful old house, then that was exactly what she needed.

Bree walked back into the living room with purpose, armed with her laptop. She looked around and suspected their furnishings were disappearing a little at a time, as Evie had taken to quipping,

"If it's made of plastic, it's not fantastic," and "Empty the home, fill the heart," from her latest book, *Minimalist Life for Dummies.* She toted things to their overflowing trash can daily; neighbors were starting to rummage at night like raccoons. Evie seemed to be missing a vital point in the minimalist lifestyle, though, because as each frying pan and dining room chair headed out the door, the UPS man brought packages of books and essential oils and beekeeping starter kits and other "minimalist essentials" now piling up in corners.

Bree moved to the couch (which she had dragged back from the street, twice) and set her laptop on her knees. She opened her browser and double-clicked on a familiar desktop document.

The List.

She had created The List three years ago, two months after her thirtieth birthday, when Cassie and her mother banded together to convince Bree to visit a career counselor.

She'd learned a lot in those three sessions. One of the lessons was to write everything down. Master the résumé, keep track of the job history, and see what sort of pattern unfolded.

Tonight she would take a fresh look at the document, pull together a direction, and go. She just needed inspiration.

If losing her job wasn't inspiration, she didn't know what was.

She skimmed down the list. First there was the apprentice job at Fanny's Floral on March 12. Had she known about her lily allergy, honestly, she'd definitely, probably, still be there today. But when the opportunity came to try the corporate life—wearing the pencil skirts, drinking from Starbucks cups at staff meetings—she switched to the paper company mid-April. It wasn't long before she realized there was a difference between the corporate life in the movies and the corporate life in Gatlinburg, at Nationwide

Paper, at a desk smaller than the ones from high school. Worse, the pencil skirts made her claustrophobic. Girls had to be out of their minds to voluntarily lock themselves into thigh corsets and make themselves completely vulnerable in the event of a bear attack. In Gatlinburg, you really had to think about these things.

On impulse she glanced toward the window, but all she saw was the dusky light reflecting off of her car. And the dog, of course, staring.

She scooted a foot to the right.

After the paper company she started taking the advice of the career counselor and wrote down what she'd learned she wanted or didn't want from each experience. So, having learned the corporate life wasn't for her, she jumped to the other side of the line. Hence the arcade supervisor job at Dollywood that started in May. And the lifeguard job at Dollywood's Splash Country through the summer. And the valet attendant, cabin inspector, pool server, and brief spell as a wax-candle store manager. Those stints carried her up to Christmas, when she took a hiatus from Dollywood life to experience the magic of childhood as a seasonal elf for Big Buck's Pros. Unfortunately, it only took two ten-hour shifts in jingly slippers to realize the attractive guy who'd hired her was probably not a real elf who was going to fall in love with her and take her to the North Pole on holidays. She never saw him again.

She felt that neck-tingling sense that somebody was watching her and lifted her head. The dog, positioned to see straight through the center of her window, panted and licked up some straying drool.

Chip was in her field of vision, too, this time. He nudged the dog to move and dug into the earth. Her gaze lingered as he shoveled three loads of dirt.

She cleared her throat.

Flicked her eyes back to the computer, read a few more lines, and looked up again. No more Chip. Dog still staring.

She scooted a foot to the left.

For several more minutes she read, jobs and descriptions trailing down page after page, head lifting sporadically to move her position left or right out of the dog's line of sight, her eyes glancing on occasion to Chip. Just to see how the fence was coming along.

Had it started to rain?

She squinted. Yes, it was raining now, and the raindrops made Chip's hair slick up and out like he was in a boy band. Which was ridiculous in a way, but also . . .

The raindrops dripped down his face, following the vein on the side of his neck before melting into his long-sleeved shirt.

No.

Ab-so-lute-ly not.

She stood to refill her mug as he started yanking out the orange wire.

She was *not* interested in that man.

She'd be out of her mind if she was interested in *that* man.

For that matter, it wasn't even *allowed* to be interested in that irritating, infuriating, unavailable man.

And yet every few minutes for the next hour, she felt her body turning toward the front door.

At every indistinct noise she lifted her head, waiting for the knock on the door. Which was a tough row to hoe, as the house was a hundred years old and creaked every five seconds. But the world out the window had become a curtain of black, and the way he had moved earlier had suggested the project should be done in a matter of minutes, not hours . . .

Yes, any minute he'd be at her door, telling her he'd finished.

She looked back to the bottom of page 7 of The List, her eyes adjusting to the brightness of the screen in the dim lighting of the living room. Kennel assistant (just one word: rabies), nanny (just one word: kids), cookie-dough scooper (the job sounded incredible, but she gained ten pounds in two weeks and started getting tendonitis in her left wrist), part-time bookkeeper, zip-line instructor—

A rap at the door jolted her. She stood.

Bree was at the door before realizing she was approximately five seconds too quick in getting there. After all, he was the one with the deadline. For that matter, she could get herself another cup of coffee and do a few pushups before answering. Heat up a frozen dinner in the microwave. Go wash her hair. He was at her mercy.

At her mercy. She liked the ring of that.

She lingered, her hand on the doorknob, then dropped it. Slowly, careful to avoid the creaking floorboards, Bree moved back to her seat. She looked at her screen.

Where was she? Ah, yes. Zip-line instructor. Had it not been for that little matter of mis-locking that man's carabiner after he had tried to feel her up on that two-foot-wide platform, she probably would still be managing the place.

But honestly, who doesn't check their own harness clips before jumping off a thirty-foot pole?

Besides, a safety net had caught him—no harm, no foul.

Another rap came on the door and she tapped a few words on the keyboard, loudly, then pushed her long braid over her shoulder. She felt the bumpy locks on the top of her head and raked her fingers through them as she stood up and walked to the door.

With a slight breath she paused, swung the door open, and crossed her arms across her chest, ready for fire.

Only it wasn't her surly neighbor in a wet, beat-up shirt wielding a shovel, but Theodore. In a crisp suit. Holding a bouquet of flowers.

Her arms fell. "Theodore?"

"I was passing by Misty's Floral and saw these."

"Oh really?"

His tentative smile started to fall.

"I mean, *oh really!*" She took the array of yellow flowers in her hand. "Wow! You shouldn't have."

"And then . . . these." He held up a bag of pickle potato chips.

"Nice!" She snatched them, then realized how barbaric her grab had been.

"I mean . . . oh, how *nice*. What a nice, supplementary thing to bring when the focus is these delightful flowers."

His cautious smile broke into an authentic one. "I thought this might be your reaction."

She smiled back, giving Theodore a sly once-over. In her two-week stint as a bridal store attendant, she had learned a bit about textiles—and she could tell the suit he was wearing, virgin wool and cashmere, was not of the JCPenney variety.

Bree, on the other hand, was barefoot, with toenails about three weeks past needing a trim, in the same leggings she wore the night before.

She tucked her toes beneath her. "Thank you, Theodore. This was so thoughtful."

A flash of light out of the corner of her eye caught her attention. Chip stood a few feet from the mailbox, wearing a headlamp as he pushed the soil back in place with his shovel.

She looked down at the bouquet.

It felt heavy in her arms. She didn't know anything about flowers. Except that these felt heavy. Ergo, expensive.

"These"—she paused, trying to find a label for the yellow things—"these are just terrific. So yellow. So happy."

"Yes, yellow. That's what I was thinking too." There was a tilt in Theodore's smile. "So, I probably ought to also admit that I'm not just here to deliver flowers, *happy* and *yellow* as they may be. I have a favor to ask."

She felt the sudden urge to smooth her hair again. "Yeah?"

"A college chum of mine is chairing the Plein Air Festival on Tuesday the ninth, and my family's tree farm is one of the sponsors, so, seeing as I'm expected to be the supportive friend and good family representative and all, I'll be going." He smiled good-naturedly. "You might not be interested in something like that," he ventured, searching her eyes, "but if you wanted to go, I can guarantee it would be a lot more fun for me. And if you don't, well, just in case you have a savior complex or something, just know it'd be a perfect opportunity to save me from an afternoon of loneliness and social desperation. But of course, no pressure."

Bree's smile grew. "My, my. For the perfect gentleman you do lay it on pretty thick, don't you? Well, as it just so happens, I do have a terrible savior complex, and"—Bree paused, blinking furiously against Chip's blinding headlamp. This time it wasn't moving. "I'd love to go—" she continued, but the light was distracting her from the rest of her sentence.

Holding a forearm over her eyes, she squinted and barely made out Chip's form. He was spotlighting the two of them.

She glared.

Nothing.

"Hey!" she called out. "The ground's that way."

After several seconds, the light moved.

Bree whipped a smile back into place as she fixed her eyes again on Theodore. Only now, with spots dancing across her vision, she could only guess she was looking at his eyes. "What time?"

"Around four?"

Tuesday the ninth. Four. She could do Tuesday the ninth at four.

"I'd love to."

A grating sound pierced her ears, and both Bree and Theodore swiveled to see Chip's shadowy body dragging his shovel across the dirt. Even from her inexperienced standpoint she could tell he wasn't actually trying to level the ground.

Well, that explained what kind of general contractor he was.

Bree spoke under her breath. "He's new."

Theodore nodded. Opened his mouth. Hesitated. "And it's dinnertime. I don't suppose you've eaten already?"

Bree paused. But of course it was insane to say she couldn't go because she had to watch the crazy neighbor shovel. And besides, she *hadn't* eaten. Two cups of coffee hardly counted as dinner.

Theodore's expression and tone dimmed as the seconds ticked by. "Unless, of course, you have other plans."

"No," Bree said swiftly. "That'd be great. I just need to change."

"You look terrific," Theo said, smiling as if he hadn't noticed she was practically in her pajamas.

Oh, but he really was a good man.

Her voice softened. "Just give me ten minutes."

It wasn't much longer before Bree had dropped the flowers on the kitchen counter, changed, and settled in Theodore's whisper-silent Tesla as it turned out of her driveway. Two pleasant hours of conversation and three courses later, she returned home to walk straight into a lecture from Evie about flowers as she clipped the limp bundle and arranged them in a mason jar. There wasn't even time to ruminate on the almost-kiss beneath the porch light before Bree found her hand—of its own stupid, stupid volition—reaching for the doorknob and breaking the moment.

Why had it reached for the doorknob?

This was the question that hounded her as she pulled the covers up to her chin in the darkness of her bedroom. Well, that and the sound of the alarm system beeping on downstairs. It reminded her of her very good point she'd been meaning to raise.

"Hey, Evie," Bree called from her bed.

Evie grunted from the other bedroom.

"You do realize you're going to have a problem when you cut the internet in your quest for off-the-grid domination."

"The internet is a black cloud blocking the light of stillness," Evie called back. "If you have a problem with *me* cutting the internet *I pay for* because of your obsession with the desensitizing clutter of your screen—"

"I wasn't talking about my computer. Cut the internet all you want. You know I don't use it." She heard Evie turn over on the creaky bed. "I was talking about your security system. Good night, dear."

She could practically see Evie in her oval-shaped bed staring at the ceiling, registering the fact that her beloved security system ran on wireless. And if there was one thing that could trump her obsession with simple living, it was her obsession with security. The woman had four locks on the front door alone to prove it.

A smile lingered on Bree's lips as she drifted to sleep, the thoughts and objects of the day floating through her dreams.

Evie drifting on an ocean in her oval-shaped bed.

Yellow flowers.

Mason jars.

Pajamas.

Shovels.

An earthquake rumbled the ground beneath her feet, the pounding growing louder and louder, jars, pajamas, shovels all falling into the growing cracks in the earth.

Quaking.

Shaking.

Knocking her head against the—

Bree's eyes popped open while she jerked up to sitting. Evie had a death grip on Bree's arm and was shaking her like a rag doll.

"I'm up! Stop!" Bree hissed.

Bree pushed Evie, who currently looked like a frightened owl in her horn-rimmed glasses. Bree pointed to the bed and whispered, "Sit," then reached behind the bed and pulled out her baseball bat.

Evie sat.

She hated when Evie did this.

At least twice a month Evie's Apple Watch started vibrating, alerting her that some intruder had set off the motion detector above the front door. Some leaf, or squirrel, or sturdy gust of wind. The first time it happened, Bree realized exactly why Evie had lived with Nana for so long. She loved Nana, sure. Who didn't? But Bree could guarantee it was also because Evie didn't want to live alone.

Bree knew Evie would morph from her night-terrified self back into her grumpy self as soon as she gave the all-clear. Bree strode through the living room, not bothering to tiptoe or avoid creaking floorboards. She disarmed the security system, then started at the top door lock and worked her way down, undoing the chain and turning the two deadbolts. She turned the lock on the handle and then twisted it open, ready to be met with nothing but the black, quiet evening.

What Bree did not expect was the black figure hovering six inches from her nose, a weapon over his shoulder.

"*Whaaaa*—" She yelped and in one motion raised the bat and swung.

The figure hollered and stumbled backward. He went down on the porch step, and after a couple attempts to catch himself, tumbled on his backside and knocked a pot sideways with his head.

The shovel clattered beside him.

Bree lifted her hand to her lips, trying to suppress the twitch as the shock, then realization, relief, and finally hysterical chuckles gave way. "I'm sorry. I just—"

Chip looked up at her and shook the dirt off his hair.

She watched the particles drift from his head, then laughed again.

"Like the view?"

"You know, I'll admit. It's pretty funny from this angle."

His frown deepened. His voice held little humor. "Line's moved. Now tell me your secret."

She extended a hand to help him up, but he ignored the gesture and pulled himself to standing.

She glanced in the direction of the median between their cars, where the streetlamp showed the line of freshly turned dirt and, of course, the dog.

By the stroke of midnight, she had said after all. A deal was a deal.

"Fine. Here it is. Mr. Richardson won't hire any contractor who can't demonstrate he's as talented with a paintbrush as he is a hammer. If you want that Barter job, you'd better brush up on your art skills." She raised a brow toward the job that should've taken far less time. "And maybe line-moving skills."

"He wants a contractor who is also an artist?" he repeated, rubbing his head thoughtfully as he took in this new information.

She turned on her heels.

"Good night, Chip."

Bree smiled to herself as she shut the door, turned the three hundred locks, got Evie her warm milk—like the toddler she was—and coerced her back into bed.

It was only as she was settling into her own bed, blinking wearily as she checked the clock, that she saw the time: 3:13 a.m.

Chapter 8
CHIP

It wasn't supposed to be this fun. But honestly, the woman asked for it.

"Midnight. Not one millisecond past."

He could still hear her condescending tone as she whipped her braid over her shoulder and slammed the screen door. As if he were that desperate for whatever she had to say. As if all of his career hopes and dreams rested in her slender hands. As if the sprightly little Barter fairy could have anything *that* valuable to tell him.

Fact was, he woke up, got out of bed, and snatched up his shovel at three in the morning for the pure joy of ruffling her feathers.

Over an hour he wasted pulling out that old phone line and dragging it through the yard as if the fence were moved. Sure, the second she was out of the driveway he dropped his shovel to do actual work—the demolished upstairs bathroom being proof, along with the Pepto Bismol–pink tub in the bed of his truck weighing down old plumbing lines, crushed Sheetrock, and shattered tile.

The reality was, he could already tell annoying her was going to become one of his fondest hobbies. He was starting to love it with every fiber of his being.

The way those pink circles rose in her cheeks. The way her nose scrunched up in disgust.

It was flippin' *fantastic.*

He had been annoyed, however, when he hadn't received so much as a "thank you" for spending hundreds of dollars on the electric fence. The water line was mandatory reparation, but the fence wasn't, and he had tried to make things right. Why? Because he was a good neighbor. To quote Mrs. Lewis herself, he was "a nice chap."

But did Bree seem to care? No.

"You've gotta be kidding me! It's three o'clock in the morning!" Bree's roar had traveled loud and clear through her wall, past the easement between their houses, and right into his bedroom. He chuckled to himself a few times in the darkness, staring at the ceiling, his hands resting behind his head.

She'd swung at him with a bat, but this reaction was so worth it.

He had to be up in three hours, and still, it was so worth it.

His head hurt a bit from that pot, and yes, it was so worth it.

But what was with that man? The guy who had stepped out of his Tesla as if his feet had never touched gravel. The way he took deliberate, slow steps to make sure his perfectly polished shoes didn't end up touching the grass. He lifted the hems of his Armani trousers like a prom girl lifting her ball gown to avoid grass stains.

So *that* was the kind of man Bree Leake dated?

You know? It suited her.

It oddly did.

He could imagine the two of them now, looking through the sunroom window of some McMansion, talking in low tones as they watched a neighbor's hired men mow the twenty-acre lawn horizontally instead of on the diagonal. How they'd *tsk* as they sipped their espressos from tiny porcelain cups, saying they really should get out of the neighborhood before it went completely to pot.

Chip pulled his sleeping bag higher over his shoulders and turned over on the otherwise bare mattress. Russell stood at the window, per usual, his breath frosting the glass as he stared at Bree's bedroom. The thoughts rolled through his mind.

Mr. Richardson wanted a contractor who was also artistic. In this town, he'd be hard-pressed to find a contractor with a hobby like art, that was certain. But then, if anyone could demand fine art in the CV and actually succeed in hiring such a jack-of-all-trades, it was Mr. Richardson. Wouldn't be long before he'd conduct a nationwide search, and the Barter would have a line stretching all the way to the Martha of men in tailored suits carrying drills in one hand and easels in the other. Well, he knew a thing or two about tailored suits. And he may not be selling oil paintings at Laurel Springs Studios, but—

Chip's thoughts stalled as he caught sight of a curious item hanging in Bree's window. He propped up on his elbow and squinted.

Sure enough, he could see a piece of paper taped to the glass.

A simple piece of printer paper with bold, black, handwritten letters:

THIS ISN'T OVER

He grinned and lay back down, putting his hands back behind his head.

This isn't over.

Well, well, wasn't that just icing on the cake?

He closed his eyes.

And slept like a baby.

♡ ♡ ♡

Chip's brother Will set his glass on their parents' dining room table. "So I told the investors, 'Guys, we can get granular about this, but just from a thirty-second look here on the Google street view I can tell you this isn't going to work. I can see overfilled garbage bins, dogs in the middle of a fight in the driveway next to what is clearly a gambling ring, asbestos siding, and a deer stand poking out from the second-story window. This isn't going to be the deal of the century.'"

Will started laughing at his own story before it ended, and chuckles moved around the twenty-person table.

Chip's mother's eyes met his, and he gave a clandestine wink before raising his glass to his lips. This was Sunday-afternoon supper at its finest: carved ham, sautéed asparagus, and 120 minutes of construction jokes and tales of heroic journeys into the land of bidding wars and project management.

Brothers Pete, Will, and David sat with their wives and babies on the opposite side of the cognac-colored, custom-made table their mother and father ordered while on a trip to Sicily. Four of his nephews and nieces dined at the children's table in the corner, well away from upholstered seating with their cranberry sauce–stained hands. With his mother and father sitting at the heads of the table, only Ashleigh and Chip were seated on the other side, flanked by empty chairs, like high school students facing the Brown admission committee.

Boy, had that been one intimidating interview.

"Pete, you didn't happen to pick up that architectural drawing for Hotel Bristol on Friday, did you?" David said. "I know we were thinking that . . ."

Chip sliced into his ham with measured precision. Because no matter how engrossed they were in conversation, they were all watching him, anxious for any indication of his state of being. Everyone down to his sister-in-law Lisa, who was in the other room nursing her baby.

Drop his knife on the ground and let it clatter against the Moroccan hand-painted tile, and Lisa would be there in five seconds, baby wailing, wanting to know what was going on. Wanting to know if he was finally talking.

Two months ago at another Sunday supper, Chip had announced he was leaving McBride Construction and starting his own business. Since then, everyone seemed to be waiting on him to make some sort of emotional declaration.

Declaring what?

Well, he wasn't totally certain. But he had heard rumors.

Some suspected he was unhappy because his salary had been lower than two of his three older brothers'. But then, after Chip's apathetic response to a stilted lecture from Pete about how he had to earn his way up the ladder—even if it was the *family* ladder—that opinion lost popularity (although Alicia, Pete's wife, apparently still favored it).

Others guessed he was jealous, that little Chip couldn't tolerate sitting in his corner desk by the copier, across the room from Pete and Will and their walls of framed newspaper clippings and regional recognition plaques. They speculated that a lifetime of walking in his brothers' shadows had slowly led to a Cain-like fury.

Which led naturally to the women's (and Alicia's life coach's) favorite hypothesis: that poor Chip was expressing his psychological need for attention. That his reserve was low in a family as large as his. That coming along with his twin brother, Jake, as a "wonderful surprise" when his mother was forty-two had led to a cycle of self-doubt and overcompensation. This was why, in Alicia's words, he wore "those lewd overalls." (She had caught him in some Patagonia cycling bibs *once*, and you would've thought she'd caught him working as a male escort.) It was all just one big ruse to be told he was loved, to receive one compliment that would bring him back into the straight and narrow of McBride and Sons.

The only story none of them believed was the real one: that he simply wanted to try things his own way again. He had spent several years on his own up north after graduating from Brown and managed his own company just fine. He didn't have the heart to mention Jake or the truth they all knew, which was that his twin brother had been the reason he'd come back four years ago. At Jake's funeral, after one look at his mother and her shaking hands—even now, as she sliced her own asparagus, they never quite stilled—he had dropped his life in Providence and never looked back.

But now? Now it was time, at last, to try to make his own way again. He'd occupied Jake's old desk for long enough.

He'd tried to explain that, yet none of them believed him.

Which explained why his mother took pains, every day, to reach out to him.

"And what fantastic renovations has my son been up to on his newest house?" Chip's mother asked above the hum of conversation.

The word *newest* was not lost on him. He was well aware of her unspoken feelings about the house she considered too ramshackle for her baby boy to call home. So what did she do? Avoid reality by referring to it as if it were just another project.

She folded and stilled her hands, and the conversation around the table quieted.

Lisa peeked her head in, then disappeared.

Even Ashleigh set her fork down and politely turned to face him.

Good grief. Did they expect him to give a speech?

He cleared his throat. "Well," he began, rubbing his lips with his napkin, "there's not a whole lot to say yet. We have a new door. I finished painting the new cabinets. I've just started in on the windows."

His mother clapped her hands together as if he'd said he was nominated for the Nobel Prize. "Oh, how *terrific*. Did you go with the Intrigue series?"

He fought the childish urge to roll his eyes. "Yes, Mom. I went with Intrigue."

She'd been married into construction for forty-one years but had learned more about the industry in the last month for his sake than all previous years combined.

"North Star? Or Interesting Aqua?"

She beamed at him, proud as ever at the fact he was willing to "experiment with color."

He hesitated, aware of the darting looks between his brothers. "The North Star."

Ashleigh jumped in, clasping his hand. "You need to come by and see what he's done just this past week, Mrs. McBride. You'd think you walked into the wrong house."

Right. The house was empty of furniture, the floors were scratched with one hundred years of wear and tear, and the upstairs bathroom was one giant, gaping hole waiting for an accident. But whoa now, people, we have cabinets.

"I'll do that," his mother replied, reaching out of habit for her calendar on her phone. When her hand came up empty, she slipped it back into her lap.

She gave him a fond smile. Ashleigh squeezed his hand with pride.

They were two peas in a pod.

Like mother, like daughter.

Er, scratch that thought.

"So is that your plan for the foreseeable future, Chip, flipping houses around Abingdon?" Chip's father spoke through his mouthful of meat. Every face turned to the man who always filled up his chair, and the room, with his presence. "Seems to me it won't take long to run out of business that way. After that fixing-upping show, everyone and their teenage daughter wants to be the next Chip and Joanna Gaines."

"Of course that's not the only plan," his mother cut in. She held her hands open. "He has the whole world where he can expand. Marion, Bristol, Kingsport . . ."

"Have to have a contractor's license for the Tennessee side, love," his father replied. "And correct me if I'm wrong, Chip, but you don't have one—"

"Well, he'll just have to get one," she replied before he could respond. She smiled through her perfectly white teeth. "Just like you did. *Dear.*"

Chip's father paused midslice and took in his wife, who was sitting in the pole-straight posture reserved for civic meetings and tea with his mother.

"Yes." He coughed. "Yes, of course he could. With that fancy education of yours, son, I'm sure you're plenty used to taking tests. Probably mastered the art of passing them without studying. You'll be spreading out to North Carolina and Kentucky before we know it."

He smiled before returning his attention to the ham.

Right. Chip was probably the only man in America whose father was disappointed his son went to an Ivy League school instead of jumping into the family business.

His mother started to stand. "Did I forget the gravy boat?"

Chip jumped up before she could. "Let me get it for you."

He pushed through the swinging doors into the kitchen. The porcelain gravy boat sat squarely in the center of the kitchen's island counter, and it took but a second to snag it and move back toward the dining room. His steps slowed, however, as he heard the conversation.

"What happened with the Lee Street estimate, Pete?" his father said.

"Too low. It was close, but we would've only hit 19 percent. Had to throw it back in the pond."

There was silence, and Chip held his breath. *C'mon, Dad. Will. David. Somebody.*

Say it.

"So who's going over to Davenport tomorrow?" his father continued.

Chip felt his heart fall.

Fine.

Nobody in his family was going to mention him, think of him, want to help him at all. Fine.

He could do this on his own. Yes. But it sure was hard to start. And though he'd never mentioned it to them, the savings he'd lost dropping his company and life in Providence cost him dearly. He wasn't searching for a handout, but his financial situation was dire enough that he had hinted separately to every man in there that if they scouted out a job that didn't hit the profit margin they wanted, they should pass it along to him. He didn't have the overhead they had. What they couldn't do, he could and then some. The favor wouldn't cost them a penny.

But had *any* of them thrown him a bone?

Chip pushed the kitchen door open.

"Here ya go, Mom," he said, then set the gravy boat beside her plate. He smiled down at her. "The potatoes are just as good without it, though."

She squeezed his hand appreciatively. "Leave it to my son to know just what to say."

"Chip the smooth-talking salesman," Pete said. "Our sales are gonna drop 20 percent without him."

The words were complimentary. The dry tone was not.

Chip pulled out his own chair. It was time to get off the subject of him. "Yeah, so what are you up to these days, Dad? I saw in the paper you all finished the King renovation last month."

King University was last year's prize build for McBride

Construction, a multimillion-dollar build of a 67,000-square-foot student-center complex. They had declined all other incoming jobs. For the construction companies in the tri-cities area that had garnered those jobs, it was a banner year. Not that there were many in the new-construction business. Anderson Builds, Gilbane, ACL Construction, and of course, now, his.

"Speaking of, Dad," Will interjected. "I saw your memo about the Barter bid. You can't be serious about passing on it."

Chip's shoulders tensed. He turned his attention to his father.

The man shook his head. "Richardson's too unpredictable. It'd be a waste of our time for something he'll probably end up giving to his cat nanny or some other oddball he meets on the street. And anyway, even if we did get the job, he'd have us hopping on one foot the whole time working out change orders."

"Yes, but a profit margin on a project like that . . . ," Will replied.

His father shook his head and started to stand. "Let some other shmuck in this town be his lap dog."

"For his *multimillion-dollar* project," Will added.

His father paused.

"At least two," Will said.

Slowly, he straightened. "Two million? But the building can't be more than fifteen thousand square feet. And it already looks sharp as a tack."

Will shrugged as if to say plenty of upscale clients spent massive amounts of money remodeling kitchens already covered in luxury granite.

His father swung his chin toward the kitchen, plates in hand. "Walk with me, Willy. What have you pulled together?"

Will jumped up and followed him into the kitchen. "Well, the way I see it, we're looking at being able to charge $150 a square foot at the very least. The demo alone should be upwards . . ."

Two million. Chip set his fork down. There wasn't a bank this side of the Mississippi that would offer him that kind of a credit line.

Conversation rose around him, but he was pulled into his own thoughts as he stood with his plate and moved toward the kitchen. He didn't have a shot in the world. And really, why on earth should he?

Redpoint had been licensed and insured a total of thirty-one days. To some extent his brother had been right; he would need to work up the ladder—whether in his dad's company or his own. He didn't have a right to be disappointed. The Barter job was just a dream.

Ashleigh put her hand on Chip's shoulder, and he turned. "Don't you think that would be nice, Chip? Tuesday the ninth?"

"Hmm?" His mother and Ashleigh were both smiling as though they'd hatched the best plan. "What for the ninth?"

"The Plein Air event with the William King Museum. You know, the one she's on the board for."

"Sorry, Ash," Chip said, a distracted eye lingering on the swinging kitchen door. "You'll have to be more specific. My mother is on the board for everything in this town."

Ashleigh gave a conceding tinkle of a laugh, as though she aspired to the same lot in life. "The Plein Air event is the art event. It's a fundraiser for the Barter renovation. She says a slew of artists will be painting along the Creeper Trail, and people can walk through and see all the fine art before it's displayed at the King Museum. Sounds like every art enthusiast in town will be there. It might be fun, don't you think?" She slid her arm around his.

"Bundled up together, strolling along the Creeper, watching the artists create all those one-of-a-kind works." Her voice gained an even silkier tone. "I think it sounds romantic."

A lightbulb in his head went off.

Fine art.

Artists were going to be perched along the Creeper Trail, next Tuesday, and the art enthusiasts in town were going to watch them work . . . for a fundraiser . . . for the Barter.

In the snap of a finger, a plan started forming.

He was not going to lie to his girlfriend.

He also was not going to lie to his girlfriend in front of his mother.

Just . . . avoid certain facts.

"That does sound riveting," Chip began, putting his hand over hers. "But I'm afraid I have a project going on for that Tuesday and will need to work late."

Technically true.

"But I hear the Tavern has a new menu coming out. We could go as soon as I'm finished and see about that stroll afterward . . ."

Bingo.

Ashleigh's eyes lit up at the new idea. A bit shamefully, he worked to avoid looking at her eyes, or his mother's.

An art event.

Tuesday the ninth.

Now all he had to do was find an easel.

Chapter 9

BREE

Bree had a perfectly legitimate reason for sitting on her porch steps, and it had nothing to do with him. Still, that didn't mean she wasn't going to make use of the time by shooting daggers from her eyes while he walked back and forth from the house to his truck, hauling bits of Sheetrock.

The real reason she was sitting on the porch steps, clutching a coffee mug between her knees and a cell phone to her ear, was because she was waiting. For them.

"I don't see—" Over the phone line, Bree's niece Anna gave a breathy pause. "—any fairies here."

"Keep digging. It's there."

Bree listened as her niece rustled through the box full of bizarre and not-so-bizarre knickknacks and collectibles, photographs, rocks, lace, and cards. Every Saturday Bree made her way to the post office and sent a package to Miss Anna Farland, 114

Haybrook Way—a box of items Bree acquired over the course of the week, items that had a story. Tangible things, a string to go the distance between them and give each one an end to hold.

It wasn't the same as being there with her. It wasn't even close.

But until she could pull herself together, until she could *get a grip*, it was the best she could do.

Evie found her postage receipts one day and asked her how on earth she managed to spend so much every week on humongous packages when Bree always claimed to be short on cash. What was in the packages? Evie had pressed. Who were they for? Were there secrets in there? Was she some sort of spy? Bree had stuffed the slips into her back pocket and redirected the topic to Evie's bizarre cat coffee mug. Evie hesitated, then went on to vehemently defend her cat mug—almost convincingly enough to make Bree believe Evie was ignorant of the fact they had changed the subject. Almost. That was the day they had turned from housemates to, in their own way, friends.

She tried not to listen to Anna's labored breathing as she sorted through her treasure box. Every breath Bree heard felt like a punch.

"Here it is!" said Anna. Bree smiled to herself as she imagined her niece taking in every detail of the photograph Bree had shot of the eight-hundred-pound, sixteen-foot-tall bronze statue of Titania encircled by Puck, woodland creatures, and her fairy entourage. When she spoke at last, Anna's voice was soft but enthusiastic. "Cute! But you circled something in this picture. What is it?"

Bree turned the mug in her hands and held the phone between her shoulder and ear. "So that's my fairy in the play. My character is Mustardseed, so I circled my fairy on the sculpture. Or what I like to believe is my fairy. I pass that fountain and the sculptures every day on the way to work."

"I like how—she's holding—the butterfly."

Bree listened as she took a sip of her coffee. Nodded. "I wanted to be the one playing in the water, but Birdie told me that was the character named Puck." Bree swallowed then, realizing she'd mentioned another taboo topic. Anna used to play in the water. Used to be passionate about swimming. Used to be part of the neighborhood swim team. But that was before the hospital visits. And the clinics. And the pain.

Now when she wasn't in the hospital Anna just sat on her bed in her filtered room, hearing the distant whistles and shouts of children playing outside.

Bree's hand slipped to her backside, where even now, seven months later, she could remember the pain of the needle pushing through her cortical bone, and marrow bone, to get to the marrow.

It was supposed to work.

There wasn't supposed to be graft failure.

And yet here they were.

Her throat stung.

Bree took a sip of her coffee to manage it.

"Did you get to the bottom of the box yet? I found the thing you wanted." She pressed her toe between the slivered crack of the porch's second step.

Anna gasped. "You found it!"

Bree smiled but also managed to shoot another eye-dagger at Chip as he passed. He wore a new hole-ridden T-shirt today and jeans covered in caulk and many colors of paint. When Bree took note of the sweat beading at the back of his neck and the little flip of his damp brown hair, her teeth clenched.

This man had woken her up at 3:13 a.m. This filthy, sweaty, disgusting man.

She turned her attention back to Anna. "If my niece wants an 1100-piece Lego Heartlake Shopping Mall set, my niece gets an 1100-piece Heartlake Shopping Mall set." Her eyes shifted to the red Buick slowly rolling down the street. "Hey, I gotta go. The folks are here. Talk tomorrow?"

Already Bree could hear the sound of cardboard ripping open. "You bet."

Bree hung up and took a shaky breath. Every good-bye, even when it would only be hours until the next hello, felt like another step toward the last one. Four months ago, she had said her last good-bye to Nana.

She never wanted to experience that again.

Not with Anna.

Stop. She couldn't let her thoughts go down that path.

Bree set her phone on the porch step, jumped up, and dusted herself off. She ignored Chip's oncoming figure as she stopped at the mailbox, waving to the car that pulled toward her house.

As if it were possible her parents could drive past her on the cul-de-sac going five miles an hour. As if they hadn't visited three times in the last six months.

Her smile broadened as she spotted her mother's face through the windshield.

Her entire life she had been told how uncannily they resembled each other. That was partly due to the narrow age gap between them, as Bree had been born when her mother was barely nineteen. Beyond that, they shared the same high cheekbones and the same wildly red, thick hair, though her mother kept hers short and tamed. But most of all they shared the same expression when they were genuinely excited about something—their eyes turned an even more brilliant, effervescent green. Their mouths puckered to form the same *O* shape. Looking at her mother right now was like looking in a mirror.

Bree bounced on her toes as the car rolled into the driveway. Her feet were nearly crushed under the weight of the rolling car as her stepfather finally put the car in park. She yanked open the passenger door.

"Happy birthday *to me*!"

Bree pulled her mother out of her seatbelt and into a hug. It was April 7 and her birthday was two weeks past, but for all intents and purposes, today was the day.

"Happy birthday, sweetheart," Bree's mother said, wrapping her daughter in a tight hug. "And look at you—you wore your birthday sweatshirt."

Bree opened her eyes in the hug and caught Chip's grin as he watched them. His eyes drifted to the colorful sweatshirt covered in scribbled birthday well-wishes from family and friends, some dating all the way back to 2000. Everything in his expression said, *Birthday sweatshirt?*

She scrunched her nose at him, frowned, and closed her eyes again.

"Now where are the presents?" She moved to examine the back seat.

"Ah. Thirty-four years old and not a day more mature." Bree's stepfather stepped out of the car with open arms and an amused smile.

As Bree was moving around the car to give Dan a hug, she heard a familiar sound. She froze midstep as she saw the dog blast through the open door. He skidded to a stop on the front porch, staring at Bree like he'd reached heaven.

He began to race toward her. She started to jump back over

the line and then realized: It didn't matter anymore. There was the fresh line of soil going all the way across the yard, a solid two feet from their cars. She had absolutely *nothing* to worry about.

Bree sighed with relief and moved to stand next to her stepdad.

If that ignorant dog jumped over the new fence line, he'd feel a nice jolt.

Was it such a bad thing that the very idea made her smile? Giggle a little inside? Have an urge to twiddle her fingers like an evil mastermind?

She reached up with one sleeve of her birthday sweatshirt and rubbed her mirthful smile down. She would not smile. But she would watch. She would stand there, offering up no warnings to the animal whatsoever, and watch with silent glee as the dog got his due punishment.

She glanced Chip's way. For such a devoted dog owner, Chip didn't seem too concerned about Russell running headlong into an electrical barrier. In fact, Chip wasn't even commanding Russell to slow down or stop. In fact . . .

Bree squinted at Chip.

Noted the way his eyes were on her at that very moment.

She looked down, noticing that the dog had not only touched the line but was now a foot beyond the line and giving no indication of slowing.

"Chip!" Bree screamed. In a single movement, she jumped, rolled across the back of the trunk, and landed on the other side. It was a Tony Stark moment born of adrenaline and terror. She could never repeat it.

"Oh, honey!" Bree's mother exclaimed with a smile. "That was splendid!"

"Dan! Watch out!" Bree cried.

Panting, Russell skidded to a stop beside her stepfather.

"Who's this fella?" Dan said, reaching down to pat his head.

All Bree could think about was the heart surgery Dan had the year prior. And Russell's paws going straight through his still-tender chest like a boot through an empty cardboard box.

"Stop!" Bree cried, leaning across the hood. "Be careful! He's—"

"Such a good boy," Dan purred at the dog, rubbing his head and ears. "What a good boy you are." He craned his head up to Chip. "How old is he?"

"Just over two, sir," Chip said.

"Practically still a baby," Dan replied, turning his attention back to the docile dog.

To Bree's horror, Dan began to kneel. "I wouldn't—"

But there he was, staring Russell in the face, both of them with slaphappy smiles. Her stepfather moved to rub his neck. The dog tilted his head and leaned into the rubbing. No drool to be seen anywhere.

"This can't be the dog you were telling us about, can it?" Bree's mother murmured. "I mean, he's large, I'll grant you, but he seems like nothing but a harmless teddy bear."

There the both of them were, beaming at Russell as if they had driven two hours east just to visit him. A dog that was evil.

Bree glared.

At the dog.

Then at the owner of the dog.

"So well-mannered," her mother added, and Bree slammed the passenger door shut.

"Ooookay then," Bree said, holding a cardboard box full of gift bags. The metallic tissue paper flapped at her face. "Let's take the party inside, shall we?"

Nobody moved. Her stepfather was starting some conversation with Chip about dog training while her mother slipped over to the dog to give him a rubdown too.

"Boiled eggs? You're kidding. Did you hear that, Ginny? He says he uses boiled eggs to get him to roll over."

"And the occasional Slim Jim," Chip added. He floated a bright smile her direction. "Russ," Chip said in a commanding tone, "sit."

Yeah, right. This was going to be one of those moments when a dog owner gave an optimistic command to his dog and made you watch for fifteen minutes while the dog started licking itself and the owner grew more and more agitated and started saying, "Oh, come on, Skipper, you were just doing it yesterday. I don't know *why* you are being shy. Paw, Skipper. Give. Me. Your. *Pawwww.*"

Russell squatted on his hind legs.

Bree's jaw dropped.

"Good boy." Chip rubbed his ears while her parents gave an amused smile. "Now. Roll over."

Immediately the dog rolled over. It stood again, shaking out its coat and looking at him eagerly for the next command. Was it just her imagination, or was the dog's coat shinier?

"Now watch this," Chip said to her parents with a wink. He pointed to the dog. "Pow."

Bree almost dropped the box as the dog staggered back three feet and crumpled.

Bree's mother clapped and laughed. "How marvelous! Bree, honey, have you seen him do this?"

"No, Mom. Shockingly enough, I have not."

Chip's eyes flickered to Bree and back to her parents. His tone lowered confidentially. "Want to see the best one? I taught him this this week."

Her parents were nodding before he finished his question.

"Russell, go find Favorite."

Without hesitation, Russell jumped up and moved around the car. He landed squarely on the driveway and looked at Bree. He started barking.

"His favorite what?" Dan was saying, looking past her with a childlike smile. "His favorite chickens?"

"No, his favorite person." Chip stretched out his hand with a nod. "Your daughter."

An eruption of laughter encircled them. Bree's mother looked like she was about to have tears in her eyes. "How absolutely precious, Bree. You're his favorite."

"I'm *very* aware," Bree said, her voice flat. She clutched the box, staring at the three of them like they were part of his family, not hers. "Well, I'm going inside now . . ."

"Is that a new bathroom going in, I see?" her stepfather said, peering at the bed of Chip's truck. "Taking down walls, putting in new vanities"—he fingered an orange wire formerly tucked beneath an old medicine cabinet—"looks like you've even got phone lines you're pulling out of the ground. Now that's dedication to the house and home if nothing else."

Halfway to her porch, Bree stopped.

Turned.

"Phone line?" she said, glancing from the line in the dirt at Russell's feet to the truck bed. "You . . . dug up . . . a phone line?"

"Well, sometimes they do get in the way of things," Dan said, as though Chip needed the defense. "Although I suspect we have more than old phone lines zigzagged underneath our house." He chuckled as he looked at Chip.

Underneath that chiseled five-o'clock shadow lining his jaw, she could see a smile that was tight. Too tight.

Chip cleared his throat. "Yes, well, you can never be too careful about phone lines."

Bree narrowed her eyes. That evil, *nefarious* human being of a neighbor. *"A phone line?"*

Dan saw his stepdaughter's pencil-slit expression and turned. "Well, we should let you get back to your work." Dan smiled, put out his hand. "Pleasure to meet you, though . . ."

"Chip," Chip supplied, meeting his hand and shaking it. "And the pleasure was mine."

The three started to separate—her parents looking reluctant—and Dan called over his shoulder as he took the first porch step. "Boiled eggs, you say?"

"Boiled eggs," Chip repeated. He raised his hand. "You all have a"—he hesitated—"well, a happy birthday party it sounds like."

Bree's mother giggled like a schoolgirl. "You too. You know, if you get tired with all that construction, we have tea—"

"No tea," Bree cut in. "We're all out of tea."

"Or coffee," her mother added.

"All out of coffee too," Bree said.

"Or water!" her mother said shrilly as she opened the screen door for Bree. "Everybody needs water sometimes!"

Bree hip-checked the door and it opened.

"You know," her mother continued, "now that I think of it, we have been having trouble with our faucets. Isn't that so, Dan—"

Bree dropped the box, pulled her parents inside, and slammed the door shut.

"All right, you two," she said and turned the deadbolt. "Let's have a chat."

When she turned around, her parents sat on the couch like children trying hard to pretend they really didn't know what happened to that broken vase. She paused, her eyes narrow.

"I know what you two are doing."

"Now, honey—"

"Shh," Bree said, shaking a finger at her.

"We just thought—" her mother started.

Bree frowned.

"He's just so friendly—" she continued.

Bree shook her head.

"And really, quite convenient, him living right next door—"

Bree shook her head faster.

"And it's not every day dashing young men move in next door, you know. Didn't you think he was quite handsome, Dan?"

Dan nodded. "And helpful to boot."

Her mother squeezed her hands together on her knees, sitting on the edge of the couch. "And I saw no wedding band . . ."

"Yes, and I'm sure his *girlfriend* thinks about that whole wedding band thing all the time," Bree interrupted, cutting to the chase.

Her mother leaned back into the couch, her brows pressed together. "Girlfriend? Oh well, those aren't always permanent, you know. Why, you've heard how Dan found me—"

"Stole you away, I did," Dan said, squeezing her shoulder with a twinkle in his eye.

Her mother let out a chuckle. "Straight from that pancake house. With him still sitting in the booth across from me—"

Bree shook her finger at them. "Shh. Both of you. There will be no dating Chip McBride. And more to the point, there will be no plotting in this house to steal Chip McBride away from his girlfriend."

Her mother flapped a hand. "Of course, honey. You have nothing but a heart of gold. But if *you* weren't the one doing the plotting . . . and perhaps someone else just so happened to get involved . . . without your knowing . . . naturally . . ." Her mother's voice trailed off, and to Bree's horror, she tapped her nose and winked.

Bree threw her hands up. There would be no convincing them. "Let me get you guys a drink."

She started moving before there could be any more winking or nose tapping.

This was the problem with being the unmarried, unsettled daughter at thirty-four.

She was twenty-four years old when they started giving her "the look" whenever they spied another single male in her presence. And at first, the list of conditions that had to be met before they gave "the look" was fairly long and rigid. Candidates had to be devoted male friends who made her laugh and clearly had a shining future ahead of them. Everyone knew the type. Med students, law students, dentists.

By her late twenties the standards lowered to charming ushers at church and nephews of esteemed coworkers at Dan's office.

At thirty-one it was the dad of the Girl Scout cookie girl who came to the house (they bought sixteen boxes and had the father deliver them personally to Bree).

At thirty-two they'd descended to ticket-stub takers whose beards had not entirely overtaken their faces.

At thirty-three she had heard Dan ask the telethon caller from the university if he was a freshman or senior. Then, after confirming he was over eighteen, he found out exactly which Mellow Mushroom he was a server at and pledged fifty dollars. Because he had a "strong voice."

Now, if anyone so much as looked at her, they gave her "the look."

Not that she didn't date. She *did* date. She'd dated plenty of people over the years. Loads. She'd even gone out with the Girl Scout dad once or twice.

But can you fault a girl for not settling? Honestly, while every other parent in the world challenged their daughters to stay strong, to not settle for any Joe Blow walking up their sidewalk with a bouquet of flowers, her parents were the opposite.

If she declared she met a guy across the country online the night before and they'd decided to elope, there'd be no demands to meet him. No background checks. No serious discussions regarding the weight of marriage. What would there be?

A plane ticket pushed into her hands and a teary wave at the security gate.

Bree walked back into the living room carrying two cups of steaming not-so-out-of-stock tea.

"Ah. Wonderful," her mother said, stepping back into the living room from the hall bathroom and taking the mug in hand. "How about you open the green one first?"

So Bree opened the presents as they jumped from topic to topic, revealing a sweater as Dan effused about the new egg beater drill he bought for his shed, three crocheted pot holders for her nonexistent cooking life while her mother talked about the new gym she just joined, and one rather stunning little black dress for all the dates her parents were scheming up with her archenemy neighbor.

All in all the gifts, and the conversation, were lovely.

Finally, with crumpled wrapping paper around Bree's feet and the mugs dry, Bree's mother reached inside her purse.

"We have just one more for you, dear."

Her mother held out a simple square box wrapped in gold foil. A red bow, like the kind a child gets on a new bike, was planted on top.

Somehow, the way her mother held it out, and the way Dan beamed as though knowing something she didn't, made Bree hesitate.

Slowly, she reached out and took it. "Y'all are making me nervous," Bree said.

They only smiled back, which didn't help.

She popped off the bow and pulled off the wrapping paper.

It was a nondescript white box.

She lifted the lid, then her brow rose as she looked up.

"A . . . key?"

Her mind flew through the options while she picked it up and turned it in her hands. She hadn't seen it before, surely? And this wasn't one of those magical "Look outside! It's your new Mercedes!" keys reserved for teenage country club kids. No, it looked more like a house key, or a shed key.

Oh no. Surely Dan wasn't about to say he was sharing the contents of his shed with her. Of course, she'd always sounded enthusiastic about tools for his sake, but *honestly.* Could anyone really care that much about tailpipe cutters?

"It's to the house."

Bree's thoughts came to a grinding halt. Her eyes shot from the key to her mother. Then to her stepfather. And back to her mother. "I have a key to Nana's house already. What are you saying?"

"I'm saying," her mother said slowly, her smile growing, "that we want to give you our *portion* of Nana's house." She paused. "With conditions."

Bree's heart started racing and, before she knew it, she was standing, the teeth of the key making dents in her palm. Her smile broadened. "You're giving me Nana's house?"

Bree swallowed the lump forming in her throat as she pulled the key to her chest.

"With conditions," her mother repeated.

"Of course. Anything." Then she narrowed her eyes. "I'm not going to get married to that guy from the post office. Don't tell me it's about the guy from the post office."

Both of them laughed, but her stepfather laughed harder. "Of course not, Bree. Who cares about"—his eyes grazed the window—"Rick? You don't need Rick."

"Or him," Bree replied, tossing her chin toward the window as well. "I take it back. I *might* consider Rick. Or a mail-order groom. But not him."

"No, no, it's nothing like that," her mother said. "Don't be silly. Just . . . come here. Sit."

Her mother guided her to the couch next to Dan. She seated herself on the other side. Quite suddenly, Bree realized she was cornered.

"We have a proposition for you, dear. We know how much the house means to you—"

That was the understatement of the year.

"And we know that of all the people she loves, she'd want you to have it."

Bree swallowed at the words.

"But—if we are going to hand our share of this property off to you, we know what a responsibility it will be. For starters, you'll need to work out terms with Evie for buying her share."

"No problem." She currently had $42.01 in the bank, but she could come up with more. Easily. No problem.

"And this house is old. It requires extra love and attention—"

Bree nodded, careful to avoid looking at the golden pothos she'd potted on top of the bookshelf that was very, very dead. "I can do that."

"And a steady income to maintain—"

Her nods slowed. "I've got a job"—she coughed and lowered her voice—"currently."

"And above all, stability."

Bree kept nodding, but at her mother's continued stare her nod petered out. "Stability. I can be stable."

Her mother began pushing nonexistent crumbs off her knees. "Yes, well, that's what we'd like to talk about."

After a pause she took Bree's hands. "You see, honey, you have this wonderful spirit within you. It's . . . spontaneous."

"Energetic," Dan put in.

"Spirited," her mother added.

Bree looked from her stepfather to her mother. "So it's established then. I have a spirited spirit. *But* . . ."

"But sometimes our greatest strengths are also our greatest weaknesses."

"And that's not unusual at all," Dan interjected. "For example, your mother's greatest strength is how loving she is."

Her mother gave a bashful smile.

"On the flip side, that means she can sometimes be a bit *too* invested. Clingy."

Her mother's smile withered. "Yes. Well. Just as one of Dan's *many* terrific attributes is his ability to stay laser focused on his goals, which also explains why he's gained twenty pounds by being glued to the couch every weekend over football season."

Dan opened his mouth to protest, but she raised a hand. "But I digress. The point is, honey, that while you are fun, and capable, and always ready for the next adventure—"

"And you can do anything you put your mind to," Dan added.

"The point is, you . . . just sometimes . . . have this tendency to run off toward the next thing. Like with your hobbies, and your sports, and the jobs . . . and the colleges . . . and all the boyfriends—"

Bree's cheeks flushed. "Okay, Mom, I get it. So I have, in the past, moved on with new opportunities. But this is different. This is *Nana's* house. There's no moving on with this. This is my dream."

"I know, honey." Her mother patted her arm. "But being a florist was also your dream. And a baker. And the general manager of Dollywood. It's just, there are a lot of things we can do with the money by selling the house. If you are going to take it, we need to know you really mean it over the long haul."

"And to demonstrate that," Dan interjected, "we have an idea."

He paused for the magnanimous moment and held out his hands. "One year."

He smiled triumphantly.

Bree looked from Dan to her mother. "One year, what?"

Her mother spoke. "One year that you stay in one place, doing one job, providing your own way, then you can have the house. Live in this fine home with Evie, keep up your terrific acting career at the Barter. One year."

"And on this day next year, April 7," Dan put in, "if you still want it, it's yours. If you decide you don't"—he cleared his throat—

"or can't, Evie has agreed to buy it out. It's the perfect housing solution."

Her mother and stepfather smiled at her as if this was the most brilliant idea they'd ever hatched.

Bree felt her blood grow cold. "One year," she repeated.

The notches in the key dug deeper into her palm as she clenched her fist at her side. One year. One year of working at the Barter—where she was approximately two weeks from being out of a job. One year of living in this house with Evie—where she was about two weeks away from living without electricity and sewing clothes from barley bags.

Her mouth opened. Paused.

The words were on the tip of her tongue: *Super, guys. No problem whatsoever. But before we start, I just gotta do one thing. It's absolutely not a reflection on my stability. Or seriousness. I just need to change everything about my job and roommate and life real quick first.*

She could hear how that sounded in her own ears.

"One year," Bree said, forcing a smile. "No problem."

Six hours and approximately three thousand calories of birthday cake later, Bree pushed her parents' passenger door shut and waved them off. The dog sat at the front of his owner's mailbox, looking like a forlorn dad watching his children head off to college as they angled out of the cul-de-sac. Russell was so compelling that her parents parked in the middle of the road and got out to give the dog several friendly rubs. Chip, meanwhile, stood at a distance on his porch, pretending to move around some empty five-gallon paint buckets.

Right. Like they really needed moving twelve inches.

Like he *ever* actually moved *anything* twelve inches.

"Lovely, again, to meet you," Bree's mother called, waving once more to Chip before getting back in the car.

"And if we have some trouble getting our dog to do that roll-over trick—" Dan called.

"You feel free to call anytime," Chip supplied. He turned a broad smile on Bree. "I'm sure Bree'd be happy to walk her phone over so we can chat."

Bree nearly collapsed then and there. Great. Just great. She could already see her parents' wheels turning. This conversation was going to carry them the whole drive home. She'd start getting calls "for Chip" by tomorrow.

"We just might!" Dan called, then settled into the driver's seat.

And here's your daughter, the one you are leaving, back here! Bree wanted to yell, but she refrained as they honked once more for the dog.

Bree lowered her hand as the car rolled down the hill and out of sight.

One year.

"Nice parents," Chip called from the porch, but she ignored him.

Her hand slid into her pocket as she felt for the key. It gave her instant comfort, instant resolve, instant—she slipped her hand out again, realizing just how much she sounded like Bilbo Baggins before the One Ring mental breakdown.

She dropped that key back into her pocket and fished for another.

A car key.

"And happy birthday," Chip said.

"It was two weeks ago," Bree replied, unmoved by kind words. Oh no. She wouldn't be falling for any of *that* again. Especially now when she was on a mission. A specific, critical mission.

She slipped into her car and five minutes later was pulling into the Barter Inn dorms, then banging on Birdie's door.

The door opened. Everything from the damp tendrils escaping Birdie's braid to the nude tights beneath athletic shorts said she had come to the right place.

"I need you to teach me to tap-dance," Bree blurted. "And maybe sing."

Birdie's eyes widened. "I thought you were out. I thought you didn't even want to try."

"I'm back in."

Birdie hesitated, clearly counting the days in her head. "But you've only got—"

"Eighteen days until the audition. I'm aware. And awareness is the first step toward success, right?"

"And you have a . . . skill level of a . . . what, would you say . . . ?"

"Level zero, Birdie. I'm at a solid level zero."

There was a short pause.

Then a longer one.

Bree's face softened. "Please."

"Perfect," Birdie said, swinging the door the rest of the way open, her tap shoes clicking as she stepped back to make room for Bree's entrance. "Absolutely perfect. You'll have nowhere to go but up."

Bree stepped inside, squeezing Birdie's hand as she entered. "Thank you."

♡ ♡ ♡

Four and a half hours later, with "Good Morning" playing on repeat through her head, Bree pulled back into her driveway. Her aching foot complained as she pushed the brake pedal and turned off the engine. She put her head on the wheel for a moment. Breathed. Finally, she pushed the door open with protesting muscles, and the door creaked at the pathetic attempt and shut again.

"Oh, come on." The words tumbled out of her hoarse throat and she pushed again. No wonder Cam and Nate—Birdie's downstairs neighbors and their District One tap-dancing competitors—banged on the ceiling so much. She couldn't even stand her own voice.

She stood and used her body weight to shut the door. Locking it, she considered how she would have to do this again tomorrow.

And the next day.

And the next.

Birdie was a good friend. She had spent a considerable amount of time showing her the basic moves of tap and song. She kept saying it was good accountability to be doing it together, that Bree's presence strengthened her, but even Bree knew Birdie's time would be better spent singing her own songs and practicing her own steps. Still, Birdie insisted. And frankly, Bree didn't have the option to turn her down—

"Russ!" She heard Chip's hiss from his porch the millisecond before the dog collapsed into the back of her knees and threw her forward. She fell to her hands and knees on the gravel, then, in a blind moment of fight-or-flight, ignored the screaming muscles in her body as she scrambled up and over her side of the line.

Panting, hands on knees, she turned.

There stood Russell, wagging his tail, well over the soil line her neighbor had claimed was the new Invisible Fence. Where he had obediently stayed behind when her parents were in view. But now, the second they were gone . . .

From the porch, she heard the chuckle. He put up his hands in surrender. "I really tried that time, Bree. I promise—"

Her head jerked in his direction. "*You.*"

Her voice was surprising in her own ears. She sounded like a teacher whose students put a tack on her chair. She sounded like Saruman calling up the orc army to war. She sounded like a woman who'd had enough.

She stared at her neighbor and made a mental declaration then and there. Her fingers slipped into her pocket for support, and she gripped the key.

When in the course of human events it becomes necessary for one people to dissolve the residential bands which have connected them and to assume among the powers of the earth, the separate and equal station to which the Laws of Nature and of Nature's God entitle them, a decent respect to the opinions of mankind requires that they should declare the causes which impel them to the separation.

Well, she had declared her injustices, and he had done nothing but mock.

So, she, therefore, Bree Leake, resident of 425 Stonewall Heights, of Abingdon, Virginia, appealed to the Supreme Judge of the world for the rectitude of her intentions to, in the Name, and by Authority of Her Sanity, solemnly publish and declare, that she ought to be free from pestilential neighbors, absolved from neighbors' crude mockery, and that all connections between herself and Iniquitous Neighbor and Loathsome Dog will, and ought to be, totally dissolved.

In other words . . .

This.

Was.

War.

Chapter 10

CHIP

Chip slipped past a slow-moving couple as he dragged the bulky easel along the Creeper Trail. Haste had not been a merry accomplice in his mission, given that there were approximately zero stores within a fifty-mile radius prepared to sell him a modern, portable easel at a reasonable price. And he opted not to steal the blue Fisher Price one from the toddler across the street.

As a last resort, and at great personal risk, he cashed in a favor from a family friend and hopped by the elderly woman's estate that morning to borrow her sturdy midcentury wooden easel. He was going for the authentic artist look, and a six-foot-high antique accessory would do the trick. He hoped the old lady wouldn't tell his mother about their little exchange at the next garden party.

Juggling the easel in one arm and a gallon of turpentine, palette, half a dozen oil paints, and ten brushes in a newspaper in the other, Chip struggled to slide his phone into his breast pocket and move on. A few art enthusiasts were already wandering the trail—men and women walking arm in arm, pointing whenever they spotted an artist as though they'd spotted a deer in the wild.

It was the day of the William King Museum's Plein Air event, and artists already dotted the dirt path every thirty meters or so. They had set up their easels to capture the picturesque farms and tree line along the thirty-four-mile route that trains once took from the elevated peak of Whitetop Mountain to the little town of Abingdon below. Every year thousands of people trekked their way to Abingdon as tourists, spent the evening at a Barter play, stayed the night at the Martha or one of the dozen Colonial-style bed-and-breakfasts, then set out for that scenic bike ride along the Creeper Trail the following morning. Even the locals strolled or biked along the trail as part of their daily schedule. Abingdon was the gold standard for tucked-away vacations.

Chip stopped and squinted down the path, searching for the perfect location to set up. Accomplishing both of his goals at once would be a challenge: first, locating a prime spot for being seen by Mr. Richardson, and second, making himself invisible to his mother or any other person who might know him. So, basically, being visible to one person while being invisible to everyone else. Right. Totally doable.

He spotted a bench somewhat obscured by two trees. Struggling, he dropped his easel down on the grass just off the path. With plastic bags of paint and brushes dangling from his wrists, he fought with the easel to pry it open. It creaked with the obstinance of a buried treasure chest. But there, at last, it stood beside the path, the creek waters rippling behind him with the rose-petal freshness of the 1648 *Pastoral Landscape* by Claude Lorrain.

Google made research too easy.

He put his hands on his hips and looked up with a smile. Five feet away a man in a maroon beret frowned, brush in his hand, yellow paint threatening to drip onto the mossy ground.

"Ah," Chip said and picked up his easel. "I'll just—give you a bit more breathing room."

The man's eyes remained trained on him until he was safely seven yards down.

Five minutes later, with easel up, brush in hand, and the colors of the rainbow spread across his palette, he was ready for action.

"Right." He looked down at the colors and up again.

A gust of wind bowed budding tulips.

He looked over his shoulder to the other painter.

The man dipped his paintbrush in—for lack of a more cultured term—purple.

Purple? That couldn't be right.

Chip looked to what the man was looking at, the stream and cow farm stretching out across the horizon.

Cows: black. Stream: blue. Barn: a dead-looking yellow and green. There was no space for purple—

He glanced over to the man's easel again.

Oh. Oh yes. Well, if you did it like that.

Chip took a few steps, angling for a better view of the man who had somehow used purple in the shadows of the hill and made it look utterly normal. As though, of course, all hills are somehow purple. How had Chip not seen that?

The man jerked up his head. His frown deepened when he caught Chip's gaze, and he tilted his easel away.

Chip tugged on his cuffs. Honestly. This was the Plein Air event. All sorts of people were about to walk by at any moment.

If the man had expected to be alone, he should've painted in a closet.

Chip returned to his easel and dipped his brush into the purple.

Yes. Purple was a fine choice.

Suddenly his breast pocket vibrated, the wail of rings breaking the song of the babbling brook. He put the brush between his teeth and pulled out his phone.

"Hey, Tim. What's up?" Chip said through his teeth, then cradled the phone to his ear to remove the brush from his mouth.

"I'm over here at Haymaker Street," replied Tim, the nineteen-year-old Lowe's delivery rep and longtime family friend. "Nobody's here to sign off on these appliances."

Chip forced himself not to growl like a caveman. This was the third time in a month his sub wasn't where he needed to be. And worse, right now Chip couldn't afford to let him go. "Okay, let me make a call. Hold on a sec."

Chip dialed Keith's number. His fingers tightened around the brush as the number of rings grew. Finally he gave up and dialed Tim back.

"Do you think you can get in?"

"I checked both the front and back doors," Tim said. "They're locked."

"You try a window?"

There was silence on the other end of the line.

Finally, Tim cleared his throat. "You want me to check for open windows, sir? You know that can be construed as trespassing . . ."

Chip pulled out his deepest, most compelling voice. "Tim. You are in Marion. I am in Abingdon. Nobody is there. I need those appliances. I just need you to go to the back window and see if you can get it open."

"It's broad daylight, sir. I can't do that again. The police—"

"I know the police caught you last time. I remember. It was a mess. But I took care of it, didn't I? I didn't leave you out to dry." Chip kicked at the dirt, realizing as he lifted his head that the artist had stopped painting and was watching him.

Their eyes met, and Beret Man jerked his attention back to the canvas.

"Just, please," Chip continued, "*please*—get those appliances to me. And Tim, if you do this"—he lowered his voice—"I'll owe you."

After a bit more grumbling, the teen relented. Chip hung up the phone and stuffed it back in his breast pocket. The phone started to ring again, but he silenced it before the second ring.

He sighed.

Looked over to shrug with a, "Work. What are ya gonna do?" but then stopped, noticing that Beret Man wasn't in his spot.

He was another ten yards off, the back of his easel now planted directly toward him, which meant the man had decided either to keep an eye on him at all times or to make Chip the subject of his masterpiece.

Good grief. You overhear someone telling a guy to break in at all costs and let you take care of the police, and you'd think he was the mafia.

There was a rustling sound down the path, and Chip turned his chin in the direction of the trail.

Here they come.

As the first couple started toward him, Chip slid a broad stroke of purple across the white canvas, as lush and moody as the velvet curtains in his parents' library. He smiled to himself and made a few more strokes here and there, zigzagging to follow the shadows of the hills beyond. Not too shabby.

Art wasn't so hard. Just a little dip here, a little stroke there, and voilà. Masterpiece.

Chip heard footsteps stop behind him and felt heat rise on his neck. With purple already coating his brush, he moved over to the blue and hovered. What was he supposed to do now? The few times he'd painted in childhood he dipped his brush into water to rinse off the paint, but—he cast a quick glance to his neighbor and didn't see any 24-ounce cup of murky water at his feet. There was some little glass bowl it seemed, but . . .

Forget it.

Chip dug the brush into the blue and made broad brushstrokes above the purple.

The people moved on.

This was fine, he told himself, trying not to pull at the neck of his suit coat as he glanced backward and saw several more people—no one he recognized, thank goodness—coming his way. This was fine.

That was the beautiful thing here, after all. He didn't have to actually *paint* beautiful art, per se. He just had to remember what to *say* about beautiful art. After all, if someone could get away with putting a red circle on a canvas and hanging it in the Smithsonian, he could certainly get away with a few—albeit crude—purple and blue strokes. Some people appreciated the abstract. He'd fit in perfectly with them, if only he could remember his research notes.

Chip flicked his wrist over and nudged his watch an inch aside with the butt of his long brush. He had scribbled notes to himself on the inside of his arm, key words like *emulsion* and *Suprematism*. He pushed his sleeve back down and looked again to his canvas.

Twenty minutes later, his brush murky brown, he heard the familiar tinkle of a laugh behind him.

He jerked his head up.

There, thirty feet down the path, was his mother taking the lead as she, with both determination and steady grace, walked the dirt in cream-colored high heels. Her long cream kimono swished around her knees as she held a clipboard and chatted amiably whenever her group paused to admire an artist at work. Represented were a few bald heads he'd come to recognize over the years, those often dragged onto the board by overzealous wives. His mother turned her head as she pointed and said something to her companions, and there, shifting into focus, was the perfectly curled blond hair of Ashleigh, who was standing with hands clasped in front of her, an eager pupil.

Perfect.

Chip dropped his brush and palette on the ground before popping up his jacket collar, jamming his chin to his neck, and striding in the opposite direction toward the bench near the trees.

How on earth was a six-foot-three-inch man supposed to hide in plain sight? He was kidding himself to even try. His mother and his girlfriend would both recognize him a football-field length away. He turned his direction by degrees as he walked and, after glancing backward, stepped off the path and came to a hedge of trees and briar bushes. A slumped barbed-wire fence followed the line of trees, and beyond that several horses stood at the top of a hill, munching at grass. With care he walked around the briars and slipped through the fence. The horses didn't look up.

This is still fine, he told himself, pulling his hands out of his pockets and wrapping them around his coat. Perfectly fine. Everything was going exactly according to plan. He'd just have to settle behind a sturdy tree and wait them out. Maybe sit down somewhere. Of course, the trees didn't obscure him all that much. If he was spotted, he could always claim to be on a contemplative walk. Yes. That was it. Work had been particularly trying, and he needed a moment to reprioritize his life. His mother, who went to one of those sensory float tubs every Tuesday, would understand.

The volume of the group grew as they strolled closer, and Chip sat at the base of the biggest tree he could find. He leaned his body a couple of inches to the left and peeked out from behind the large oak tree. They slowed at his easel. A couple glanced around as if to spot the artist who'd abandoned his station. One man squinted as he took a step nearer the easel, examining it with a frown. Somebody else pointed at something in the center, and the man nodded. Finally, they moved on.

Chip pushed himself off the grass and was dusting himself off when he saw his mother step up to his neighboring artist.

Her voice drifted with the breeze.

"Sir"—she paused and scanned the clipboard—"Mr. Harding. Do you know who set up their easel there? I don't have anyone on the map listed for this spot."

Mr. Harding took off his beret and coughed, his milky blue eyes dodging toward him in the trees and back.

"Mr. Harding," his mother repeated, "is that a yes?"

Mr. Harding coughed again.

For some reason the man wasn't ratting him out. For some reason, he looked terrifically red around the neck as he clutched his beret.

"Mr. Harding," his mother said a third time.

If the guy was going to be paranoid, Chip might as well use it to his advantage.

The next time Mr. Harding shot a glance in his direction, Chip mustered his best I'm-an-unstable-man-and-conflicted-artist-alone-with-you-in-the-woods stare. Chip raised his brows as if to purr, *Just wait until they leave, buddy.*

Bingo.

"No, I . . ." Beret Man fumbled with his supplies, dropping his brushes and paint in his bag. He hoisted his easel under one arm, wet canvas and all, and returned his beret to his shiny bald head. "I was just leaving."

"Now, now, Mr. Harding, please stay!" Chip's mother called after him. But he was already kicking up dust on the trail.

They all gawked silently as they watched him stalk off.

His mother gave an upbeat pivot on her heels. "Well," she said, tucking the clipboard under her wing, "that's the wonderful thing about artists. With them, there's never a dull moment. You never know when their next inspiration will strike. Let's move on. Next up, we should see a lovely work in progress from our young prodigy Ms. Tiffany Marler, one of Laurel Springs Studio's own protégées."

Several heads nodded in studious spirit, and together they moved on.

He held his breath as he watched the last pair of heels slip out of view. Already two other groups had passed while he'd been out of sight, and there was no way he was going to be stuck behind some briars in a horse field missing his moment with Mr. Richardson.

If he could just—he looked down at his pants, snagged by

some thorns—get past these surly bushes. He pulled his leg up, and the thorns dug in deeper.

Male and female voices came up the path.

The woman laughed a nice feathery laugh, and he grabbed a briar between two fingers and pulled it away from him. He seemed to have stepped directly into the center of the thicket, and like a fly caught in a Venus fly trap, he seemed to be the briars' prey. Without hurting himself further, he worked to unwind each briar wrapped from his ankle to his thigh.

The voices were growing louder and, with them, his sense of determination and anxiety. He was not going to have wasted the workday stuck in a briar patch. If he could just—he pulled the fourth briar off—hurry up the stupid things . . .

Losing all patience in one snap moment, he ripped his leg forward. His leg burst free, and he high-kneed several steps over the rest of the bushes, cantered down the small embankment, and took one final leap over the sodden ditch to get back onto the path.

His feet landed squarely in the center.

There was a disconcerting feeling of airiness about his thighs and he bent down to examine his pants.

A couple of stubborn thorns still stuck to the fabric. He swatted them off, but there was no major damage.

He straightened, tugged on the cuffs of his nicest suit coat, and walked back to his easel.

Now. Where was he?

He picked up his brush and gave the canvas several brown strokes.

"Taking a bathroom break?"

Chip recognized her voice instantly.

That voice.

He forced up a casual smile and turned.

With parallel expression Bree smiled back at him, hands clasped in front of her. She looked absolutely—no, *ravishing* couldn't be the word—*startling* as she stood beside her companion. Her long red hair was in neither a braid nor a bun, and the slight waves rippled to the waist of her yellow pea coat that appeared to fit her to a tee. Maybe he hadn't seen her complete wardrobe in the past few weeks, but it was no secret that on the rare occasion she wasn't wearing sweatpants, she was borrowing an outfit from her short roommate.

But here, now, well, there was no doubt about it. Those sleeves reaching to the tips of her slender wrists, that collar, those seams resting perfectly on her shoulders: that coat was entirely meant for her.

Which meant Bree had bought it.

Recently.

For this occasion.

With this guy.

The purring Tesla guy.

Chip overcompensated with a bright tone of voice. "Why, hello there, neighbor. I heard your voice a minute ago but, surprisingly enough, didn't recognize it." He creased his brows as he looked into Bree's eyes. "I can't imagine why, though. I should've recognized that happy-go-lucky laugh anywhere. I mean, Bree Leake. Happy happy happy."

He clipped on a bright smile to match his eyes.

Bree's grin dampened.

Then she recovered.

"So?" she said at last, nodding to the bushes.

"Oh. That?" Chip swiveled backward, pointing toward the

trees with his brush. "I just wanted a little one-on-one time with the farmland. In order to truly get into a picture, I must let it communicate with me. Whisper in my ear, so to speak."

"And did it whisper?"

"Oh yes."

"And what did it say?"

"Oh." He put his hand across his heart. "That I cannot share."

"So then, tell me, why is your easel pointing the other way?" Bree put her finger beneath her chin, as if examining his work closely. "And correct me if I'm wrong—"

"I'd be happy to do that for you."

"But where are the horses? And the barn?"

Tesla Man coughed politely. "I'm sure Mr.—" He hesitated.

Chip supplied "McBride" and the man's brows rose.

"Yes, well, I'm sure Mr. McBride has it all under control. After all, it's only been, what—an hour?—since you've begun."

"Correct. Like Da Vinci laboring over *Mona Lisa* for four years, anything I pour my heart into gets my undivided attention."

The man nodded as if impressed. "So how long does one of your paintings typically take?"

"Three hundred days."

"Oh," the man said, his brows rising.

"I insist that every single stroke is perfect. I won't be satisfied until even the tiniest speck swims in harmony with the others."

"I see. That's some dedication."

Chip smiled to himself. This was good practice. He had used the line prepared for Mr. Richardson, and it was good to see it make an impression.

The man stepped forward and stretched out his hand with silky, efficient motion. "Theodore Watkins, but please, call me

Theo." The words fell off his lips with as much practiced perfection as his movements.

Chip shuffled his paintbrush to his other hand and took it. "Chip McBride. Good to meet you."

Theo seemed to hesitate as he let go. "Tell me, are you related to the McBrides of McBride and Sons?"

Ah. The all-too-common question. "I'm actually one of those sons."

"Fascinating." Theo turned his attention back down the path, still clasping his hand. "I would love for you to meet someone. Mr. Richardson!"

Mr. Richardson?

Chip felt his pulse rise. A meaty man in a wool mohair suit and open overcoat strolled down the path beside a woman in feathers. From the white feather hat to the ostrich feather coat, the couple was impossible to miss.

They stopped behind another painter at work, Mrs. Richardson craning her neck over the man's shoulder as if she'd never seen such captivating work in her life. Mr. Richardson turned at the call of his name, and his eyes caught sight of Theo's raised hand. He murmured something to his wife and she nodded, keeping her eyes on the painting. He tapped his Stetson an inch up his forehead and moved on.

Chip felt his fingers tingling.

The moment had come. Hard to believe, a bit, but the plan had come to fruition. Nearly as seamless as he'd imagined.

All he had to do now was remember a few of a dozen key words. *Reinhardt. Montage. Monochrome.* Deliver the lines as he slid effortlessly into a discussion of his construction achievements, and—

"You're holding your brush wrong."

Chip stiffened at the sound of Bree's voice, then looked to the brush in his hands.

Theo looked at her with a startled expression, and she backed up with a blossoming—and if he hadn't known better, well-meant—smile. "It's probably because of all that hammering you do all the time. Your hand seems to be stuck in that position. Like it's . . . hmm . . . ready to attack the canvas, maybe?"

Chip's cheeks tightened as he smiled back.

Except for her.

This was the opportunity he'd waited for, but for her.

He loved Bree.

More specifically, he loved how incredibly fun it was to ruffle her feathers. To drive her mad. And to be fair, he'd tried the nice route. He'd offered up a prized Frisbee with a kind note. He'd saved her from theatre disaster that one evening, for goodness' sake. He'd already helped her parents *four times* when they'd called. Once for dog-training tips. The other three about their leaking faucet and other home-related inquiries.

Could he have offered her parents his personal phone number so Bree didn't have to be a liaison? Yes. Could they have asked for his number for the same reason? Yes, but they all seemed to find joy in communicating through her instead.

And the scowl on Bree's face every time she had to march over to Chip's house, phone in hand, so her stepdad could ask Chip a question about insulation upgrades? Absolutely priceless.

But *now*? Torturing each other *now*?

This was *not* the time.

He wanted to whisper, "Leave it alone, Bree. We will carry on when we get home!"

His neck itched beneath the fancy wool scarf he'd stolen off his brother at the last family supper. *Maybe this,* he hypothesized, *is why artists are tortured. They're not suffering from lack of money or food or shelter. Their scarves are choking them to death.*

"You're spot-on about the tool analogy, Bree. That position is called the screwdriver," Theo said, raising his brow first at her, then him. "I hear it's quite useful for expressionist painting. But of course, you could enlighten us on that, Chip?"

"Hmm?" Chip said, dragging his eyes from Mr. Richardson back to them. "Oh yes. It's quite difficult for some artists, at first, but those who keep at it tend to agree it's useful."

Theo nodded as though this made perfect sense. But Chip saw something else in the man's eyes, a cloudy expression. "So. How long have you two been neighbors?"

"A little over three weeks," Bree replied. Her doting smile turned Chip's stomach. "But already it's starting to feel like a lifetime."

The wind rippled through the blossoming dogwood trees as Mr. Richardson made his way over.

"And . . ." Theo looked with uncertainty back to Chip. "How's the neighborhood, Chip?"

"Oh, it's terrific," Chip said, feeling the need to rearrange the paintbrushes. "I can honestly say I've never had more engaging neighbors." He turned toward Bree. "You know, I just realized I was supposed to call your parents back. Can you call *right now* and tell them I'll be a little late today?"

Bree smiled. "Of course I will, but can it wait? I wouldn't dream of missing out on this meeting. And how funny it is that you were *just telling me* how nice it'd be to meet the man behind the Barter. What a coincidence."

Theo's ruffled brow conveyed he felt the undercurrent of tension. Mr. Richardson stepped into the circle. "Mr. Richardson, meet Chip McBride."

The older man turned by degrees as he held out his hand to Chip. Theo said, "Chip here was just telling me about both his professional interests as well as his extracurricular passions. I think you'll be interested to hear about them both."

Right. It was time to pretend Bree wasn't standing there, staring, knowing he was a complete fraud.

Chip pivoted to crop Bree out of his line of vision.

"Oh, painting is never an extracurricular passion," Chip said as he took Mr. Richardson's hand. "Art is the lens through which I see the world. Art is in everything, from the monochrome land conveyed in this pastureland to each brick of the Village I built at Emory and Henry last year. It's just a matter of the medium. Nice to meet you, sir."

"Mutual," Mr. Richardson said, his eyes shining as bright and blue as the sky. "Tell me, you're Art's son, right?"

"I am, sir," Chip said. "But I've launched my own construction company in the last year," he added. Technically, thirty-four days. But that was inconsequential. "Redpoint Construction. You may have heard of it."

"No, I don't think I have," he said. Mr. Richardson's eyes dimmed. "What sort of work have you done?"

"Oh"—Chip waved a hand, his paintbrush darting daringly toward Bree's coat—"this and that. We specialize in new construction, remodeling and renovation, historical restorations—"

"You specialize in historical restoration?"

"Oh yes, sir." Chip had added that specialty to his business cards the evening prior.

"Interesting." Mr. Richardson stepped forward. "Where are you located?"

Chip took a small step back, inclining his chin as far away from Bree as possible. "Just a few streets up from the Barter."

Out of the corner of his eye, he saw Bree lift a finger. "Oh," she said innocently. "The one by Plumb Alley?"

He hesitated. Darted one polite but swift glance her way. "Yes. I believe somewhere near there."

"Just off, say, North Court Street?"

Chip paused to think while his face tightened. "I think so," he said, tugging lightly around the collar. "I'd have to say, Mr. Richardson, restoring an old property to its original glory is the highlight of my days."

Bree opened her mouth.

"Here"—Chip rushed to stop her from speaking again—"I think I have a business card somewhere if you're interested." Before Mr. Richardson could reply, Chip reached into his breast pocket and whipped out a card. There was one in each pocket of his trousers and in about ten locations in his bag, just in case he forgot where he'd placed it for this critical moment. "Are you doing some remodeling, sir?"

"I am, actually," Mr. Richardson said, peering at the card in his hands.

Maybe it had been too much to put pictures on the back of both *The Last Supper* and the new Emory buildings side by side.

"Thank you for this." Mr. Richardson tucked the card in his pocket and looked up to the easel. "And what do we have here?"

"Oh," Chip began, trying not to clam up. "I was just working on my"—he mentally scanned the words scribbled beneath his watch—"crosshatching."

That word worked here. Brushstrokes crisscrossed one another to create a web of mixed colors. He laughed politely. "But you know how it goes."

"Seems like a lot of brown here, not a lot of colors," Mr. Richardson mused, resting a finger on his chin.

"Well," Chip began. What was that artist's name again? He moved his hand behind the easel, pulled back his sleeve, and scrolled through the few words. "As an avid fan of Albrecht Dürer's style," he said, tugging an invisible stray thread from the canvas, "I like to follow in his footsteps for landscape scenes like this."

Mr. Richardson frowned. "Dürer. I've never been too fond of his work. All so eerie and disapproving."

"Did I say Dürer? I must've just had his name on my mind after my nightly reading. I meant Johns. Jasper Johns."

Mr. Richardson pressed his lips together in a thin line. "Johns. I've never liked any of his works either. Like any young, untrained man could just—just—"

"Stand out here pretending he's a twenty-first-century Da Vinci with a few zigzag brushstrokes?" said Bree.

The group turned to look at her, holding her hands clasped at her waist, smiling with all the innocence of a wolf hidden in Grandma's clothing.

"Exactly," Mr. Richardson replied, shaking his finger at her as if noticing her for the first time. "You're one of ours, aren't you? A fairy in *A Midsummer Night's Dream*?"

She bowed her head. "Mustardseed at your service, sir."

His eyes softened. "I'm so sorry about the trouble at the Barter lately. I must say, in all my years we've never had a mix-up like this." He patted her arm. "At any rate, my dear, I certainly hope the cast cut won't affect you."

Theo took a protective step toward her. "I'm sure it won't, sir. Not with a talented fairy like herself."

Mr. Richardson smiled up at him, a twinkle in his eye. "Yes. Well, as we all know, Theo only spends his time with the best. Professionally and otherwise." He winked her way. "You're fortunate you keep such fine company, Ms.—"

"Leake," she replied, but Chip noted the falling smile.

So. Tesla man was going to work behind the scenes to keep his fairy girlfriend in the next show. It wasn't surprising. And certainly not something to be embarrassed about. Still, the look on her face told him this was news to her. She blinked his direction, the color in her cheeks deepening.

Mr. Richardson adjusted his hat and turned back to Chip. "Mr. McBride, if you're available, I'd like to come by your office sometime tomorrow to discuss some plans we have for a renovation project we're about to get going at the Barter." He'd brought the business card up to his eyes, peering for some address. "Although, I may have to avert my eyes if you have any Dürers around." His lips twitched at his own joke.

Chip stumbled to respond. "Oh—I'm sure I couldn't give you my best thoughts without walking through the site in question firsthand."

Mr. Richardson was nodding before Chip finished his sentence. "True. True. How about this. I'll call you tomorrow around noon and set up a meeting for this week. I'd like to have eyes like yours on it, see what you think, before we start taking bids."

Chip nodded. "I'd be delighted, sir," he replied. "Here." Only after he handed him the second card from his trousers did he realize he'd done it already. "In case you lose the first."

Mr. Richardson hesitated, then smiled. "You know, I like a

man who's prepared." Mr. Richardson tapped his pocket and the business card tucked underneath. "I'll be in touch."

Chip couldn't help his ballooning smile, though his brothers had warned him it had the look of a six-year-old Boy Scout proud of fitting six marshmallows in his mouth. Hundreds of thousands of dollars were at stake! He turned his attention back to the canvas, dipped his paintbrush, and gave the canvas a flourishing brown curlicue as Theo and Mr. Richardson shook hands and made their farewells.

Voilà.

He stepped back, admiring the squishy brown circle.

A few more curlicues later he felt a presence behind him. He looked over his shoulder.

Bree had her arms crossed tightly over the chest of her yellow pea coat, that look in her eyes as she stared at Theo.

Ohhhh, Chip recognized that look.

He would know that look a mile off.

Considering the way Theo was casually typing on his phone, he had no idea what kind of storm was about to blow his way. Poor chap. Chip almost felt like tapping him on the shoulder and whispering in his ear, *Run*.

Theo finished tapping and slipped the phone into his pocket. He looked up, saw Bree's burnishing glare, and frowned.

"I'll have you know, Theo, that I am a terrible fairy."

His mouth opened. It shut. It opened again. "Of course you're not—"

"I am. You know I am. They could've bought a mannequin to replace me and saved a few thousand dollars."

"I don't know what you're trying to get at here. Are you affronted that I complimented you?"

"Yes." She nodded her head firmly. "And I resent it."

Theo looked dumbfounded.

Chip's Boy Scout grin sprouted.

Theo took a step toward her. "I just thought you would appreciate a nice word to the chief administrator—"

"A nice word? That wasn't a nice word. That was an embarrassing display of favoritism. How do you think I'll feel if I get cast into that role in two weeks?"

"Relieved? Pleased?"

"Cheap."

"Cheap?" Theo's eyes flickered to Chip, who directed his attention to his canvas. His voice lowered. "Come now, Bree. This is just the art of business, not some sort of prostitutional barter."

"I see what you did there—" Chip began, grinning, but the look on both of their faces whipping his way made him cough and turn back to his easel.

Theo reached for her arm. "This is what I do. Leveraging networking relationships to achieve the optimal outcome for both clients and businesses. I assumed you'd appreciate a little help in a time of need—"

"Because I need it?" Bree replied.

"You just said you did!"

Bree turned her chin away. "I never said any such thing."

Theo, dumbstruck, held out his hands. "Can you tap-dance, Bree? Do you have alternate employment options between shows?"

Chip grinned wider as he listened, his throat tingling with the urge to laugh as he watched the quarrel from the corner of his eye.

Bree's face was flushed as she shoved her hands into her pockets. "Whether I can tap-dance is unimportant here. The point is, there's no honor in awarding someone a job they aren't qualified for. I can't imagine the rumors that would go around."

Theo raised a brow. "About you and Mr. Richardson?"

"No," she retorted. "About you and me."

He smiled. Saw her expression. Stopped smiling. "And that's . . . a bad thing?"

"If people believe I'm using you, yes!" she sputtered. Without pausing she pointed at Chip. "Stop smiling."

Chip put his free hand to his chest, fighting his smile down. "Forgive me, neighbor, but I believe I'm the one stationed here, incapable of moving my conversation elsewhere—"

"Chip?"

The three of them stopped.

Oh boy.

Twice today he'd heard a woman's voice he didn't want to hear.

Wincing, he turned around, all jovial spirit gone. "Heyyyy, Ashleigh."

And there Ashleigh stood, gawking as the head of his mother's little tribe. His mother stood behind her to the right, the group lining up like bowling pins in formation.

Ashleigh looked from him to his easel. "I'm . . . confused. I thought you had work today."

He felt his own neck starting to flush. "I did. I do. I just had a quick side project going."

Her frown deepened. "Painting? You never told me you painted." Everything about her face and voice was like a soft, fluffy white kitten with a hurt paw.

Out of the corner of his eye he saw Bree's frown turn. Her posture straighten. One brow twitched ever so slightly as if to say, *Trouble in paradise, Chippy boy?*

They all split up quickly after, Bree and Theo continuing their stiff conversation on one side of the Creeper Trail, Chip taking on Ashleigh and her endless questions on the other. Chip's mother directed the tribe to a spot beneath the canopy of some trees while covering her son's lapse of judgment with phrases like, "My youngest son has always carried the mysterious virtues found in such men as Picasso and Kandinsky. I'm not surprised, honestly, that he's expressing the cerebral needs of his right brain through the lens of the canvas. Much like Van Gogh, in the 1800s, who was misunderstood by so many in his time . . ."

♡ ♡ ♡

Chip paid for his little lie to Ashleigh. By that evening, he'd ignored twenty-five work calls, sixteen text messages, and fourteen emails so he could focus on fifteen thoughtful apologies, mostly in the form of "I'm sorry" and "No, I don't have a hidden alternate lifestyle." It also cost him one exquisite, covered-in-guilt-and-gravy dinner for two at the Tavern.

Finally back at home, Chip pulled himself out of his truck and shuffled to his own dark house. The street was silent, void of signs of life from the parallel-parked cars and lightless houses. But Mrs. Lewis's porch light glimmered.

Beneath the caramel full moon, Chip dragged himself up the porch steps and sat down. Soon Russell lay beside him with his head on his paws, drooping eyelids slowly closing off the midnight-blue world.

He felt the jab in his pants pocket and pulled out his business card.

He twirled it around a few times between his fingers.

He was five days overdue paying four subcontractors.

Six hundred forty-two dollars away from the business account dropping into the red.

Twenty degrees from freezing in his fixer-upper home.

But, he thought, spinning the business card around and around . . .

He had his dog.

A girlfriend who was better than he deserved.

A house with a terrific view of the Appalachian Mountains.

And perhaps, just perhaps, a date with destiny.

Now all he needed was a bank crazy enough to lend him two million dollars.

Chapter 11

BREE

"Yes, Cass, I have walked through my options. And this is the only logical plan of action."

On the other end of the phone line, Bree heard a sharp whistle and the telltale noise of sneakers squeaking against the linoleum flooring of a gymnasium. Bree pulled the phone from her ear while Cassie yelled, "Go, Star!" before her voice shifted with scary speed. "Sorry, Bree. Anyway—this idea is completely insane. Surely you have more sensible options."

"You tell me then," Bree replied, holding the phone to her ear with her shoulder while pulling up the workout leg warmers Birdie had supplied. She pulled the phone away from her ear to check the time: 11:42 a.m. Almost game time. "You try. Tell me what *you'd* do in my position."

"You could sit down with him and have an honest conversation."

"I have. And by the end of that conversation, I was balled up on the floor of his kitchen trying to hide inside my own jacket. Then he laughed, and then he promised to move that fence, which he didn't do, and then he laughed some more—"

"C'mon, Ref! Fine," Cassie said, cutting off Bree's rant. "Then just do whatever every neighbor on the face of the earth does. Ignore him."

Bree hopped down the porch stairs. "I do that already. Regularly."

"No, I mean really ignore him."

"I did. Cass, he got a card in the mail from my parents—and he *sent one back*. They're corresponding now. They're planning a trip here in three weeks to bring *their* dog to *his* house for 'dog-training camp.'"

Bree flung open her car's passenger door, twitching away when Russell presented himself beside the vehicle. The English mastiff stood on the line, barking. She frowned at him, slipped into the passenger seat, and popped open the glove box.

The dog kept barking.

"Honestly, Bree, how bad can this guy be if your parents love him so much?"

"You know their value judgments mean nothing. Remember Flapjack Jack?"

Cassie went silent. Neither she nor Bree could forget the man her parents tried to set her up with at an IHOP. The man whose face suddenly popped up on the restaurant's corner television with the headline "Escaped Inmate from Louisiana State Penitentiary Last Seen in Stolen Blue Civic Heading North on I-81."

They all looked from the screen, to the matching man, to the parking lot. And the blue Civic he'd parked there ten minutes earlier.

For at least two years, her parents pressed pause on setting up their daughter.

As she and Cassie talked, Bree slid a CD into the car player, her eyes ticking up to Chip's farthest right-hand window while she did so. She could see Chip sitting there at a plastic pop-up table. The room was empty of everything except his computer, chair, and a slew of papers covering his makeshift desk. He was on the phone. He stood, and she scooted out from her seat and shut the door.

The dog's barks grew louder, in rhythm with his vertical jumps.

"Hush," Bree said, her ears crackling with his reverberating barks. She moved back to the porch, excitement rising as she slipped on her tap shoes.

"For the record," Cassie said, "my official statement is that I am not in support of any of your decisions here and henceforth regarding this situation."

"Noted and appreciated." Bree spotted Birdie's car coming down the street.

"See, I don't think you understand what *appreciated* means. Appreciated means you see my logic and will change—"

"Gotta run," Bree cut in. "Shake your fist at the ref for me!"

Bree set the phone on the porch railing and danced down the steps once more, ignoring the clap of her heels and toes as she strode down the sidewalk. Her face broke into a wide smile as the car's doors opened and out spilled Myra, Evan, Luke, and Birdie, all dressed in warm-up attire.

Luke, who preferred the millennial man-bun look, eyed the property. "So this is the notorious Evie's house. I've always wanted to see the inside of this place."

Bree frowned, and Luke amended, "And your house."

She motioned to the cleared front porch. She had meticulously moved every pot and plant to the yard. Thankfully this was not a typical Virginia April, when the sky eked out one final, surprise blizzard before giving in to green trees and mossy undergrowth. The sun hovered overhead, the sky rich and blue, the air a crisp fifty-four degrees.

The group looked at the freshly hand-mopped porch, the stack of water bottles, and the folded hand towels. Bree was ready.

She checked her phone again: 11:48 a.m.

They spent the next five minutes slipping on their tap shoes, warming up, and lining the porch walls with the props they'd need, mostly umbrellas and fedoras. "This is really nice," Myra said, stretching one leg on the porch railing as if it were a ballet barre. "Built-in studio, fresh air, lots of space. Good acoustics. Man, if you'd let us, Bree, we could practice here every day."

"Let you!" Bree practically barked. "I'd like to *force* you!"

Their expressions tempered her tone. "Because I'm committed to us getting cast in this play."

"Musical," Luke corrected.

She shook a finger at Luke. "Right. Musical."

"Let's be honest," Myra said, lifting her foot off the makeshift bar. "The chances of all five of us getting a spot are pretty much nil." She turned to Evan, the one who, amazingly enough, was even less talented than Bree. "Have you guys made plans for if you don't get cast?"

"Why does everybody look at me when you ask this question?" Evan retorted.

"All right, guys, we don't have time for another pity party." Birdie released her leg from a stretch that looked debilitating. "Bree, where can we play the music?"

Bree dropped her phone on the pack of water bottles. The time now: 11:56 a.m. "My car. I'll go turn it on."

Birdie put her hand on her hip, her arm slender like that of a prima ballerina. She raised a quizzical brow. "Your car?"

"Yeah," Bree called behind her as she stepped off the porch. "The stereo will be perfect."

Birdie moved to the railing. "Won't that be too loud for the neighbors?"

Bree waved away her question. "Stonewall Heights couldn't be more loyal to the Barter. They'll probably all come and watch in support. It'll be like a free show for them."

Bree threw her car door open just as Russell, again, jumped out from behind the car and started barking.

Even at this distance Bree heard the group take in a breath, several hands flying to their chests at the sight of the murder dog.

Bree turned the key and pressed Play. Then lowered all four windows, releasing the music from its captivity.

"Perfect," Birdie said, giving her a thumbs-up as the group began to move into formation.

Bree cranked up the volume to the max.

Birdie shouted something back, but Bree could only read her lips as the music poured through the neighborhood like a flood. She jumped out of the car, walked around to the back, and popped open the trunk. There, two fat subwoofer speakers plucked straight from the 1990s took up every square inch of trunk space. The world was completely overcome with the music of "Singin' in the Rain." No other sound could compete. Not the birds on the electric lines overhead, who were flying away en masse. Not the chickens clucking and clamoring to get inside their henhouse. Not the enormous beast of a dog who had turned tail and run toward the backyard. She smiled at the speakers like they were her newborn twins.

She put raging tailgate parties to shame.

The cast had taken to shaking umbrellas at her to get her attention, but she just kept smiling blissfully.

Why?

Because it was 12:01 p.m.

Perfect. Absolutely perfect.

"Are you sure it's not too loud?" Birdie shouted into Bree's ears as she hopped back up on the porch and took her place in the back of the group. Bree shook her head, her slap-happy grin glued to her face.

"Good stage smile, Bree!" Birdie yelled again into her ear with another thumbs-up. "Too big, maybe, but good to see you've been working on it!"

Birdie moved to the front of the group. She raised her hands and rested them on her waist, feet in position, chin raised. Everyone else followed.

Birdie waited four beats and gave a sharp nod.

And as if it couldn't get any louder, the mass tap dancing began.

And singing.

They were a level 8 earthquake in tap shoes.

Out of the corner of her eye she saw Mrs. Lewis step onto her front porch in her bathrobe. She gave Bree a little wave.

Bree waved back and kept tapping.

Flap-flap-step-step-brush-hop-step

Flap-shuffle-ball change-brush heel

Flap-flap-brush-hop-step-ball change

Bree followed along with the steps, stumbling every few beats as she strained her neck to look into Chip's window. Every time she managed to catch a glimpse of him, she lost her place and needed at least eight beats to get back into rhythm.

"Brush hop left," Luke said after Bree missed her turn and they collided.

Bree stumbled back to position.

It didn't matter though, because through the window, she saw what she'd been hoping to see. Her smile widened as he moved to the window. With a perplexed expression, he watched the performance.

Their eyes locked.

Bree saw curiosity in his gaze. Some daring. As if he wanted to say, *And what are you up to now, Miss Bree Leake of 425 Stonewall Heights?*

And then, to her utter delight, she saw him reach into his pocket. Pull out, at exactly 12:03 p.m., his phone.

And, with recognition snapping into place, stare at her.

Chapter 12

CHIP

Chip fumbled for the Accept button on his phone—the movement he'd been waiting to make all morning. Right now he could barely hear himself think, let alone concentrate on a potentially life-changing phone call. He was supposed to be an organized and successful businessman. But what about the insane, musical-twist-on-a-tailgate-party currently shaking down his house?

Chip stared at the group sashaying in a circle full of jazz hands. How would he ever explain this?

The phone rang a second time. He moved away from the raging party and toward another part of the house, dodging paint buckets and chop saws and panels of Sheetrock he had yet to install in the dining room. He stopped in the corner of the dining room, standing at the farthest square foot possible from the noise. When it rang a third time, he pressed Accept.

And magically, as if God and His angels had thrown down the Cone of Silence over his house, the music stopped.

"Chip McBride here," Chip answered in his most clipped-yet-friendly, easygoing-yet-professional voice.

An eruption of trumpets and drums and tap shoes blasted through the walls again. He slid toward the kitchen.

"Chip, it's Clarence Richardson. How are you?"

"Oh, Mr. Richardson," Chip said, scrambling to open the refrigerator. He opened it and stuck his head inside, next to a gallon of milk. "Doing well. Glad you called."

"Yes, well, I'm sorry to say I missed seeing your painting at the King Museum yesterday evening. I know some young artists can get bashful about an unfinished product on display, but still, I had hoped you would understand the spirit of the event."

"You missed my painting?" Chip replied, pushing orange juice aside to stick his head in farther. "Oh, that's too bad. It was just beside the"—he closed his eyes for a moment, trying to remember the old building he'd been to so many times as a kid—"water fountain," he said. "It was beside the water fountain."

"Beside the water fountain?"

Chip nodded, and his head knocked against the fridge ceiling. "Just above it actually. To the left. There was a plant there though. Lots of people. Easy to miss. Anyway, what can I do for you?"

"Well, I just looked at my schedule this week and it's a bit dense. What do you think about—I'm sorry, what is that noise in the background? Are you . . . is that . . . music?"

Chip jumped out of the fridge and slammed it shut. He didn't want to move closer to the abysmal noise, but the only place he hadn't tried hiding at this point was in one of the three bedrooms upstairs. Unfortunately, that would mean getting closer to the source of the noise before going up.

He had no choice.

He jogged toward the stairs, covering the phone with his hand as he did.

"Yes," Chip said, pulling his hand off momentarily as he took the stairs three at a time. "Let me see"—he covered the phone again—"if I can turn this down."

"Is that . . ." Mr. Richardson said, suspicion heavy in his voice, "'All I Do Is Dream of You'?"

Chip ran inside his room and shut the door. The windows vibrated with the noise.

He snatched up his pillow and all but dove for his closet.

Yanking the door shut, he dropped on the floor in the blackness, stuffing the pillow between the cracks. "Yes," he said, catching the muffled but still audible chorus. "Yes, I believe it is."

Chip hung his head.

There was a pause.

"Splendid!" Mr. Richardson remarked. "I've been listening to that same tape all morning. You know, we'll be doing that musical for the next lineup. *Singin' in the Rain*. You'll have to come and sing all the songs from the audience. I know I will!"

Mr. Richardson chuckled on the other end of the line, and Chip, only too heartily, joined in.

"Tell you what. Were you planning, by chance, to attend the finale of *A Midsummer Night's Dream* Sunday afternoon?" Mr. Richardson said.

"Was I?" Chip gave a half laugh, half cough. "Where else would one rather be this coming Sunday?"

"Excellent. We'll mix business and pleasure. I'll tour you around before the show then. See you around noon?"

There was another pause in the music outside.

Chip stood, then cracked open the door. Slammed it shut as a new song began.

"Perfect," he said over the trumpets. "I'll see you then."

Chip sweated through the slew of polite parting statements, then set the phone down in the darkness of the closet and exhaled. He could feel his hot face in the darkness, knew that if anyone opened the door on him in that moment they'd find a grown man sitting cross-legged on the floor, grinning like an ape who'd found his lost banana.

Because Chip McBride had weaseled his way into a meeting with the chief administrator of Abingdon's renovation project of the year. The very same Chip McBride who—after days of strategic internet research—knew more about domed ceilings, sweeping archways, and embossed gold wallpaper than the architects and manufacturers of old.

He let his imagination run wild for a moment. He pictured himself in a brand-new workspace: a historically renovated office building with an original Degas painting on the wall, offering Perrier to his clients.

Chip moved to the window and gazed down. The chorus to "Singin' in the Rain" spilled out of the speakers. The dancers clumsily twirled a variety of umbrellas as they danced in the congested area. Floral umbrellas, tattered umbrellas, not one but two oversized umbrellas with "First Tennessee Bank" printed in gold. He smiled, seeing Bree nearly poke out the eye of another girl as she, a beat behind the others, spun in a circle.

He watched Bree put her hand up and step back, evidently in

the midst of apologizing when she glanced up and caught his eye. She paused, her umbrella drooping.

He smiled with everything he had.

Then, just for the fun of watching her umbrella drop completely, he waved.

"Nice try, Bree," he said, and even though she couldn't hear him, he could've sworn from her expression she knew exactly what he'd said.

Several hours and several dozen calls, problems sorted, estimates created, and dollars juggled later, Chip whistled to Russell as he made his way upstairs. His legs ached from the dinnertime run. His knees ached from the two hours he'd spent sanding the floor. Still, the house was slowly coming along.

Russell pushed ahead of him through the door of his room and jumped on his bed, circling as he scratched at the sleeping bag. Chip was on the cusp of telling Russ to stop when the dog dropped with a belly-flop thud, jaw slack and panting.

After double-checking his alarm, Chip set the phone facedown on the table, switched off the light, and lay on his bed. For one solid minute he stared up at the ceiling, replaying the scenes of the day.

Watched the highlight reel fly by.

Captured the key moments.

Smiled to himself as he paused on one moment in particular.

He switched on the light.

Sat up. Pulled out his phone.

One text message to her parents, and he'd secured her email.

Now came the fun part.

Sixty-two blissful minutes later, after signing her up for a variety of e-newsletters, he was clicking Complete on the tenth catalog subscription for a Miss Leake, 425 Stonewall Heights Drive. Within days everything from *All About Mastiffs* to *Potato Review* to (his personal favorite) *Rage Be Gone!* would be making its way to her door. He even started a special subscription for Evie: *Beyond Off-the-Grid*. With any luck, Evie would yank the AC out of their house just in time for summer.

He scoured under his bed for his journal and a Sharpie, yanked out a piece of paper, and wrote his neighbor a message.

Four minutes later he pushed his feet back into the sleeping bag and flicked off the light. Chip turned on his side, watching her window through his.

He smiled to himself with one final glance at the sheet of paper he'd taped to the window.

And fell asleep.

Chapter 13

BREE

YOU'VE GOT MAIL

It took three times reading through the glass to register the words. She rubbed her tired eyes, peered through the dawning world outside, and read again.

At the bottom of the simple piece of scratch paper, there was a secondary note.

She squinted, and the blurry words came into focus:

PS: THANKS FOR THE SERENADE

Every muscle from her pinky toe to hip flexor cried out as she tenderly made her barefoot way down the stairs and to the front door. Why was she even doing this? Surely this was a trick, some rude power flex. She should ignore that note in the window and walk right back up the stairs.

Bree pressed her lips together. Turned the first lock. The second. The third.

Quietly, she cracked the door open. Peered down at the fraying doormat.

Mail? She had no nefarious packages from him. No evil surprises dropped on her doorstep.

He was just messing with her, per usual. Maybe now his plan was to include mind games.

But thirty minutes later, as she sat at the dining room table and opened her phone email, it clicked.

Her eyes followed the stream of new spamming emails, nearly all starting with "Congratulations! And welcome to our . . ."

Mail.

Oh, she definitely had mail.

Bree munched on her second plate of eggs and sausage as she clicked through the email catalog subscriptions with one thumb, deleting them one by one.

Her gaze shifted, though, with the sound that was becoming so familiar down the street. She stopped. Perked her ears.

"Evie," Bree called over her shoulder to the kitchen, where Evie was fighting to choke down some kombucha. "The UPS guy is here!"

She danced to the living room window and heard Evie drop her glass on the countertop. Bree opened a curtain and peeked through.

Yes. It was definitely Gerald.

There was an upside and a downside to the UPS man's appearance these days. The downside was that it meant Evie had ordered something else. Again. There were only so many candle-making kits one could squeeze inside an eighteen-hundred-square-foot-house. The upside was that the interactions between him and Evie were priceless. Bree liked to think of them as a bumbling version of a Hallmark movie on her doorstep. Every single time Gerald dropped off a package, she wanted to hide behind a curtain and watch the awkward sparks fly.

"But I haven't ordered anything," Evie said, rushing into the living room like there was a school fire drill, she was in charge of it, and she had no idea where the exits were. She pushed her hair up as though by mere force she could make the high bun higher.

But then—oh. Well, apparently with enough hair spray, she could.

Bree raised a brow as she helped Evie untie her apron. "*You* haven't ordered anything, Evie? *Really*?"

"No, I've ordered things, but—" Evie seemed defensive. She lifted the apron off her neck and over her head. "I'm just not expecting anything to arrive *today*."

Bree took one look at her panicked roommate. She'd been watching them bumble along for months. Last week she had decided to step in. It was time to assist, to intervene in this romantic plateau.

"What could it be then? If I didn't order anything, and you *never* order anything . . . Where's my lipstick? And my lashes?" She started patting down her face. "And the cookies! I didn't have time to make the cookies—" Evie was clutching her chest.

"Calm down, Evie," Bree said, taking her by the shoulders.

"I told him last time about the cookies. I *said* I'd make them—"

"The man doesn't need any cookies. He isn't Santa—"

"But—"

The doorbell rang, loud and clear, and they both shut their mouths at once.

Evie's eyes roved around the room and landed on the tube of bright red lipstick sitting on the windowsill.

The doorbell rang again.

She took a step toward the lipstick, and Bree grabbed her by the back of the shirt and turned her around. "You look *great*," she whispered. She gave her a little shove toward the knob. "Now go get 'im."

Evie approached the door like a sloth. To move things along, Bree gave the knob a twist and darted behind the door. She yanked it open, exposing Evie batting her lashes.

Bree tiptoed backward toward the window and inched the curtain back to see through.

Gerald held a five-foot-long package. "Mornin', Evie," he said, his voice more gravelly than usual.

She pinked.

"Mornin', Gerald. That's . . . quite a package you got there."

"I was about to say that myself. I couldn't help but notice the label on the box—" He looked down at the Quest logo stamped along one side. "So, you got a fishing reel after all." He paused, then awkwardly placed the box in her arms.

When he stepped back again, he rubbed the back of his neck. "It was just . . . nice to see you ended up getting one . . . after all. After we talked about it that one day . . ."

"A fishing pole?" Evie said, surprise clear in her voice as she looked at the illustration of the rod on the cardboard box.

Bree coughed discreetly.

Evie jerked her head to Bree. Had Evie penciled in her eyebrows properly, everyone would've seen them fly to the sky. "Oh yes! The fishing reel! For trout fishing. Yes, indeedy. I did buy that." She clutched the box to her chest. "Because I want to fish. So badly."

They stood silent for a moment, Gerald rubbing the back of his neck while it turned red, and Evie batting her lashes at him at 90 miles per hour.

Good grief.

Bree had put the bait in their hands. In their literal hands. All the two of them had to do was take the next step.

Say it.

Bree squinted through the window, willing Gerald to say the words.

Seconds ticked by.

C'mon, man, say it.

SAY. IT.

Bree exhaled and pushed herself off the window. She walked to the stairs, then loudly hopped off the bottom step and marched through the living room like she hadn't a care in the world. Halfway through, she stopped as though noticing the two of them for the first time. Her leg halted in the air, and she pivoted toward them.

"Oh? What's that, Evie? Looks like a . . . fishing pole?" Bree set her hands on her hips. Put on her serious face. "Evie, have you got someone to show you how to fish? Don't tell me you're thinking of going out to the Holston all alone, when you can't swim—"

"You can't swim?" Gerald interjected.

"Of course I can swim—I'm just—" Evie began.

"I can take you out sometime," Gerald said, quick as a beat and then halting as though realizing what he'd said. "I'd just . . .

uh . . . I'd hate to see a lady such as yourself out there, stuck in high water."

Bree nodded, fingers pressed to her lips. "But can I trust that you will keep my dear, *dear* friend Evie safe?"

"Oh." Gerald was nodding. "The safest."

"I don't know," Bree said. She folded her arms across her chest. "Maybe you ought to get some good swimming lessons under your belt first, Evie."

"Lessons? Oh, well . . ." Gerald had his hat off now and was playing with it in his hands. "I don't mean to puff myself up, 'course, but I did happen to be on the swim team back in high school. We got third place in state."

Bree popped her hip out as her eyebrows rose. "Oh really? Is that so?"

"If we could, maybe, find a pool—" Gerald began.

"Like the one that's open at Virginia High Tuesday through Friday from four to seven and every Saturday from nine to one?" Bree said, and then shrugged. "Because I've heard that's a good one."

Bree left the two of them and moved to the dining room, knowing her job was done. They could handle the details of their date without her hovering.

With one major checkmark on the day's to-do list done, Bree snagged her plate from the dining room and moved to the kitchen. She leaned against the counter with her plate and glanced through the window. Chip stood there inside his own house, moving around his own kitchen.

She would've surrendered some of her frustration with him, even just momentarily, had the sign not caught her eye.

Still there. Mocking her.

YOU'VE GOT MAIL.
PS: THANKS FOR THE SERENADE

Of course, she was well aware she started the paper-to-window memos. If THIS ISN'T OVER for Bree, then apparently it wasn't going to be for him either. Bree took a brooding sip of the now lukewarm coffee and began to list Chip's faults in her head. First the rude driving, then the water line, then the repeated assaults from his dog, then the fact he lied to her about the Invisible Fence, then knocking on her door at three in the morning to give her the fake message that he had moved it, then daring to chuckle to himself *every single time* something bad happened to her because of him . . .

She wasn't losing her mind, was she? He really had put up that sign, even if no one else was there to see it. He was toying with her. And what had she done so far? What had been her act against him? Nothing. Just a single, tiny little episode involving music and tap dancing.

If she could just figure out how to drive him half as crazy as he was driving her.

For that matter, if she could only get that man to *leave*.

After all, he was one of those McBride sons; he probably owned dozens of properties all over town. If she could just get him to change his mind about his so-called treasure of a home. Just make him flip the house to some far less annoying owner—like a family with eight kids, or an aspiring tuba player—well, she'd be doing everyone a favor. He could make loads of money selling it and find himself a nice residential house somewhere far, far away. He with his holey T-shirts and alluring five-o'clock shadows could marry Ashleigh, and they could move together into the country.

Where they could have perfect shiny-haired, brown-eyed babies together.

If only there were some way to make *him* less comfortable—

Bree's eyes narrowed as she watched him. The way he stood at the sink the last several minutes, staring out thoughtfully, coffee in hand, like her. The way he looked at the mountains. The—her eyes followed his—*perfect* panoramic view of the Appalachian Mountains.

Bree set her mug on the counter so hard the coffee jostled and spilled a bit.

"Where are you going?" Evie said gruffly, moving into the kitchen. "We've got some talking to do—"

"We'll talk in a minute," Bree said, snatching her keys off the key post and yanking the door open. She turned quickly to Evie. "Evie. What does your lifestyle book say about planting trees?"

"Trees? How are you going to pay for trees?"

"I'm not!"

Chapter 14

CHIP

Chip woke up Friday morning smiling.

He went down the stairs, whistling "Singin' in the Rain," smiling.

He hummed along as he made his breakfast, smiling.

And when he opened up his email at the start of the workday to find the inbox sitting at eighty-two new emails from places like *Women's World* saying, "Thank you for joining our daily newsletter! See below for 52 Easy Steps to Melting That Belly Fat Away," his smile grew into laughter.

"*Touché*," Chip murmured, taking pains to scroll to the bottom of each email and unsubscribe. And the ones with the dodgy unsubscribe buttons . . . Oh, it was clever.

Chip paused halfway down one. Scanned the paragraph. Paused on the phrase, "With our 100 percent natural clay and seaweed hair removal cream, you can remove stubborn, overgrown hair from your legs in minutes." Clicked Forward. Swiftly typed in her email.

Wrote beneath the subject, "I think this one was meant for you? I'm so glad to see you are doing something about this."

Hit Send.

It was truly a wonderful world.

Until, glancing up to her window, he saw the newly posted sign.

And then heard the rumble of the truck down the road.

Chip stared out his kitchen window at an excavator making its way toward Bree's backyard. Then his eyes ticked over to the sign taped to Bree's window:

OH, CHRISTMAS TREE.

He knew something was up. He just didn't know how high.

He began to get the sense of it when he saw a semitruck bearing three fifteen-foot fir trees following the excavator, which started digging right on the other side of his fence.

A while later he saw a hard-hatted man peer down and say, "About two more feet should do it."

The excavator responded with another dip of its massive claw.

The man put a hand up and the hoe stopped.

Chip was still staring, thirty minutes later, as the trees were transferred from the back of the semi into his neighbor's backyard. They thudded into the ground, tall and green. Solidifying his new reality: his million-dollar view was obliterated.

♡ ♡ ♡

"Ms. Littleton is just finishing up a meeting at the moment. She'll be on a work trip for the remainder of the week, but she'll be happy to give you a call back when she returns."

"Next week?" Chip's attention fell away from the hideous trees and refocused on the phone conversation. Never in the four years he'd worked at McBride and Sons had Ms. Littleton, bank manager of Third Bank and Trust, ever put him on hold, much less told him she'd have to call him back *in a week*. Sure, he was on his own now, but seriously?

This woman wasn't ignorant. She had to know that he knew what he was doing. Chip pushed an open door on his new slow-close cabinet. It was a bit off balance and slammed.

He pressed the phone to his other ear. "I just need one minute of her time. Please. This is *Chip McBride*."

"I know, sir. I relayed your message: Chip McBride wants to speak with you regarding upping his line of credit for a new project."

"Did you add the urgent part? Did you say it was urgent?"

He popped the screen door open—it creaked loudly—and moved down the rotting back steps.

"I did, sir. I'm sorry. She's tied up the rest of the day."

In the past four years, whenever she had been "tied up" and unavailable to someone else, it had been because *he* needed her time. Back then, Ms. Littleton would halt whatever meeting, drop whatever call, and throw whatever customer into whatever sitting area, plying them with coffee and lollipops, in order to accommodate *him*. The woman—the bank for that matter—tripped over their feet for *him*. Oh, how the tables had turned.

Chip swallowed hard. Fine. If this was how they were going to treat him when he was on his own without Daddy's dollar bills, it was better to know now.

His phone indicated an incoming call from one of his subcontractors.

"I see. Well, I'll look forward to her call next week." *If I haven't found a new bank by then.*

He switched the line.

"What's up, Andy?"

"We're not going to be able to drop off that dumpster to Kingston Road on Tuesday. Johnny said they're going to need to keep my last one for another week, and . . ."

Chip listened as Andy went down the rabbit trail of explaining who needed which one where, and for how long, and why.

Half listening, Chip stopped next to his fence.

Looked up to the towering firs.

Half of his mountain view, gone. The entire right half of his perfect, panoramic view of the Blue Ridge Mountains, ruined. Decimated by three fat, overstuffed Christmas trees spanning the length of their fence line.

Chip's shoulders tensed as he heard her voice.

"It's absolutely perfect, Theo. I can't thank you enough."

He turned slowly toward her elevated back porch.

There she was, leaning on the rail, slender and tall in loose, threadbare jeans and a pale beige sweater. Tesla Man stood at her side; Evie sat on a chair behind them. Bree's hair was shinier than he'd ever seen it, a loose bun high on top of her head. There was a shimmering pinkness to her cheeks, and he was fairly certain it was the first time he'd seen her in makeup—real makeup, not of the green Shrek variety. But the thing that was shining most of all were her eyes. They positively glittered.

That woman.

As if sensing his stare, she turned her head and refreshed her smile like she was noticing him for the first time. She put her hand on Theo's arm.

"Well, hello, neighbor. What do you think of the new and improved backyard? I felt so stimulated by the hard work you were pouring into your own home, and then was so inspired by that natural beautification article in the *Beyond Off-the-Grid* magazine that popped up at our front door. It got me thinking."

She looked over her shoulder to Evie. "We should seek to . . . revitalize our world with the raw, simple materials of nature's bounty. Isn't that how it goes, Evie?"

Evie nodded and gave two thumbs up.

Bree turned her grin back to him. "So when Theo thought of his quaint family Christmas tree farm in Damascus, and all those lonely oversized Fraser firs too big to get cut down and stocked for Christmas—"

"Actually," Theo interrupted, "I believe you were the one to bring up the farm—"

"I just knew we had the perfect opportunity to give them a new home," Bree continued. "Wasn't it generous of Theo's family to donate them to our cause? And aren't they just divine?"

Her profile shifted toward them, a picture of innocent happiness. "I could just stare at them all day. Couldn't you?"

"Andy, I'm gonna have to call you back," Chip said and dropped the phone from his ear.

His eyes shifted from her to the hideous trees.

In that moment, things changed.

The woman had gone too far.

♡ ♡ ♡

Saturday night Ashleigh stood at her usual spot beside the door while Chip got ready for their dinner date. The pile of magazines on the floor beside the door—no doubt just a fraction of the ones to come—however, was anything but usual.

"Chip? Are you having any . . . health troubles?" she said, eyeing the magazine with the headline, "Witch Hazel! The Magical Homeopathic Way to Clear Up Hemorrhoids."

"My back has been killing me since that fall on my bike last week," Chip called over his shoulder as he worked on his tie in the mirror of the open bathroom.

Through the reflection, he saw her nudging the magazine with her shoe to reveal the one underneath. Her eyes widened like one of those anime cartoon characters, her cheeks flushing a rosy pink. "And . . . do you know, I happened to pop into Jared jewelry store the other day with Gracie—"

His brow furrowed. "Jared? Isn't that out in Knoxville?"

She waved a hand. "She was getting her ring cleaned—"

"She had to drive to Knoxville to get her ring cleaned?"

"Anyway, I saw this stunning French-set halo diamond ring. I was actually so surprised it was in store at such a value . . ."

His fingers paused on the tie, and he swiveled around to look at her. Then the magazine at her feet. Ah. The Diamond Nexus catalog.

He turned back around.

"You know, I just really, really like that"—she enunciated each word—"French. Set. Diamond. Halo. Style." She started nudging the stack with her toe again. "Of course all the bands are beautiful, and it's the sentiment that counts, but if I were so lucky as to pick a ring, I would go with the—Chip?"

She stopped. Her tone was higher than usual, which was truly saying something. "Chip? Is there something we need to discuss? Any . . . area of your life that is out of control?"

Terrific. He knew what she'd seen. His fingers finished up his tie.

"No," he called over his shoulder. "I do not have an addiction to eating chalk." He turned and gestured to the special-edition psychology magazine for people struggling to overcome all addictions. The one in bold scribbled chalk across the front was "Pica Addiction: Your Nasty Secret."

"I believe that one belongs to my neighbor."

"Really?" She nudged the magazine halfway covering it aside. "It has your address."

"It was a mistake."

"It says right here, Chippy the Chipmunk McBride." She paused, her perfectly formed eyebrows tweaking up. "That's odd."

"Believe me, Ashleigh, I can spell my own name. And I don't make jokes better suited for third graders. But if you'd prefer to investigate the house and pull together an intervention group . . ."

It took several more minutes of defending himself and declaring he had not ordered the magazines before she let the matter go. Still, as they drove into town and walked across the sidewalk and into Rain, he couldn't help noticing Ashleigh rubbing the ring finger of her left hand with her thumb and casting a few wistful looks down. Good grief. The woman was genuinely disappointed he wasn't actually a man with a chalk problem, in need of hemorrhoid cream, obsessed with tropical birds, in search of an engagement ring.

It was impossible, but it was almost like Bree *knew* he would've dropped the magazines by the door in his haste, and she *knew* Ashleigh would stand there by the front door, waiting on him, and see it. He could never prove it, but he'd bet everything those magazines hadn't been for him. They were for *her.* To get to *him.* And that fact was both irritating and impressive.

♡♡♡

The next day, standing in front of the Barter, he was still ruminating on how she did it.

It was a temperate Sunday afternoon, cars inching along bumper to bumper on Main Street in the post-church rush to get out of ties and dresses and whip up potato salad for Sunday family suppers. Weekenders slowed to take pictures of the iconic Barter building with its charming exterior and medieval-looking flags. Or they gawked at the sprawling estate of the Martha Washington Inn and wondered who was in the mysterious limousines that deposited guests at the lobby.

Chip hadn't told his mother why he couldn't attend that afternoon's supper, opting instead for a vague explanation. "Something's come up, Mom," he said. She used her time-honed mothering skills to express disappointment over the phone without saying one word about her disappointment over the phone, and frankly, he wasn't sure what she was more disappointed by: that her baby boy wasn't able to make it, or that they would have to go without the cornbread he usually brought.

"Mr. McBride," Mr. Richardson said, stepping off the Barter's bottom step toward him.

Chip hopped up from the crosswalk and met him beneath the sign containing the words *A Midsummer Night's Dream*. He moved forward to shake Mr. Richardson's hand but received a hearty slap on his shoulder instead. The administrator turned on his wingtip heels and guided him inside.

It was a pointless maneuver, but Chip ducked his head slightly into his collar to hide his face. If his father wasn't calling him by the end of the evening, asking why he'd been spending time with Richardson at the Barter, it would be a miracle.

"I want to preserve the basic layout of the lobby here," Mr. Richardson began, stepping onto the decorative red plush carpet between racks of souvenir candles and T-shirts. "But we'll update the café area to offer a more accessible array of fudges, wines, and coffees during intermission. As it is, you can see the space gets congested. Anyway," he said, waving his hands, "black granite, quarter-sawn white oak. I've had my eye on a carpet from Brintons for a while—a rich, red broadloom classic, a perfect blend of the Persian and Amerindian motifs—you know how it is. But in here"—he opened a set of double doors with a flourish—"I see everything different. Here is where I envision *the magic*."

The doors opened onto Gilliam Stage, the main theatre, which sat under a forty-foot ceiling and was saturated in red: rows of rich red seats with the embroidered crest of the Barter shimmering in golden thread, pallets of red damask along the walls, and more elaborate maroon damask carpeting the aisles. The room was royal and rich and, if Chip were quite honest, utterly *not* in need of updating. But then, Mr. Richardson wasn't asking him to be honest.

"Tell me, Mr. McBride, what do you see?"

Mr. Richardson took his fedora off as he gazed up to the two chandeliers dangling from the high ceiling. Chip looked up too.

Ceilings. Okay. This was a bit of a stretch from double-hung windows in ranches or carpet tiles for university gymnasiums, but there were some similarities here. Like, this was a building. And he had worked in a building.

So far so good.

Chip racked his brain for something inspiring. Ceilings. This was a domed ceiling, with two chandeliers . . . Of course, he could suggest a new chandelier.

Maybe a bigger one.

A much bigger one.

With a lot more tiers of those gold, glassy bulbs.

Mr. Richardson shifted his weight to his other foot. "Of course, we could go with some gilded ceiling murals. Those would go nicely with the updated chairs and amber Kashan carpeting for the floors. We'd stick with the crimson color, of course."

"Of course." Chip nodded and started to lower his chin but noticed Mr. Richardson still gazing up.

"But then, even with those murals—should we consider a nautical theme?—we'd still have to do something with the center, and I hate the way the Chicago Theatre just peters out with that milky blue. Such a waste of good space."

"Mmm," Chip said noncommittally toward the sky. "It would be nice to have a center that really pops."

"Exactly. Pops. That's what I envision here. That's what I want."

Chip stood next to Mr. Richardson, craning his neck backward, wordlessly staring at the ceiling until his neck started to ache.

"You know," Mr. Richardson said, hushed and with a touch of giddiness, "I've had dreams where I'd walk into the Barter, like it was any old day, and look up to see it had become"—he lowered his voice even further as his eyes darted toward Chip's—"the *Fox Theatre.*"

He lowered his neck at last and Chip followed suit. Mr. Richardson's eyes were watery, either from emotion or because all the fluid from his neck up had been stuck for the past five minutes with nowhere to go. Regardless, they held a child-like shine, as though he had just told Chip his most sacred secret. "Wouldn't that be something?"

Chip resisted rubbing his neck. The Fox Theatre. It wasn't even worth trying to scroll through his mental cavities. But now, at least, he had a name. And something to spin. Chip summed up his most enthusiastic yet professional voice. "It certainly would. And I want to dig into that thought deeper. But if you could just excuse me a moment, I need to find the gentlemen's room."

He waited for a reply, but Mr. Richardson only looked back up to the ceiling, lost in his own boyhood dreams. "The Fox Theatre," Mr. Richardson murmured. "Wouldn't that be marvelous?"

Chip opened the lobby doors and turned down the hall. As he walked, he pulled out his phone and started typing *Fox Theatre ceiling.*

Chip pushed open the door to the men's room as the website began to load.

He stopped inside the doors.

"Well, well, if it isn't our favorite guy in town."

A steady stream of Google images flooded his phone, but Chip's eyes flickered upward.

At the sink stood Dan, Bree's stepfather, washing his hands beneath a steady flow of water.

"Mr. Leake," Chip said, lowering his phone. "What a pleasant surprise."

"Likewise," he said, turning the faucet knob and reaching for a paper towel. He ripped one off with a glimmer in his eye. "So you're here to see Bree's finale. That's awfully neighborly of you. What would that make this? Two performances in the past four weeks?"

"Oh. Um. Yes. Yes, it is."

Had Bree told them he'd been to her show?

Why would she do that?

What else had she said about him? And perhaps most importantly, why on earth did that give him the urge to smile? What sort of bizarre, sadistic man was he? *The woman ruined your view, man. Don't feel pleased that she's talking about you to her parents.*

His eyes fell back to his phone and pictures of a theatre with an impressively realistic-looking blue sky for a ceiling. The text fell down the page titled, "The Landmark Fox Theatre: An Adventure in Lights."

In truth, Chip had planned to slip out after the meeting with Mr. Richardson. He might get to his folks' in time for the dessert his mother made for family supper. It was cheesecake week. He never missed cheesecake week.

Regardless, he had no intention of experiencing *A Midsummer Night's Dream* a second time.

"I actually plan to—" But then Chip stopped. He looked up to Dan. Grinned. "You know what? I was just about to buy a last-minute ticket. You wouldn't mind if I snag a seat by you, would you?"

"By us?" Dan's eyes lit up. "Oh, of course. That'd be *great*."

Two minutes later Chip hummed to himself as he moved back down the hall, skimming the Fox Theatre article along the way:

> The historic 4,768-seat theatre of Atlanta, Georgia, has thrilled thousands of entertainment-goers since its erection in the 1920s. Since taking on the whimsical task of creating a skyline effect in 1929, with its sky-blue interior paint and ninety-six 11-watt incandescent bulbs . . .

When he swung open the door to Gilliam Stage, he found Mr. Richardson in the exact position he was in before, staring up at the ceiling as though it truly was a night sky.

Chip slipped beside him, hands clasped behind his back, resuming his position as he looked up. "Now, just thinking here, if you were to go with a trompe l'oeil ceiling simulating that starry midnight sky, I think you would want something special to set you apart from the rest of the world. Have you considered, perhaps, the touch of a sunset?"

"A sunset?" Mr. Richardson's brow furrowed for a solid minute as he stared up at the ceiling.

"Yes. Perhaps a changing sunset?"

Mr. Richardson pursed his lips.

Finally, uneasily, Chip said, "Or perhaps—"

"A sunset," Mr. Richardson repeated. "The movement of dawn to dusk." He dropped his head and stared at Chip. "The changing of the stars. An Appalachian sky."

"Well," Chip began.

"And the murals across the walls would represent the changing of the seasons, the local life of the town." He dropped his head. His voice fell to a whisper as he looked into Chip's eyes. "But do you think it's possible?"

Chip recognized that look. It was the look all his clients had when they thought something they wanted was within reach. And all they wanted was to hear their dream was possible.

Chip gave his most confident smile. The smile that nine times out of ten solved whatever problem was standing in his way. "Absolutely. I think that is a terrific idea."

And frankly, it was. It really was.

"Absolutely," Mr. Richardson repeated, as though hearing the words but not yet registering them. His eyes shifted to the stage, where cast members were gathering. "Absolutely."

Suddenly Mr. Richardson swept up Chip's hand in a hearty grasp and started pumping. "And of course, with a ceiling like that we'd have to change the color of the seating—"

"The seating?" Chip's smile dimmed.

"And the carpet, and the walls, the lobby, and . . . We'll have to start from scratch!" He let go of Chip's hand and started moving backward. "Mr. McBride, thank you! I've got to get on this directly!"

"You're doing what?"

"Jotting these notes down! Calling the architect!" He nearly tripped on one of the seats as he backpedaled up the aisle.

"But—"

"You will be in attendance for the bid meeting on the twenty-fifth, won't you?" He was already at the back row. "You think you can make it?"

Chip's smile melted. "The bid meeting?"

"Yes. The bid for the renovation," Mr. Richardson replied, barely pausing at the door. "You'll make it, I hope?"

Chip tried his best to hide his disappointment.

The man wasn't going to offer him the job.

The man was still going to make him sit around a table with the other top businessmen of the area—and perhaps beyond—forcing him to compete against the best in the industry.

Against his father and family.

"I wouldn't miss it for the world," Chip replied, forcing himself to sound at ease.

"An Appalachian sky!" Mr. Richardson shouted this time, then pushed the door open.

Chip stuffed his hands into his trouser pockets, then turned at the sound of voices on the stage.

"No, it's *flap-heel-toe-heel*, *flap-heel-toe-heel*, and then *Maxie Ford*."

Chip lifted his chin as he saw Bree and Birdie, the other girl who had frequented her porch the past week for practice and went over for the weekly card game at Mrs. Lewis's.

They both strode across stage in full fairy regalia.

For a moment it jolted him, seeing her dressed like the first time they'd met. Like she was a completely different person. Like she had transformed back into that fun, spontaneous girl walking light on her toes without a care in the world. The first version of Bree.

"Yes, but I thought that was after the *leap-toe-heel*—"

Bree halted.

He caught her eyes and her face shifted into a scowl. An impressive transformation.

As her face was crumpling, his brightened. A genuine smile crossed his face as an idea, fully formed, popped into his head. An idea so delicious Bree would never see it coming.

♡ ♡ ♡

Three solid hours later, the curtains rose for the final applause. As the crowd stood and cheered, Chip watched Bree come in on the fairy train behind the queen and take her place on the stage beside Birdie and the rest of the cast.

Chip waited as Bree, with green-glimmering cheeks and eyes, clasped hands with everyone and took a bow.

She scanned the room, looking for her family.

And her eyes stopped on him.

He wished he could capture the look on her face as she spotted her stepfather and mother, clapping and standing next to Chip. He held up the sign just below his chin.

GUESS WHO'S COMING TO FAMILY DINNER?

♡♡♡

"Oh, Chip sweetie, you don't have to wait here. I don't know why she's taking so long."

Chip and Bree's parents had stood in the theater's foyer for forty-five minutes, making small talk while waiting for Bree to appear. Forty-five minutes was all it took to upgrade him from "Chip" to "Chip sweetie." He could only *wait* to see Bree's expression when her mother laid that on him at dinner.

"Really, Mrs. Leake," Chip said for the fifteenth time. "And I can't express this enough. There is nowhere else I'd rather be."

And it was true. Oh, so cosmically true.

Chip had to admit he was enjoying himself. For one thing, Bree's parents had been nothing but kind, engaging, and encouraging from the moment he met them. They said things like, "Well, aren't you so smart!" and were impressed by even his most basic skills. He explained how to seal a pipe? Impressed. He discussed a bid he put in at a town auction? Impressed. He shared how to add two-thirds cup of sugar to the jalapeno cornbread recipe to give it that perfect combination of savory-spicy-sweet? Super impressed.

To be honest, he would head to dinner with her parents even if Bree didn't show at this point. It was nice just to be encouraged.

Chip felt his trousers buzzing and slipped his hand into his pocket, withdrew his phone.

His father's name flashed across the screen.

"Excuse me a second. I'll just be outside."

The pair nodded as he slid the phone to his ear.

There was no greeting.

"Chip. What the *heck* have you done?"

He pushed open the doors and stepped into the fresh air.

"I'm sorry, Dad," Chip replied. "You're going to have to be more specific."

"I'm looking at an email from Richardson's engineers saying they are doing a complete rework of the original drawings for bid. Do you have any idea how much more it'll cost to make just *some* of these things happen? I don't even know what some of these items are, much less how to get them." A paper rustled in the background. "'Forty-foot illuminated replica of night sky?' What *on earth* is he talking about?"

Chip felt his throat tightening. "Why do you think *I'm* to blame for this?"

"Because you and I well know you were with him at the Barter today. And because every other businessman in this town has been trying to limit Richardson's sky-high fantasies for weeks. But one hour with you and suddenly everyone is scrambling. And only *you* would come up with something as crazy as this."

Chip felt the pressure in his chest as he exhaled. "I'll have you know that the Fox is a landmark theatre that has maintained similar designs since the 1920s," Chip retorted, then winced. He walked right into that confession.

"That's fine and good, but do you know how much profit Pete estimates losing for these alterations with this grand new plan?

Three percent. *Three percent*, Chip. On a profit margin already as thin as a rail tie. Because, sure enough, unlike blue paint by the five-gallon bucket, Lowe's doesn't stock"—he paused and read from the sheet—"'ColorCast 14 lighting luminaires' to make up any 'bright night skies.'" There was a heavy pause. "You aren't seriously considering throwing in a bid for this, are you?"

Chip moved aside for a family to pass and meandered in the other direction. "I don't see why not. I live in the area. I own a construction company." He nearly found himself adding a tongue-in-cheek, *I specialize in historic renovation*, but resisted. "I have the experience."

"Nobody's asking about your experience, son. Or where you live. Do you have the money? The resources? Taking on a job like this out of the gate could kill you."

"It won't."

"But if it did?"

"It won't," Chip repeated.

"Chip, I'm going to say this once, so you'd do well to hear me and hear me now. The risk is too much. And I love you, but you can't expect me to catch you, or your company, from a fall like this."

Right. Because that's what this was about, wasn't it? Making sure his father didn't have to come save the day when he failed. Well, he wasn't a child anymore. Chip wasn't a twelve-year-old kid signing up to sell too many fundraiser chocolate bars that his parents would have to buy in the end.

As if reading his mind his father continued, "You know, your mother still has a box of your chocolate bars in the basement."

He frowned. "They're twenty years old, Dad. She needs to throw them out."

"She keeps them for sentimental purposes. I keep them as a reminder of situations like this."

Good grief.

This was exactly why he had decided to branch out on his own. The McBride men were always so methodical, so emotionally detached from everything but the calculator. Everything came down to a number. If the profit margin came to a certain level, it was safe. Move ahead. Just one hundredth of a percentage point off, and they'd pass no matter how else the job mattered. Not even if it was a good networking move. Not even if it was an exciting project.

Unlike them, Chip saw the value in the intangible aspects of their work. He didn't want to spend his whole life managing yet another standard three-bedroom, two-bath, gray-walled ranch. He'd rather take on the challenge of making that choppy, poorly laid-out, rusted old Victorian off Main Street sparkle. He dreamed of not just changing out brown kitchen cabinets for owl-gray, but of doing something bold, something electric.

Fact was, he had been an excellent son at McBride and Sons. An excellent employee. An excellent coworker. He just didn't want to spend the rest of his life as a cookie cutter. Not when he knew what it was like to enjoy the freedom of owning his own company.

Chip lifted his chin. "If you're asking me to stay out of this bid because you're afraid I'm going to underestimate the costs of labor and supplies and come running to you for financial support when I fail, then you can quit worrying. I've learned a thing or two in ten years of business."

"And I've learned a thing or two in the forty years of mine."

Chip opened his mouth, then shut it again. Had his father any clue, *any inkling* of how well he had done up north? How much better he could've done if only . . .

"How about you just worry about your bid, Dad, and I'll worry about mine."

There was silence, and he found he was holding his breath, waiting.

"Fine. If that's really what you want to do."

Chip paused on the sidewalk. "It's really what I want to do."

"Then I wash my hands of it. Whatever comes."

Chip pursed his lips. Nodded. "Noted."

His heart felt heavy as he hung up, turned around, and stared up at the theatre looming above him.

Fine. He didn't need his father to believe in him. He believed in himself, and that was all that mattered.

Still, as he turned back up the steps of the theatre, he couldn't help feeling the void in his chest.

Chapter 15

BREE

Bree had charged offstage the second the curtains closed.

While everyone else clapped each other on the back and hugged and said sweet nothings about the special time they'd experienced together performing *A Midsummer Night's Dream*, Bree pushed through the clusters of actors until she made it into the empty dressing room and back to her station. But she didn't peel off her eyelashes or wipe off the thick green makeup like she usually did. She dug deep into her backpack until she found it.

Her phone.

Fifteen minutes later, she finished writing a fuming message and hit Publish.

She had known he would do something. She knew the second he saw those Christmas trees drop into her yard he was going to fight back. But her parents? Dinner? This night was going to kill her.

"And here are the dressing rooms." Titania's voice wafted

across the room as the star herself floated in, her posture and air monarchial even after the show was over.

Bree dropped her phone onto the vanity and let it clatter, letting them know she was there.

Titania's (or rather, Kayleigh's) hand flew to her chest. "Oh. Bree. You startled me."

"Sorry," Bree said, her tone only half apologetic as she yanked out her braid.

"This is . . . my friend Selena. She's visiting from New York."

"Hello." Bree dragged her brush through her tangled, overly hair-sprayed hair. "Did you come just for the play?"

"Oh, just wanted to visit Kayleigh's slice of the world," Selena said, her eyes roaming around the room. "See what kind of setup you have down here."

Her voice fascinated Bree. It was as unique as her vibrantly red, heart-shaped lips and pistachio-colored heels. It was deeper than she usually heard in a woman, each word pronouncing itself slowly, appraisingly, like she had nowhere else to be. It purred.

Bree's brushing slowed as suspicion rose. "And are you . . . an actress too?"

She laughed, but it was the unkind type that seemed to say, *Like you? Oh, honey, we aren't in the same league.*

"I'm making my way," Selena replied.

The woman delivered the humble words with her purring, northern voice while making it clear she was doing far more than simply making her way. How could someone talk in such layers?

Selena touched Kayleigh's elbow and, as if the movement was their own private language, they swiveled on the balls of their feet. Bree heard Selena ask in a discreet tone, "Were you going to show me the green room?"

And just as they glided in, they glided out.

Bree's gaze was still on the open door when Birdie, wide-eyed, rushed in with the rest of the cast. Words of panic danced in conversations around them as Birdie spoke. "Did you see her? That woman Selena?"

Bree set her hairbrush down, calm despite the anchor falling in her stomach. "Yes."

"Did she say anything to you?"

"Only that she was an actress from New York and came to visit."

"Visit," Birdie repeated. She took a deep breath. Her eyes darted around. "That's all it is. Maybe just a visit."

"Oh please," Cara said from the other dressing table, pulling off her beige slipper. "She's a classically trained actress *and* a Rockette. She just came back from an Off-Broadway tour, and Kayleigh's trying to convince her to stay and audition for *Singin' in the Rain*."

Birdie took another deep breath, then pressed her fists to her hips and swiveled back to Bree. "Oh. Well, that's fine," Birdie said in clipped, upbeat notes. "That's fine because we can still land a role—even with one less slot."

Bree stood there while Birdie started on her best we're-gonna-get-through-this-we-just-have-to-practice pep talk. Bree nodded mutely while she scrubbed the makeup off her face and changed into jeans.

But all she could feel while she transitioned from theatre clothes to street clothes was the world closing in. All she could hear was the door slamming.

It was time to call it.

"—because if *anyone* knows this theatre it's *us*, not her, and just saying she was in Off-Broadway means nothing. She could've been a mute servant girl who gets killed in the first act and has to lie onstage the rest of the play until the audience figures out who did it—"

"Yeah, well, I gotta run, my parents are waiting for me," Bree said, breaking into the middle of Birdie's speech. She tried to give Birdie's hands a heartfelt squeeze, but even she could feel the limpness of her own. She looked Birdie—dear, sweet, nearly mad-eyed Birdie—in the eye. "I know you can do it, Birdie," Bree said, her voice low. "You're going to do great."

Bree let go of Birdie's hands, snatched up her bag, and hurried for the door.

"*We're* going to do great!" Birdie called out after her. "*We both* are gonna do great!"

Bree's legs felt like a thousand pounds as she dragged herself down the hall, the voices from the dressing room chasing her.

"Comin' through," a man said, and she turned sideways, hugging the wall to make room for a rolling tree prop.

Her fingertips held on to the beige cinderblock a moment longer than necessary before she let go and resumed walking.

She wouldn't have admitted it to herself before, but she was going to miss this place.

The frantic dress rehearsals.

The collective energy just before the show began.

The feeling like wherever you were in that moment onstage was the most important place to be, and you were doing the most important thing to do.

Sure, she would've wanted to do more than lounge against trees one day. Maybe land a real speaking role. Maybe even—in her newest, wildest dreams—get to sing a song or two.

If she was honest with herself, she had actually started to hope. Over the last few days of all-day, late-into-the-night practices at her house and with Birdie at the warehouse, she had begun to believe a future at the Barter just might be possible.

But now . . .

Bree cleared her throat as she pushed open the door and walked onstage. She stopped dead center, holding her backpack on one shoulder as she looked out over the auditorium. The lights were low. The room empty. A single spotlight still fell directly where she stood. Where she was bound to stand for the last time.

On this stage.

Soon enough, in Nana's house.

She imagined spending the rest of her life bouncing from job to job, home to home. Driving by Nana's house sometimes just to see if the red-and-green-striped bathroom wallpaper she'd helped Nana hang that day had been painted over, or if the creaky wood porch swing had been replaced with something shiny and metal. Exactly how long would it take to tear down a thousand memories that were the foundation of her childhood, the foundation of her very being?

If only she had walked in earlier that morning to check on Nana. Maybe if she hadn't slept in . . .

Would it have made a difference?

Bree felt her throat burn and gulped down the sizzling pain.

She tucked the thoughts away and dropped down off the side stairs, strode up the aisle, and, without looking back, pushed her way into the foyer.

"Ah, the woman of the hour!" Dan's voice boomed as she emerged. "Here's our star."

Dan stood beside her mother, whose arms were full with the largest bouquet Bree had ever seen.

"Thank you!"

Bree inhaled the flowers' scent as she and her parents exchanged hugs and stepped outside.

"Where's Chip?" she said warily, feeling at least some of her tension release. Maybe he had just come to the play. Maybe he had thought taunting her with a sign was enough for one day.

"Right here," Chip said, slipping his phone into his pocket as he rounded the corner. There was a hardness to his brow Bree recognized at once—his Work Brow, she liked to think of it—but no sooner had she seen it than it dissolved.

His brown eyes caught hers and he smiled, as though remembering how much fun this was going to be. "Your parents said you settled on Bone Fire. If that's still where you want to go."

She couldn't do this. She couldn't sit in a restaurant across from this man, this wolf in sheep's clothing.

"We skipped lunch, actually, when we got caught in traffic," her mother supplied, a smile on her face. "So we're starving! Whatever you pick, we're game for! The night is all about you!"

Bree fought the cold, hard lump in her throat trying to block her from speaking.

Actually, I just want to go home.

Actually, I just need to lie down.

Actually, if Chip stands there one more second beside you guys, smiling at me like we're in a Hallmark movie, I'm going to bring out the claws.

"Bone Fire is perfect," Bree said, fastening a smile on her lips. "Let's walk."

Five minutes later, the four of them were directed toward

the only empty booth in the restaurant. The bar stood a few feet across from them, and a band was setting up beside them, the banjo player hitting a string and turning the tuning key as he went. The air was heavy and thick with barbeque sauce slathered over smoking pork.

"Mom, you can sit by me—"

"Nonsense," Chip said, looking toward her parents. "You two lovebirds stick together."

"Oh, aren't you sweet," her mother said, just as Chip dropped into the booth and sat on Bree.

The scents of cedar and pine overwhelmed her—not unpleasantly—and she exhaled sharply under his weight and moved to her side.

"Sorry, thought you'd already scooted over," he said, smiling as he tugged on the red scarf overlaying his black sweater.

She squinted, knowing exactly the last time he wore that ridiculous thing and exactly how many times he had scratched at it in front of Theo and Mr. Richardson like a man on the edge of sanity. When she glanced at her parents, they were looking at the two of them like he had just called *them* the lovebirds.

"I love that scarf, dear," Bree's mother said as she picked up her menu. "Nice to see young men who can dress up on occasion."

"Oh, this?" Chip said, glancing down at it as if noticing it for the first time.

"It's awfully hot in here," Bree said, glancing at the crowded bar. She scratched her neck. Blinked in Chip's direction. "Feels like it must be ninety degrees. Don't you think?"

For three full seconds Chip's innocent brown eyes stared back, his winning smile frozen on his face. "Not at all," he replied. "Not. At. All. You know," he said, snapping his attention to her parents, "I've been thinking about getting some floodlights for the house."

Dan's attention lifted from the menu. "Really? What's the cause?"

"Oh, just a security measure. I feel no matter where you live, you can never be too safe."

Her parents started nodding like this was sage wisdom from an old man. You could see the approval flooding Bree's mother's eyes. "That's just what I tell Bree all the time. You never can be too safe. I say that, honey, don't I?"

"Well, I'd be more than happy to install some at your house, too, Bree," Chip said. Her mother's eyes were now practically bursting with heart emojis. "Of course," he continued, swinging back to face Bree, "the floodlights I'm getting put up tomorrow should be more than capable of covering us both. They're the same 500-watt commercial-grade lights I used on the exterior of a gymnasium I helped build last year." Chip picked up his menu and began a loathsome fake scanning motion.

Bree squinted. So Chip was going to put in commercial-grade motion-sensor floodlights tomorrow and no doubt have them face directly into her bedroom window, where she could be blinded at random, insanity-inducing intervals throughout the night. Every night. Terrrrific.

"That sounds expensive," Bree put in.

"A little over five hundred dollars when I first bought them," Chip replied. "But can you put a price on safety? . . . Especially *yours*?"

Bree's mother put her hands on her chest.

"Five hundred. Talk about an investment."

Bree was going to have to break out the BB gun Evie hid under her pillow.

"That is just *so* thoughtful," her mother said.

"It's nothing," Chip said.

"You are our answer to prayer," Bree's mother persisted.

Oh, good grief.

Mom's eyes were starting to water. Bree felt like ducking under the table and squeezing between their legs for the exit.

Her mother leaned in. Her voice was low as she looked at Chip. Her Bible-Belt, foothills-of-the-Smoky-Mountains accent grew as thick as the preacher's of her mama's country church. "And are you . . . well . . ." She shrugged to finish her words.

He lifted a questioning brow.

"Are you a religious man, Chip?"

Bree almost hid under the table.

This was excruciating.

"Yes, Mom," she answered for him. "He goes to Abingdon Community Church, and he's got a Bible at the head of his bed. You don't need to add him to your prayer list." Sure, she was 99 percent certain he was praying to God to destroy her, but still. "I feel like we can safely avoid you trying to convert him in this conversation. Okay? Okay. Who's thinking brisket?"

Chip's and Mom's heads swiveled in her direction.

"How did you know I go to Abingdon Community?"

"Why have you seen his bed?"

Both asked their questions at the same time, with the same expressions. Terrific.

"You go every week to sit with your family before heading to family supper," Bree said hastily. "Phone conversations carry. And I've seen his bed because he *happens* to have a bedroom directly across from mine." She shifted uncomfortably. "And I've just *happened* to notice it. Once."

Her mother pursed her lips then, and Bree knew she was struggling between chastising her for looking into men's windows and celebrating that they were one step closer to matrimony.

Apparently she settled on glee, as her eyes started glimmering. "Well. Chip. Isn't that nice to hear you're so connected to your family. Family supper. We have those as well, only on Saturdays."

"Really?" Chip said. "So you had one yesterday?"

Clearly it was the wrong question, because her mother's and Dan's expressions shifted. "Oh, not yesterday. We had a bit of a"—her mother's eyes darted away from Bree—"family emergency."

Bree stopped halfway in the act of unrolling her napkin.

"But we're confident that it will all smooth out soon." Her mother paused. Bit her lip. "Lord willing."

"What's wrong?" Bree said, her words swift and low.

Bree watched as Mom took a breath. Exhaled. "Anna's back in Knoxville. They're considering . . ." She hesitated. "Transferring to Memphis."

"To *St. Jude's*?" Bree felt panic and release at the same time. She'd been trying to get her sister-in-law to transfer Anna to St. Jude's since the diagnosis. For six months Daria had fought it. Saying Anna's condition was serious but not *dire*. That traveling to Knoxville's Children's Hospital would be hard enough. That it was better for Anna to recover at home, where she belonged. That keeping her life as close to normal was important, more important than traveling across the state and turning their lives upside down, far away from everyone.

But what was happening now? What had happened that was so awful to make Daria change her mind?

The thought made Bree sick, and the stench of the food around them was too much.

"I'm actually feeling a bit under the weather," Bree said, the booth suddenly claustrophobic.

"Oh honey," her mother began. "We didn't mean to—"

"I'm fine," Bree said, nudging Chip's shoulder. "It's fine. I just need to lie down. I'll call Daria when I get home."

Chip slid out of the seat, moving well back in order to let her stand. He opened his mouth as he looked to the door, and if she hadn't known better, she might have said he had true concern in his eyes. It was clear he had no idea what was going on.

"I can drive you home."

"No." Bree shook her head. The crowd swelled. Bodies were everywhere. The banjo player struck a chord, and the speaker screamed in her ears. "No, you guys go on and eat." Bree was walking backward now. "Thank you for coming tonight. This was really—" She bumped into a waiter.

Finally, Bree spun toward the exit and escaped.

A breeze rolled down Main Street and lifted her hair, and she took what felt like the first breath in two minutes. Her phone was buzzing in her pocket, but she turned it off. And began to walk.

Chapter 16
CHIP

Chip sat across from her parents through the meal, each of them mumbling a polite yet awkward word of sympathy about Bree's sudden sickness, then proceeding to talk ten minutes longer than Chip would have thought possible about the type of barbecue sauce they preferred on their meat. When that topic ran out of steam they turned to tools, and for the rest of the meal Chip and Dan went through every tool in Dan's shed, down to the Japanese ryoba saw.

The three of them did everything in their power to pretend the situation did not exist, but when they walked back to Mr. and Mrs. Leake's car, Bree's mother crouched down and tucked herself into the passenger seat.

"Here," Dan said, pressing his business card into Chip's hand. "This is my number. It's always good to share your family's emergency contacts with neighbors."

Wow. They really were worried about her.

"Of course," Chip said, putting it into his pocket and reciprocating with his own. "In case you ever need to reach Bree and are having trouble."

A smile slipped up Dan's face. "Or I need some more dog tips."

Chip smiled back. "Sure. Or dog tips."

A few minutes later, Chip pulled into the cul-de-sac and then his driveway. As he turned the engine off, he saw that Bree's place was completely dark. The porch was lightless, and even Evie's car was gone, leaving only a shadowy spot of driveway in its place.

He unlocked his door quietly. Moved toward the kitchen.

It was eight o'clock, but his hands found themselves digging spoonfuls from the coffee bag. Pouring water into the coffeemaker. From the kitchen window he could see the glow from the lamp in her bedroom.

Later, in the darkness of his bedroom on his bed, he sat. Took a sip of his coffee as he looked from his window into hers.

And contemplated.

What was going through Bree Leake's mind while she paced the length of her room, talking into her cell phone? Who was she talking to? The girl Anna? Her mother?

She had changed clothes since dinner. Her jeans replaced with sweatpants, the soft-spun pink sweater, which he couldn't help noticing as he'd rubbed arms with her at dinner, replaced with a holey *Gatlinburg-Pittman High School* T-shirt.

Chip pulled the scarf off his neck and dropped it on the bed.

There was something beautiful yet strange in the number of expressions flying across Bree's face as she paced. Her eyes were free of the annoyance they held whenever he was in her presence.

Dropped was the wall she put up whenever they stepped outside in the mornings at the same time. And yet something stiff, complex, creased her forehead as she walked, her mouth tipping up and down in what appeared to be attempts at smiling. Like she was trying to keep herself together while her face stated clearly: she was not okay.

She stopped pacing. Turned her back to the window. Started to nod vigorously.

When the heel of her hand started wiping at her temple, he realized he was standing.

He shouldn't be watching this.

Chip flicked on his bedroom light and moved downstairs, finishing off his cup before he hit the landing. He should let Bree handle her own affairs. She had plenty of people in her life who could swoop in and assist if needed. Plenty of people she'd *want* to talk to. Who was he, anyway? He was probably the last person on earth she'd ever discuss her life with.

He felt pent-up energy (no thanks to the caffeine) and dumped his coffee mug in the kitchen sink. He could go on a run, sure, but his calves still ached from the long mountain-bike trail he'd done yesterday with Russell. One glance around the room confirmed at least three house projects he could be doing, but his eyes just roved from one to another without enough interest to stop. He could reply to his mother's group email discussing Easter plans. Yes. This was the perfect time to finally get to it.

Chip moved to his office and pushed his desk chair out.

As he sat down, he felt a jab at his thigh.

He reached into his pocket, pulled out Dan's business card.

Set it on his desk beside his computer.

Looked at it.

Frowned.

She had her parents. She could talk with Evie. The girl Birdie, who was at her house daily these days. Mrs. Lewis.

Even after only a few months in this town, Bree had a thousand shoulders to cry on.

Not his.

There was *no way* she'd cry on his shoulder. Even if a part of him, a strange, small part, wanted her to.

He tapped on the computer and waited as the monitor woke up.

The cursor flashed at him on the password line, waiting.

His fingers hovered over the keys.

He glanced out his window.

Exhaled.

Stood.

He walked back up the stairs and peeked through the bedroom window. Bree was no longer on her phone but sitting on the edge of her bed. Alone. Her head sunk into her hands.

Within seconds, he was out the door and standing on her doorstep. He rang the doorbell and waited . . .

Chip pushed his hands into his pockets and rocked back and forth on his heels.

Listened to the quiet clucking of the chickens inside their henhouse.

Watched the windmill at the top of the henhouse turn.

He rang the doorbell again.

"Bree. It's Chip," he said through the door.

He inclined his head to the door. Heard nothing but silence on the other side.

He rang the doorbell once more, and after one more minute of silence, he walked until he hit the crunchy area of her driveway. He peered up to the second story. Picked up a piece of gravel. Rolled it in his fingers. Tossed it up to her window.

It clinked against the pane and fell to the driveway.

Silence.

He tossed another.

And another.

Bree came to the window.

He caught her eye.

"C'mon, Bree. Open up."

She hesitated but then pulled up the pane. "I'm not in the mood to fight, Chip," she said, and started to shut it again.

"I didn't come for that." He put up his hands in surrender. "Honest. I just want to talk."

Her long braid fell over her shoulder and a few inches out the window while she stood there. He almost saw the gears turning in her head.

He bounced on his toes, looking back at her. "Just for a minute," he said.

Even from this distance he could see the red around her eyes.

"Just for a minute, then," she repeated. A moment later, the window slammed shut.

As her figure moved out of sight, he walked over to the front porch. Listened as several deadbolts unlocked behind her front door. The door swung open.

Bree stood beside it awkwardly. Nodded as though she had no idea what to do. "I would say I was sorry for leaving so abruptly, except I didn't invite you."

Chip cut to the chase. "Who's Anna?"

Bree pursed her lips.

When she spoke, her voice was carefully controlled. "She's my niece."

Chip nodded. For the first time since he'd moved in, there was no sarcastic tone or hidden meaning between them. "How old is she?"

"Eight."

"Cancer?"

Bree seemed to have to swallow before she answered. "Yes."

Chip nodded again as he stood there on her front porch, his hands dug into his pockets. He nodded more toward the doormat this time, bouncing on his toes for a few moments before settling back on the ground. "I had no idea."

"I can't imagine how you could," Bree replied, her voice as stiff as her posture against the door.

For several seconds they both stood there, each staring down at the mat, she looking as uncomfortable as he at this new type of communication between them. Teasing was easy. Silent mockery had been fun. But honesty? Authentic feelings? Pulling down their guard?

"I'm sorry," he murmured.

She nodded.

It didn't feel like enough, though. He found himself standing out in the cold, having dragged her out of the privacy of her own home, just so he could pry out the facts of why she was so upset. It wasn't enough. What he'd said wasn't enough.

He had to say more.

He cleared his throat. "The fact is, Bree, I know a little something about loss too. Being afraid of loss." He hurried on with the words he so seldom shared. Facts everybody in this town knew except her. "My twin brother passed away four years ago. It's . . . why I came back to Abingdon."

He watched as she blinked, and her hard expression softened. "Oh."

He hated sharing this. He hated what followed every time someone found out. Condolences. Slanted, pitying eyes. Trite, pithy sayings to fill the void of silence.

And now he was standing there, waiting for her to say something about the most defining event of his life. If she said something mocking, it would kill him. If she said anything sarcastic at all, he'd walk away and never return.

Even Ashleigh had tried to talk with him about it a few times, but he just pressed his lips together. Cracked a joke about something completely irrelevant. Turned her attention to something else. Fact was, Jake wasn't just a brother. He was half of Chip's heart. And even on the best of days, there was never a moment he didn't feel like half his heart was missing.

He swallowed as he looked up at the stars.

"I'm so sorry." Her voice drifted quietly to his ears. Soft. Undemanding.

And suddenly she was at his side looking up at the stars too.

"I really am, Chip."

Chip felt his jaw clench as her soft hand wrapped around his. It was a fleeting touch, a momentary squeeze of his calloused palm before her hand dropped back to her side. She said more in that gesture than words could express.

Something about her tender touch, the stillness of the evening, the revealed secrets and sorrows under the milky moon made his throat sting. "Jake was a good man. And a great brother."

He heard the small intake of her breath, practically felt her groping for the helpful response that didn't exist.

"I didn't know."

He raised a brow, one side of his mouth hinting at a smile. "I can't imagine how you could," he repeated softly.

Both of their eyes crinkled in the start of a smile as they looked at each other. The soft start of a first shared joke, but their smiles couldn't bear the heaviness of the moment, and their expressions faded.

They watched the headlights of a car rolling by.

Quietly stood side by side until the brake lights turned off and the couple walked inside.

"Anna has been a trouper this past year." Bree's words came so lightly they seemed to dance on the breeze. "She's been through it all . . . even"—her voice cracked slightly before she composed herself—"even the marrow transplant that led to GVHD. But the phone call I just had with Daria . . ." There was a second's hesitation before she inserted hastily, "I mean, the doctors haven't said there's no hope. Daria's trying to stay upbeat. But, but . . ."

Her words seemed to fail, and her fingers flew to her lips.

He watched the moonlight shine dimly upon her profile, her lips pressed tightly against each other, her left hand clenched at her side. She looked like every muscle in her body was taut, as though any moment the scream she was holding so deep inside was going to break open and pour out into the night air. He knew that look. He lived that look, breathed that look, had watched that look on every member of his family at one time. Sometimes still saw that look in his reflection in the mirror.

And he'd seen firsthand what it looked like when a person finally let go.

Without hesitation, Chip wrapped one arm around her shoulders, squeezing, helping her to keep it in for that moment—if that was what she wanted.

Grief was a cruel jack-in-the-box. Sometimes it popped out at the least desirable moments: at the codes department, just when you're stepping in for a building permit. In front of your mother, just when you see her dry-eyed for the first time in months, just when she's thinking of something else for once.

But of course, there was never a time, really, that Jake wasn't in the back of their minds. Standing there in the corner as they talked about recipes for egg salads and his niece's latest achievements. Jake was always there. Over time, Chip had accepted and integrated that fact into his life. This world wasn't all he had grown up to think it was. Nothing was stable. Not the years of playing make-believe in the backyard with his brothers, the barbecues and fireflies, the comfort of warm duvets on soft beds. Not his family, friends, money, possessions, intellect, status, abilities. None of it was secure. None of it could he stand upon and know it would hold his weight.

Because someday, some awful day, the ground *would* shift beneath his feet. The ground *had* shifted beneath his feet.

As he'd learned four years ago, the world was good, but it wasn't wholly good.

The world was beautiful, but it was also worse than his worst nightmare.

That worldview shift was what first broke him.

But now? Now it was what he clung to.

He stepped back. Gave her room. "Are you going to see her?"

Bree shook her head. "I can't go to the hospital. I can't see her on that bed, watch her struggle to breathe. And I can't be there to see the worst happen. Not again. I can't."

His brow furrowed until he remembered what Evie had said one day about their living situation. "You were here when your grandmother passed?"

Bree swallowed. Nodded.

"I was the first one there that morning. I was surprised she hadn't opened her door yet and so I went into her room, talking nonsense about what kind of eggs Evie was making, pushing open her curtains . . . all without a clue until . . ." She paused. Collected herself. "Until I turned around." Bree held one hand to her lips for moments that stretched to minutes, pushing her fingers against her teeth as if to build a dam. Finally, she turned to face him. "How can you bear it?"

Her voice didn't wobble as she said it. Instead her words flowed as though, for the first time, she was really seeing him. Bree Leake seeing Chip McBride. And person to person, she wanted to know.

There was no way to sum up four years' worth of experience. Four years of cycling through the injustice, the emotions, mentalities, worldview shifts, and then cycling through it all again. He wasn't like the strangers with their pithy words. He could never sum up what he'd learned in the waiting, the aching, the seeking. But he did know one thing.

"I once heard it said, 'If I find in myself a desire which no experience in this world can satisfy, the most probable explanation is that I was made for another world.' I live in a world where I find myself with desires for things that don't exist. The only logical conclusion is that they must exist somewhere else, and I was made to live there." He smiled slightly as he looked into her eyes. "I used to not understand it. Now I've said it to myself so many times I've memorized it. And I think, the longer I live, the more I'm able to appreciate the good as I experience it here, but also look forward to moving on from this beautiful, horrible rest stop to something more."

His expression softened. "You should go see her."

An infinitesimal nod escaped from Bree, but she didn't say anything. There was silence as her gaze moved from him back to the moon. They stood quietly for a minute more.

Finally, Chip turned to face her. "Hey, so, I'm not 100 percent certain, but I believe some rude man fourth-wheeled on your family dinner and, unless I'm incorrect, you're hungry. Now, I don't know about barbecue, but I can whip up some chili worthy of at least a B+ rating."

"Oh." Bree looked startled as she pulled her hair behind her ear. "No, Chip. I couldn't. But thanks—"

"I'll even throw in some cornbread I made last week. It's only four, maybe five days old."

"Five-day-old cornbread. No. That's okay—"

"There may even be some two-week-old cheesecake I forgot about in the back of the fridge," Chip continued. "The fridge is a bit wonky, so it might have frozen up a bit, but—"

"Half-a-month-old frozen cheesecake. Wow. While that is appealing—"

"Not to mention I know where you live," Chip pressed, finding the urge to have her over growing by the moment. "And I can just watch you like Russell does through the window until you give in."

"Stalking now," Bree said, her mouth starting to curve into a smile. "This whole conversation is just getting better and better."

"But I mean, that's fine if you want to stay in," Chip said, flexing his fingers. "I can just work on installing those floodlights instead . . ."

Bree cracked into a full-on smile, the twinkle in her eye giving off an uncertain dare. "You wouldn't. Surely you wouldn't."

"Wouldn't I?" He shrugged. Tilted his head toward his house. "C'mon. It takes about thirty minutes for the space heater to heat up, but it'll be great."

"Wow, you really are a salesman, aren't you?"

Despite her words, she followed.

Russell, who was, per usual, panting at the line, barked a couple of times as they neared.

Chip whistled. "C'mon, boy. Let's get you a Slim Jim."

The dog perked his ears at the words, and with one final bark at Bree, he turned and trotted inside.

"Just give me one sec," Chip said, raising a finger as he slipped through the door.

He found he was jogging when he hit the living room.

"Slim Jim," he said, throwing open the pantry door and scanning the items inside. He snatched one from the open box, ripped it open, used it to lure Russell upstairs, and threw it in his bedroom before shutting Russ inside.

A sudden fear that Bree would slip back to her house if he didn't hurry propelled him down toward the landing. His eyes roved the space and, quick as a flash, he danced around the paint buckets, tidied up the toilet paper rolls in the hall closet, tossed a crumpled pair of athletic pants and T-shirt in the bathroom vanity, and snatched up his tennis shoes. Dropping the shoes side by side by the door, he exhaled, smiled, and whipped the door open.

She was still there. Hesitancy deep in her eyes.

"Coast is clear," he said, smiling as though he'd been lounging around all day.

Smiling as though she was just a friend who'd come by for dinner.

A neighbor swinging by for a quick bite.

Like normal people did. Normal, non-mortal enemies.

"C'mon in," he said and swung the door open wide.

She looked down at the threshold as though he'd asked her to step off a ledge.

His brow rose. "Tell you what. You come in, and I promise we can resume hating each other tomorrow if it'll make you feel better." He lowered his voice conspiratorially. "You know, just to keep our options open."

This tipped her face into a smile.

She took one tentative step in.

They both looked down at her foot appreciatively for a few moments.

"All right then." Chip clapped his hands together. "Let's get you some food."

Bree followed Chip, her head swiveling back and forth as she took in the house. She looked as uncertain as he felt. "So . . . you feed the dog Slim Jims on purpose now."

"I admit, I had a hard time finding it on the doggie food pyramid, and the vet informed me in no uncertain terms that I'm an irresponsible doggie parent if I let him eat them too often. So don't worry. I am well-informed of my bad parenting." He dragged a kitchen chair beside the space heater and waved to it.

"Oh." Bree cracked a smile as she sat on it. "Well, I'm glad to hear you're admitting it at least."

"And that's the first step to recovery, I hear. Sorry—" He leaned over her, reaching for the power button on the space heater squeezed between Bree and the kitchen wall. He clicked it on, then pushed the heat to high. Even without touching her, he could sense her stiffness. Feel his own.

He stood upright. "There. That should just take a couple minutes."

"What? Not thirty? I was promised thirty."

He looked up to her face as he moved to the other side of the counter. Heard the playfulness in her tone. Good. She was starting to relax. Even if just barely.

He swiveled around. Pulled open the fridge and ducked his head in. "Okay then. Chili. Moderately decent chili . . ." He plucked a couple of tomatoes from the bottom drawer. Grabbed the jar of minced garlic with the other hand.

"Minced garlic. Wow." Bree stuffed her hands beneath her legs. "I did not expect you to be a cook."

He raised a brow. "You mean you haven't seen me chopping up onions from the kitchen window?"

And for once, she looked abashed. "Well . . ."

He smiled as he set a few cans of black beans on the counter. "You know, while brooding with a steaming cup of coffee at your lips?"

She rose her brow innocently. "Has that ever happened? Surely not—"

"And mouthing words at me? What were those words . . ." He tapped his finger on the counter as he shut the cabinet. "What were they? . . . I. Hate. You?"

"Oh look!" Bree pointed to the cabinet. "It slow-closes now. Isn't that just lovely?"

The comment, intended to distract, brought the conversation to an abrupt stop. He opened his mouth, tripping to find a good reply, while the thoughts flashed across his mind in bold: She paid so much attention to him that she knew his soft-close cabinet had been broken at one point. And that he'd fixed it. She'd watched him enough through the window to observe the pace at which his cabinet closed.

And had just admitted it.

To him.

He found himself looking for a reply that would make the red creeping up her neck dissipate.

"Well, it's not anything near the vintage-modern style of your open cabinetry, but I'll take the compliment," he said nonchalantly. "By the way, what is *with* your mismatching appliances? I'm not picky, but a stainless-steel dishwasher with a white fridge . . ."

"You," Bree retorted, "not picky? Every single room in this house is *the same color.*"

He laughed. "Yeah, yeah, my gray walls don't have quite the charm as your wallpapered ones. But at least I don't have creepy children on the wallpaper of my dining room."

She smiled as she crossed one leg over the other and laughed in an indignant way. "What they are is *adorable. Adorable* little kids running down a hill carrying baskets."

He pulled out the knife and began chopping a tomato. *"Creepy* little kids chasing a poor old man down a hill while carrying baskets."

"He's not an old man."

"He's bald."

"It's a boy with a baseball cap."

"He's a bald old man being harassed by the village children." He pointed his knife toward the window. "You see it from my angle."

While the pot of chili simmered, and after much argument,

the experiment began. She went back to her house, flicked on the light switch to the dining room, and then came back so they could stand side by side at his window, observing as if they were in an art gallery.

"I still don't see it," she said, her fingers pressed to her chin as she squinted from his kitchen window to hers.

"Turn your head," he said, tilting his head a few inches.

She watched him, then did so herself.

Waited a few moments.

"Nope."

"Squint a little," he said.

She squinted, then tilted her head the other direction and squinted again. "Nope. Just an adorable little boy followed by his clan."

"You'll see it better from this window," he said and moved toward the window above the counters. She followed.

They ended up trying every window facing her house. And then, when she had finally conceded to a *slightly* disturbing image, she dragged him over to her house to see the wallpaper for himself—where he then conceded to it not being as creepy as it seemed from a distance.

Thirty minutes later, Bree sat with bent knees up to her chin as she dragged the last of the crumbly cornbread across the bowl of chili. They'd talked more of his family, her family, how she felt about life since leaving Gatlinburg, how he felt about the Barter bid. It was easy, talking to her. Almost as easy as it had been that first night. And for the first time since moving in, the house started to feel like a home.

She popped the last bit of cornbread into her mouth as she looked at the freshly painted wall.

"Do you think there's something wrong with me?"

He raised a brow. He spoke around his mouthful of cornbread. "I'm sorry. Is this a trick question?"

Her eyes turned from the wall to him. She made a face. "Really, Chip. Do you think there maybe is something wrong with me, that I can't find *anything* that makes me happy? *Really* happy?"

"You seem to be happy with lots of things. Heck, you look like you're having the time of your life with that chili."

Bree, who indeed looked both happy and relaxed, rubbed the last of the crumbs off her T-shirt. "No, I mean beyond the chili—which, for the record, is a solid A-minus. I mean with jobs. And experiences. And life in general. I just feel like sometimes I can't enjoy the moment as fully as I'm supposed to. I just wonder if maybe something's wrong with me. Like I just can't get filled up to the top like everybody else."

"Oh." He shrugged. "Well, I don't believe anything in this life can fully satisfy. Not in the way we were designed to feel."

"But why can everybody else be content and not me? Look at you. You seem perfectly content having this house that you're always working on."

He nodded. "That's true. To the extent that I can be, I am."

"And your job. You are *passionate* about your job. It's obvious. Just like Birdie's passionate about theatre. And my best friend was passionate about her job and now about parenting all of her kids. Everyone around me seems to have found something that makes them want to get up in the morning. But me?" Bree tossed her crumpled paper towel on the table. "I've tried so many jobs at this point, Chip. I feel like at some point I have to admit that maybe it's not the job's fault. It's me. There's gotta be something wrong. With me."

She pressed her lips together as she looked at him, and it was clear in her eyes that this topic was important to her. It meant something. To give a flippant reply that she was perfectly normal, that everybody felt this way sometimes, couldn't do it justice.

And really, he wanted to do it justice.

"Well. Let me think." He set down his spoon.

Thought for a moment before choosing his next words.

"You're a lot of things, Bree, but I've never looked at you and thought *impossible to satisfy* was one of them. Hardheaded, yes. Stubborn. To. A. Fault."

She frowned. Crossed her arms over her knees.

He put up a hand. "But also spontaneous. Adventurous. Fun. Your loyalty to your friends and family is inspiring. You have a gift in seeing the outsider and drawing them in. You are the person people want to be around." He grinned. "Even I fall into that category. Even if it's been for the pleasure of driving you crazy."

He thought he saw her blushing as she drew her knees up until they covered her chin. "But I don't *love* a job. *Any* job. And I've tried—"

He shrugged. "So unlike half of the population, you love yourself too much to settle for fifty hours a week doing something that doesn't spark you. You value your time more than possessions. I think that takes bravery."

She shook her head. "But more than jobs. It's hobbies. A lifetime of ridiculous hobbies. And even with guys—"

"So you keep moving on because you haven't found the one who makes you want to stop." He smiled slightly, then felt the heat creep up the back of his own neck. "I know a little bit about that struggle. It's not the end of the world to wait for the right person."

He paused for a beat, then put out his hands. "Look, everybody longs to capture that picture-perfect moment when their hearts are bursting with joy around friends and family and achievements and whatever else, and then live in that frozen, perfect snapshot forever. Well, it doesn't happen here. But I think the fact we long for that means it's going to happen somewhere else. Otherwise, why would we all want it so bad?

"So maybe you need to lower your expectations a little bit on what you think this life 'should' look like 24/7. Maybe you need to recognize that there is no way the job you pick or people you're with are going to be easy and fun all the time. Or"—he shrugged as he picked up his plate, then hers—"maybe you just haven't found the right job, or hobby, or person, and need to keep looking. Or, and this is what I'd bet on, maybe you need to do a little of both."

He paused before he took a step toward the counter with plates in hand. "You tell me, Bree. What do you want *most*? Right now. What's one thing you think you want *most* right now?"

He felt a flurry in his chest as he said the words.

In that moment, looking at Bree sitting on that chair with her knees pressed to her chin, he knew what his answer would be.

And it was startling.

"What do I want most, right at this moment?" she repeated, her evergreen eyes on his.

He saw the perfect crease between her brows.

Fought the desire to reach forward and smooth it.

What would he do if she said *you*? What madness would he have stumbled upon if the woman who had brought him such mirthful misery over the last month said his name?

She exhaled softly. "Nana's house."

Chip felt his own chest deflate. He pushed aside the ridiculous thought, and even more, the ridiculous disappointment that came with her answer. The house. Of course. She wanted the house.

She shrugged. "I know. It's not much. It's not even a passionate, life-or-death desire. But right now, I just want Nana's house. I want to own these memories. I want Anna to see Nana's house and to love it. I want to preserve all of the good things that happened there."

He nodded. "I get it." He patted the counter. "I want this house too." He set the plates in the sink and started up the water. "So get the house."

"Yeah. It's not that easy."

"Is anything worthwhile ever easy?"

Chip picked up the scrubber. Started scrubbing down the plates.

Bree stood. Took the paper towel and started sweeping off the crumbs from the table.

When she finished, she tossed the paper towel in the open trash can. Shifted her weight uncertainly. "Well, hey, this has been . . . really nice. Thanks for the meal. And the company."

He dropped the scrubber and fully turned, realizing he wasn't quite ready for her to leave. "Oh. Oh sure. I'll walk you to the door."

She gave an appreciative smile as she pushed both chairs in and followed him.

He opened the door and stepped onto the porch.

For a few moments they stood there, saying nothing. The moon hung over the house above them, stars twinkling as they'd twinkled for the millions before them. The billions around them. But at this moment, the display seemed only for them.

He jutted his thumb toward her house. "I'd say 'drive safe' but . . . I figure you can manage pretty well."

She gave a soft laugh and wrapped her arms around herself. "Thanks again. Chip. This was really . . . nice."

He opened his mouth to give a casual, frivolous reply, then stopped. Because this wasn't casual. Nothing about this conversation, or this night, was trivial. Even her calling him by name, just then, wasn't casual. All of it meant something.

Maybe even a whole lot of something.

"You're welcome, Bree. And I agree. We should . . . do it again," he said, looking straight into her eyes.

And then she did something he didn't expect. In fact, she did something that, five hours before, he would've bet his house and business on never happening.

She hugged him.

He felt the squeeze of her arms around his torso, her face pressed against his collarbone. Her hair tickled his nose and rubbed against his five-o'clock shadow. The air suddenly smelled a little more like strawberries. For the first time ever, he felt the impulse to rest his cheek there, to feel her soft hair against his rough jaw. But before he had the chance to wrap his arms around her, she pulled back.

A flicker of movement came to his right, and his eyes followed the source to the glow of Mrs. Lewis's living-room window. He saw the woman's face peeking from behind the curtain.

Bree bounced on her toes, looking more than a little embarrassed by her spontaneous display of affection. "Right. Well, I'm going to head back now. Thanks."

He nodded, trying with all his might to keep the smirk from running up his cheeks. "Sounds like a good plan if you want to keep those legs of yours from freezing off before your audition next week."

Her embarrassed expression dropped immediately. She lifted her brow. "Okay. I can concede to kitchen stalking. But how did you know?"

One side of Chip's face lifted in a smile. "To defeat your enemy, you have to know them. And believe me, Bree, I know you better than the back of my hand."

Bree released a sliver of a smile. "Well, all I can say is, that game plan is mutual."

She hesitated, then ducked her head and hopped down the stairs.

The gravel crunched beneath her shoes as she crossed over his driveway and onto hers.

"Hey, Chip," Bree called once she reached her porch steps.

"Yeah?"

"For the record, I hope you get the job next week too."

♡♡♡

It didn't take but two minutes back inside his kitchen to make Chip drop the plates into the drying rack and snatch his keys off the counter.

He drove straight to Ashleigh's house without calling. No text. No heads-up to set her mind spinning.

Oh, the transformation on Ashleigh's face as she opened the door was painful. It took only seconds for the initial look of pleasant surprise to shift to a crease of concern above her sky-blue eyes.

But he had to say it to her. Because he had been right in what he'd said to Bree.

You need to keep on moving until you find the one who makes you want to stop.

And he had never quite stopped for Ashleigh, though she had waited patiently at the door for him all those nights while he worked, had waited patiently for him every step of the way.

She wasn't meant for him, but for someone who appreciated her much, much more. Who didn't just *know* she was wonderful but *felt* it.

That was not how Ashleigh saw it, and she made this painfully, tearfully clear over the next two hours. After he explained to her the reasons they should break it off—she insisted on hearing each one—the full force of Ashleigh's oratorical skills came out as she paced and talked, wearing down a line on her Persian rug.

Several times key phrases such as "time I invested in you" and "waste all that work" came up, but he didn't interrupt. Eventually she ran out of words, and he ran out of apologies, and she did the only thing a respectable southern belle like herself would do: wrap herself around his neck with one hard, final hug, peck him on the cheek, straighten her blouse, and tell him she appreciated the strength he demonstrated in talking freely with her.

Honestly, she was going to make a terrific senator's wife.

Back at home, Chip lay on his back in the quiet of his room, the same milky moon watching him from the window. Quietly he lowered his hand and rubbed Russell's ear.

Russell inched his head up and leaned into Chip's palm, then dropped down again on his paws.

For several minutes, he lay there in the quiet, thinking about the bid and the Monday morning meeting he'd *finally* secured with a bank to talk about a credit line. Thinking about his crew and the ongoing schedule changes and needs. Thinking about the bathroom wall he had meant to paint that evening. Thinking about the strange way a man had to keep living in this world, making plans and goals and priorities, knowing how fleeting it all was. Thinking about Jake. Thinking about Bree.

Chip pushed his sleeping bag off and planted his bare feet on the cold hardwood. Russell lifted his head while Chip went over to the new dresser, where a legal pad lay open in the center next to a Sharpie. He uncapped it. Wrote the message.

SLEEP WELL

As he settled back down on the mattress, his eyes didn't stray from her large, dark window.

He watched the window as the minutes on his watch ticked on and the milky moon rose higher in the sky.

Eventually Russell fell asleep.

Chip's own eyes started to take longer and longer blinks.

And then, from one moment when his eyes closed to the next when they opened again, her response was there.

YOU TOO

Chapter 17

BREE

"What did you do?"

Bree opened her eyes slowly, blinking as light flooded her retinas. Slowly, she registered the hands on the hips of wildly flared bell-bottoms. The keys, with attached donut keychain, clutched in one hand. Her gaze lifted as she watched Evie's chest rise with an impatient breath. By the time her eyes lifted to Evie's face, she didn't expect any less than the heavy purple-lipstick frown.

Evie put more effort into her scowl and furrowed her brow deeper, but she only succeeded in looking a little more like a peeved squirrel.

Bree winced as she raised herself on her elbow. She began rubbing her eyes with one hand. "What's wrong, Evie?"

"I've got a car blocked in and a meeting in ten minutes. And I'm not sure exactly what's going on, but I have a feeling you can tell me."

Evie moved over to the window and pulled back the sheer white curtain. She pointed. "Tell me, Bree, might you know why our street is covered with farm trucks and chickens?"

As Bree crossed to the window, the events of the evening before sprang into her mind. In reverse.

Bree answering Chip's note in the window. Dinner with Chip. Chip beside her on the porch beneath a clear sky, as she shared things about her life she hadn't even told her oldest and dearest of friends. Gravel tapping her window while she stood in her room, overwhelmed with the news. Anna in the hospital. Anna getting transferred. The New York girl. Chip sitting in the audience, holding up the absurd sign about family dinner—

Wait.

Backtrack.

There.

Just after the play.

When she made it to the dressing room, she had swooped to her phone with the deftness of a vulture alighting on its dead. As she clicked open Craigslist, her fingers never paused or faltered. She had published a post.

The fate of her job, the news about Anna, the bizarre evening beside Chip had eclipsed her memory of the little, insignificant post.

The post she had assumed would amount to nothing but a few annoying phone calls—at best, a random visitor.

Bree spied out the window.

Tried to swallow but felt her throat too dry to do so.

She had done an excellent job—too excellent—getting revenge.

Her eyes bounced from the cars to the trucks covering the cul-de-sac.

One impatient driver honked at a truck trying to parallel park in too small a space.

In front of Mrs. Lewis's, a family stood at the open back door of an old Camry, tugging on the rope of an unwilling goat in the back seat.

"Oh no." Bree reached for a sweatshirt hanging on the door of her closet and yanked it over her head. She tripped over a stack of whittling tools on her way down the stairs as she checked the time.

6:59 a.m.

"Shoot. Shoot. Shoot. Shoot. Shoot. *Shoot*."

Her advertisement said to come at seven.

She yanked the door open and ran out barefoot. The gravel dug into flesh as she jogged toward an old red pickup. She grabbed the driver's side mirror as the door shut. Lifted a finger to the man in Carhartt overalls in need of a good wash.

"Sir, I think there's been some mistake." Her head jerked up to Chip's second-story window as if expecting his glowering face to tower over them. But there was nothing. Nothing besides the lingering note saying SLEEP WELL in the window.

She glanced back to the farmer. "If you could move out of my driveway, *and quickly*, please—"

With a bit more prodding the farmer gave up and got back in his vehicle. The engine turned and he backed up, but just as Evie was hopping into her car, another car smelling of dozens of freshly baked strawberry swirl, chocolate chip, and asiago bagels swerved in like a shopper taking the last Macy's parking spot on Black Friday.

"Ma'am," Bree said, knocking on the person's window. The woman had apparently decided to pretend this wouldn't be a problem. "Ma'am, you need to move. My housemate needs to leave."

The woman—looking everywhere but at Bree—started digging in her purse. She pulled out her phone and put it to her ear.

"Ma'am," Bree said, knocking again at the window.

The woman nodded and started talking.

Bree exhaled impatiently. "I saw your phone. *You. Aren't. Talking. To anyone.*"

A hum of commotion grew behind her, and Bree whipped her head around to see the crowd forming into a pushy sort of line to his front door.

A woman on his porch peeked through his living room window.

Panic rising, Bree heard a door slam and swiveled her head to see that the bagel woman had slipped out the passenger door and was now running toward his yard with her basket of bagels.

"Hey!" Bree yelled after her, just as her eyes glimpsed a man raising his fist and knocking heavily three times on the door.

Oh no.

No, no, no.

Bree felt herself slipping toward her own porch, but Evie just stood there, arms crossed with her keys dangling from her clenched fist.

Bree moved backward toward the bagel woman.

"Ma'am!" she called, but the woman either didn't hear her as she pushed her way to the front of the crowd or—and Bree would've wagered her own house on this—was ignoring her with the deftness of a toddler wielding a cleaver.

Bree slipped past two men holding chickens.

Maybe she could just yell to everyone that this was a mistake. All a terrible, terrible mistake and they needed to go on home.

There was nothing to see here. Just a typical, neighborly spat gone wrong.

Hi, everyone. Let me take a moment to explain. I'm Bree Leake, totally out of my mind and accidentally terribly clever, a person who will manipulate the lot of you to get back at my neighbor with my seditionist needs. Now, please, if you could just pack up your cattle . . .

Or maybe she just needed to go back inside and feign ignorance.

Yes, that was it. She had no idea what this was all about.

Nobody had seen her do the Craigslist post.

Nobody knew it was her.

This was all just a mistake. A bizarre little mistake. Just one of those funny things.

They could laugh over it during breakfast.

She'd stay inside until the last car was leaving, walk out onto the porch, and pretend she'd slept through the whole thing. Listen with dismay and pent-up amusement while he reenacted the bizarre morning. Eventually coax him to calm his nerves over breakfast. Because . . . perhaps she would ask him to breakfast.

She could.

He'd fed her dinner after all.

Just a few hours before.

Bree started inching her way toward the front door. She avoided Evie's furious gaze as she started to cross the driveway, tiptoeing on gravel.

But then his door opened.

People started shouting.

"I have a 2010 John Deere 3520 tractor, only 480 hours on it!"

"I can make you a custom board-and-batten, seven-by-sixteen chicken coop. You pick the color. And I'll throw in twenty-five beautiful Rhode Island reds like the one here for you."

"Care for a bagel, sir? We have plenty!" the shrill woman who had parked in Bree's driveway said, holding up her basket.

The crowd surged and Chip—holding a coffee mug and looking clearly undercaffeinated—sloshed coffee all over his hand as he stepped backward.

"I have a variety of animals to get your hobby farm started!" A man holding a leashed goat and pot-bellied pig called from beside a tree. "And a twenty-four-page PDF book to get you going."

"I'm sorry, I just—" Chip raked a hand through his hair, bug-eyed.

His attire was different, more polished. He wore a suit that looked as though it couldn't possibly have come out of that residence so dust-free. The five-o'clock shadow that typically accompanied his face was shaved clean.

"What is it you all are here for?" Chip's eyes grazed the crowd.

Caught like a deer twenty paces from the blazing vest of a hunter in the bare winter forest, Bree halted. Held her breath. Prayed he wouldn't notice her among the crowd.

She watched as his eyes roved over them one by one. Her chest tightened as the spotlight of his gaze drew closer. Closer and closer, bouncing off farmers' hats and livestock and children and bread baskets and—

They stopped on her.

She stood in a scene surrounded by farmers and cattle, mowers and livestock. And she might as well have been naked.

Chapter 18

CHIP

Unbelievable.

Simply unbelievable.

Whatever shred of belief he'd had that Bree Leake was a decent person after all was gone. The woman was out of her mind, sitting-in-a-stock-barrel-down-the-Niagara crazy.

Everywhere, as far as the eye could see, vehicles were pulling in. The cul-de-sac was lined on both sides with cars and trucks, the street congested with people and, bizarrely enough, farm animals. Stonewall Heights looked like the newest location for the Appalachian Fair. All that was missing was a Ferris wheel and a place to bob for apples.

Oh look, there was somebody with a basket of apples.

The man closest to him pressed closer still. He held up his guinea fowl. "I've got a hatchery with as many of these as you desire." He eyed the living room. "They're one-a-day layers, no finer fowl in the county."

Chip noticed two men inspecting his bushes, another two giving a scrutinizing look at the gutters.

Two full-grown Old English Sheepdogs barked when Russell appeared at Chip's leg.

Chip grabbed at Russell's collar just before he lunged.

"I'm sorry," Chip began, grunting as he planted his feet against the doorjamb and fought to hold Russell back. "Whatever you are talking about, I'm not interested."

The man looked taken aback. "You're—you're not interested?"

Chip spoke firmly. "No." His eyes cast over the group, landing squarely on the large man in suspenders. The insane woman hid behind him. "Please share the news."

Chip yanked Russell back and tripped over him trying to push the door closed. Quickly, Chip twisted the deadbolt, cursing himself for putting the installation of blinds lower on the priority list.

In his pocket, Chip's phone began to ring.

He didn't have time for this.

The people stared through the window at him, and the man with the guinea fowl started to shout, "It's a crock deal. The man's changed his mind."

A wave of disappointment and a few cries of injustice swept the crowd as they started to disperse.

One woman holding a duck under each armpit stared unnervingly through the window at him.

It was time to hide.

Holding firmly to his coffee, he snatched up his computer and went up the stairs to the safety of his room.

He peered out the window at the group below. It appeared

that for each truck and car leaving, there was another pulling in. What on earth had Bree done?

Another loud knock sounded on the door downstairs.

He ignored it and opened his computer.

Frowning, he checked his email. Aside from about thirteen work-related emails, there was nothing.

He glanced down to the growing crowd and typed into Google, *Abingdon VA Livestock Trade April 15.*

The first few hits involved the weekly Abingdon cattle auction market report, and the Virginia Cattlemen's Association covered the rest.

His phone began to ring. He ignored it.

Frustration building, he typed *Insane Abingdon Neighbor Bree Leake* and, surprisingly, nothing showed up.

Trying to hang on to his composure, he avoided banging the keys with his hands.

The time on the phone said 7:16 a.m. He had approximately fifteen minutes to sort this out before he had to be in a meeting with the Bank of Abingdon—the only bank of the five he'd contacted interested enough to want to meet. Could he leave his house unprotected from these people?

From *her*?

In the yard, a woman was kicking his gutter lightly with her shoe. The elbow joint fell off.

His phone rang again, the number unavailable.

He snatched it up.

"Hello?"

"Yeah, I'm calling about your ad on Craigslist."

An ad. On Craigslist.

He swiftly began typing as he spoke. "What about it?"

"I'm just wanting to make sure this isn't some sort of joke." There was rustling in the background. "I got several cattle here that I could trade, but I don't want to haul them out if this isn't legitimate. You mind confirming before I load up?"

Load up. Cattle.

"Um." Chip typed in his address. Sure enough, a result popped up clear as day on his screen.

Bingo.

He sat back. Stared.

Unbelievable.

"Sir?"

"Right. Um, no, this isn't legitimate. And if you talk to anyone else, please tell them."

He hung up, and his phone drifted down from his ear as he took it all in.

There, on the screen, under the Housing Swap tab, was the headline "Livestock Trade for House in Need of Massive Renovation."

Massive. He took offense at that.

He scanned the ad:

Will Trade House for Livestock

Single man in over his head with financial burden and no marital prospects has decided to give up suburbia for hermit living. Wants: livestock for his hobby farm. Willing to trade: decrepit house in otherwise nice Abingdon, VA neighborhood. Great neighbors. All offers considered. Note: Please bring at least one example animal from livestock offered for demonstration and inspection on offer. Will be considering offers until midnight, April 15.

She had included his phone number.

Simultaneously, his phone started to ring and knocking resumed.

He buried his head in his hands.

Well, the way he saw it, he had two choices. Make the bank meeting and risk the real possibility that his deranged neighbor might auction off his home, or cancel the bank meeting, forfeit his microscopic chance of winning this Barter bid, and spend the next six months watching McBride and Sons tackle the renovation that would've launched his career.

He had to sacrifice something here.

He dropped his hands from his head when he realized what he had that could turn these events around.

Neighbors.

There was more than one kind in the world.

Mrs. Lewis.

Chip made his way outside. People were milling around, and several looked up at him expectantly, a few lifting their chickens as though they were raising handfuls of hundred-dollar bills. Chip held up his hands.

"Sorry. There was a miscommunication. I am not selling—or bartering—this house."

While most faces fell and people who hadn't heard his first announcement started to depart, one man trailed him as he walked across the yard.

"Having a case of seller's doubt?" he said in a voice that made Chip almost certain he sold used cars for a living. "I don't blame you. I haven't seen much here that I would take in exchange for a promising home such as yours either."

"I'm not moving," Chip said firmly, navigating around a family who was starting to break down their tent. "And even if I was, chickens aren't the kind of thing I trade in."

"Of course not," the man replied, keeping step beside him as they moved onto the congested street. "Chickens are too easy to find. Why, even I could get you five hundred chicks no problem."

He paused, the question in his eyes.

Chip waited for an RV to complete a painful three-point turn. "I'm not interested."

"Of course you're not," the man continued without skipping a beat. "That's precisely my point."

The RV moved on, and Chip started walking again.

"No," he said, "what someone like you needs is a trade of equal value. Now, let's take that house for instance. I know that in these tumultuous economic times, it wouldn't be easy to get the kind of value you're looking for. Realtor fees. People coming in and out, invading your personal space for showings. House inspections"—he raised a hand to the side of his face and leaned in, lowering his voice—"and we both know you'd be in a lot of trouble there." He straightened. "Months and months of nothing but debt piling up at your doorstep as you wring your hands, waiting, begging, pleading for the tides to change. And you deserve more."

"I don't want more. I want my house."

"But tell me now, have you ever considered"—he held his hands out, practically purring—"a house*boat*?"

So Chip was wrong. It wasn't used cars. It was houseboats.

"I've got three now, gently used, but with a unique flair. Right now I have an outstanding 1971 Nautaline with your name on it. A newly painted upper sun deck, loads of room in the galley and upper helm. They patched the hole last year. It should float again just fine—"

Chip stopped abruptly at Mrs. Lewis's front door. He turned. "Please go."

The man stopped midsentence. Put up his hands as he backed away. "Listen. I'm just trying to get you a good deal. Have I mentioned the Nautaline comes with a seventy-five-inch flat screen?"

Chip's eyes narrowed.

"I'll just leave you my card."

The man slipped a business card on the step between them, then raised his hands as though caught by the police as he moved backward. "Call me."

Chip turned and rang the doorbell.

The door swung open immediately.

Mrs. Lewis tightened her robe around her, her hair in rollers.

"Mrs. Lewis. I've run into a bit of a problem—"

"Honey," she said, peering over his shoulder, "I believe you've run yourself into a zoo."

"Yes," he said swiftly, his mind on the clock. Ten minutes. He had ten minutes to get to the bank. "I've told them it was all a mistake and to go home, but it looks like we may have people coming in and out for a while."

Mrs. Lewis fixed him with a stern expression. "What do you need?"

He hesitated. "Do you mind keeping an eye on my house for a bit and making sure nothing extreme happens? Like, oh, I don't know"—Chip threw out a hand—"an unbalanced woman showing up with a megaphone taking bids for the house? I should be back within an hour."

Her brow rose at his suggestion, but she just nodded. "Sure thing, honey. Leave it to me. I won't let anyone start messing with your house." She paused, peering over his shoulder. "Or your new landscaping. Hey!" she called, flapping a hand in the air. "You there! Step away from the man's hydrangeas!"

Chip gave her a grateful smile. "Maybe you're the one who's going to need a megaphone."

Mrs. Lewis cinched the belt of her robe with a determined air. "Don't you worry about a thing. You go on. You can count on me."

"I appreciate that." He really did. "You're a good neighbor."

Despite how wonderful a neighbor he truly had, nine minutes later, at precisely eight o'clock, Chip gripped his steering wheel with the unleashed power of a python. He stared at the back of a 1971 Nautaline houseboat at an utter standstill in the middle of the road, animals and barterers all around. And as he did so, Chip held on to one, and only one, thought.

Bree Leake was most definitely *not* a good neighbor.

Chapter 19

BREE

Nearly a week passed in virtual silence.

Quiet, terrible days.

Saturday afternoon Bree did a series of *flap-ball-change* steps in her socks as she cradled her phone to her ear and moved to the sink with her coffee mug. Roughly four days ago her feet had started to tap-dance without her approval. Also, if she was not belting out the words to "Good Morning," she was humming it every hour around the grandfather clock. This was what she got for practicing with Birdie twelve hours a day. If she didn't get the part, at least she could perform on the sidewalk for tips.

Her sidewalk stage name could be That Girl Who Used to Be That Fairy for Barter. She'd do great.

"I *tried* talking to him, Cass. Honestly. Later that day, I *tried*."

"Tried telling him you were sorry?"

"So sorry. I even wrote a note and put it in my window."

"Pause. You put a note in your window?"

"We do that sometimes."

"You exchange notes in your windows. *Sometimes*?" Cassie exclaimed.

Bree shook her head as she popped open the microwave and set her mug inside. Her legs took her into a *shuffle-hop-step-flap-step*. "Nothing like that. We dabble mostly in I-hate-you notes. Cheap and convenient taunting."

"But he forgave you," Cassie countered. "So now the notes are . . . ?"

"Nonexistent. I haven't gotten any note in a week. And believe me, Cass, that feels worse than the I-hate-yous."

She set the time for thirty seconds and pressed Start.

"So you said you were sorry and wrote a note. What did he say?"

"That's the worst part." Bree dropped her head. "He pulled an incredibly polite voice, said he accepted my apology, and . . . nothing. He went inside and we haven't had a conversation since." The microwave beeped as she twirled while tapping. "I didn't mean for him to miss whatever thing he was going to. I didn't *try* to plant that houseboat on the road."

"Bree. You summoned everyone from Virginia, East Tennessee, and West Virginia, claiming you were a desperate man trying to get rid of his house for a few chickens."

"I didn't force them to come. Or stay—"

"You posted the ad on Craigslist for five different cities."

"I thought I would get a few people crazy enough to believe it," Bree said firmly. "I mean, honestly, who would believe a man would trade his house for *chickens*?"

"Are you kidding me? I've seen ads on Craigslist for rentable ducks who wear money hats so party guests can pick up dollar bills while they walk by. Nothing is out of bounds on Craigslist."

"So I underestimated the overwhelming number of unrealistic dreamers in the world—"

"Do you *know* how many people waste their money on the lottery? Do we live in the same universe?"

Bree frowned as she did a *shuffle-hop* over to the microwave and popped it open. "The point is, I didn't mean to make him do that erupting-volcano face. For heaven's sake, I didn't even *mean* to do it that morning. *Any of it.* If I could take it all back, I would." Bree popped over to the window yet again and looked out. No note in the window. The grass and trees were a muted gray beneath overcast skies, the street an eerie quiet. "I'm fairly certain I heard a Jekyll-and-Hyde laugh coming from his bedroom window that night though. What do you think that meant? Do you think I actually made him lose his mind?"

"If you're asking if you are capable of making someone mentally unstable, then yes. I think we've been over that topic."

Bree took a thoughtful sip of her coffee and started to hum.

"Bree, if you are actually worried that you ruined a genuine opportunity for him, why don't you try something really novel?"

She set her coffee down. Her voice came out more desperate than she'd intended. "What?"

"Go out of your way to do something nice."

Bree looked out over the distance between her house and his and considered the silence between.

It was ironic.

She had finally gotten what she wanted all along. Peace and quiet. A neighbor who minded his own business.

And it was more maddening than ever.

Bree started humming again.

"Stop," Cassie said.

Bree stopped and took another sip. "I've gotta go. I have a dinner date."

"*What?* With who?"

"Theo."

"Theo? You've been dating a man named Theo and you've spent the last month giving me agonizingly long details about the *neighbor's dog*?"

"Because it's not as complex. Look, I'll tell you all about it when I get back if you really want to know," Bree said, and after a few more parting words, she hung up.

An hour later, seated at the Peppermill with Theo, Bree found herself transfixed by the butter dish sitting on the white tablecloth.

Chip never could have fit a business card onto it. The plate was too short and narrow.

"I'll have the Shem Creek Sauté," Theo said and handed the waiter his menu.

They both looked to her expectantly, and she looked up from her own menu, realizing she'd been sitting there for long minutes without reading a single item.

"Same," Bree said, giving a slight smile.

"Without the shrimp," Theo added swiftly.

"For yours, sir?"

"Hers."

The waiter looked back to Bree, who was watching a woman slip off her coat of feathers. What if she botched up his opportunity? What if Chip had been going to something important Monday morning—she'd seen his face, his fresh suit, he had to be—and she had ruined it all?

The thought had visited her frequently—and with each visit, killed her—the past week.

There was a discreet cough and Bree jerked her head up. The waiter was still there, looking at her. "No shrimp for you, miss?"

"Oh. Yes. No shrimp. Thanks."

The waiter gave a prim nod and drifted away. Bree turned to Theo. She attempted an easy smile. "Thanks for catching that."

"No problem. I've heard those shellfish allergies are easy to forget about," Theo replied. Though his smile was mirthful, his eyes held hers.

"So," Bree said, trying to sound upbeat as she pulled down the hem of her dress again. "Tell me, what's new in the great grand world of corporate finance?"

It took a moment before Theo blinked and stirred. He seemed to put his thoughts aside to take up the unexpected conversation. "This week one of my clients did make an interesting decision with one of his de novo banks in Asheville. It's not final yet, but . . ."

Even as she stared at his face and focused on his words, she felt his voice starting to grow distant. His perfectly shaped mouth spoke, paused, took a sip of red wine, and continued speaking, but all she could focus on was the rhythm of his movements. Speak, pause, sip, repeat. Speak, pause, sip, repeat.

Her feet started tapping silently on the old hardwood floor beneath her, sliding to the steps.

Flap-flap-step-step-brush-hop-step, repeat.

Flap-flap-step-step-brush-hop-step, repeat.

Which reminded her: she had an audition in a matter of days. She had to wear tap shoes. Which were currently in her house. Across from Chip. Whose dreams may or may not have been destroyed. By her.

"But what do you think?"

Bree's toes halted halfway through a scrape across the worn hardwood. "Oh," she began, trying to replay the conversation she had missed. "I quite agree."

His face was deadpan. "Really. You agree."

Bree felt herself hesitate, as though she was one foot away from stepping in a trap. Her metaphorical foot lingered over the hole. Felt the draft. Pulled back. "Well, not always. You'd know much more than me. So . . ." She cast her eyes around, searching for anything to talk about. They floated across the dimly lit room full of flickering white votives, white linens, and waiters sliding around couples while carrying trays of Cajun-fried crawfish tails and crème brûlées. They landed on his sharp suit, impeccable, as it always was.

Why had Chip been wearing that suit that day? He never wore suits. A crisp dark blue that showed off the amount of time he spent in the sun out with his dog, biking through the pines between earth and sky. His neck looked particularly tanned. Especially—she swallowed, burning with fresh embarrassment—as he jerked at his tie in frustration, staring at that houseboat, stranded behind the wheel.

"Here we are," the waiter said, setting down bowls of soup she had no memory of ordering. She looked down at the mystery soup, seeing what appeared to be noodles, and picked up her spoon.

"Bree, is there something you'd like to talk about?"

She realized she was grimacing over her soup.

She looked up.

Theo sat there with his hands folded, a smile playing on his lips. The kind of smile she had a feeling psychiatrists used to coerce conversations out of patients. Slowly, she put her spoon down.

Should she tell him she had been in the middle of a

neighborhood war? That there had been a cease-fire? That she had botched it by bringing in a zoo?

He'd think she was crazy.

Maybe she was.

No.

Yes. Absolutely. Positively. Was.

Bree pursed her lips as if thinking.

"I can't think of anything," she said at last, then reached for her water glass. As she picked it up she meant to deflect with some fascinating conversation point, but her eyes fell on a man at a table on the other side of the room, raking a hand through hair that looked about a month overdue for a trim.

Like Chip's. She'd never quite noticed before she stood beside him on her porch that evening. He had smelled of sawdust and coffee grounds when he shocked her to the core and put his arm around her, pulling her deep into his side. Cocooning her from the outside world for a few brief, safe moments.

She had processed and reprocessed that gesture well past midnight.

"Is there . . ." Theo paused significantly. "Somewhere else you need to go?"

Bree shook her head, picking up her soup spoon.

Of course not. She was here. Dipping her utensil into something—she wasn't sure quite what—made of coconut milk and cumin.

"Perhaps someone else you'd like to be meeting tonight?" Theo pressed.

"No." Bree dropped her spoon in the bowl. "Of course not," she said, forcing herself to meet his eyes. "I can't think of anything nicer to do tonight than this."

That was true. Theo was one of the most pleasant men she knew.

Theo's brow dropped, his onyx eyes saying silently, *Then what aren't you telling me?*

She pressed her lips together, but her resolve withered under his patient stare.

"It's just . . ." Bree reached for a bread roll. "Just . . . I may have been involved in an adolescent war on my neighbor and crossed a line."

There. She'd said it. She was a child.

"You . . . are in a war. With your neighbor," Theo repeated, a smile beginning to rise. He was looking at her like the parent of a kindergartener listening to his child's complaints about the rainbow erasers being sold out at the book fair.

"You don't understand," Bree said. "I'm not talking mature, adult-level, hate-your-neighbor stunts. I'm talking spending hours scouring the internet to subscribe him to every bizarre magazine on the planet. I'm talking about running up an eBay bid for 250 live eastern subterranean termites to place on his property."

"You have . . . an eBay bid running for 250 subterranean termites?"

Bree shrugged defensively. "That one was just a backup plan."

He settled back in his chair for a moment. Pensive.

"Is it that single man who lives perpendicular to you? The one with the leering expression?"

Bree's forehead creased. She didn't even know the man perpendicular to her. "No."

"The woman with the toddler?"

Bree shook her head. Picked up her roll. Started shredding a piece here, there.

"Is this the elderly neighbor I met the other day who lives across from you? The one you have game night with?"

"Mrs. Lewis?" Bree furrowed her brow. "No. She's a saint."

"Pity."

There was silence for a moment while Theo sat back in serious contemplation. She continued to shred her roll until it was a pile of tiny bits on her napkin.

Theo leaned forward, his voice tentative. "Is it the new man we met on the Creeper Trail the other evening?"

Bree felt her chest pinch. Nodded.

"The tall one?"

"He's got a few inches on me."

"Athletic?"

"He's not allergic to working out."

"With the casual-Californian air, who is taking phone calls with your parents to provide complimentary dog-trick training?"

"That's the one. Wait. How did you—?"

"You've been talking about your neighbor quite a bit. Sometimes directly. Sometimes under your breath." Theo shrugged. "I listen."

Bree felt her neck flush. She pushed away the bread pile at her fingertips. "Sorry, if you could just see what all has happened the past few weeks . . . It's been so chaotic . . ."

He smiled, but his smile seemed to be soft, vulnerable. "Well, I must say, I do wish it was the elderly woman."

Bree laughed. "Oh sure. Because you would prefer to hear your date's in a ruthless war with misfit senior citizens?"

"No, I just prefer not to hear that my date's consumed by her handsome neighbor."

Bree's smile fell.

They were quiet for several moments as the waiter discreetly served their dinner plates.

Theo reached for his fork. "Have you ever heard of Allmont Industries?"

"No, I haven't."

"The owner was a client of mine five years ago. They supplied nearly every gas station on the West Coast with snack products. That is, every gas station but BP, which used Hathaway. The two companies hated each other. Bickered at every chance meeting, were an absolute disgrace at every public event. I could hardly keep them apart."

He paused to reach for his wineglass.

"What happened?"

"The thing that always happens. They got married." Theo shrugged. "In my experience, both personally and professionally, it's the thorn in our side that gets the most attention. Not"—he smiled softly, a bit sad—"the average man taking you out to dinner."

"What?" At last, Bree found her voice. "No. No. Let me be clear. I in no way think you are an average man, Theo. You are absolutely *not* average."

"Then tell me, Bree, when you call that friend of yours back home, who is it you talk about? Me? Or him?"

Her silence was his answer.

They finished the rest of their meal, a touch speedier than normal but overall a nice pace. She made a point to ask about his newest ventures and listen to his answers, and he in turn made friendly inquiries about her upcoming audition. They both politely declined dessert. Then they said their good-byes at her doorstep in a way that meant, *I'll be looking forward to meeting again. As friends.*

Before he stepped away, she found herself reaching in for one last hug. "I'm so sorry, Theo. You deserve someone much better than me."

"Nonsense." He released her from the hug and gave her hand a light squeeze. "I'll settle for someone half as wonderful as you. You just point me in the right direction."

She waited and watched as his Tesla pulled out of the driveway. As the car drifted from sight, she turned back toward the door. Put her hand on the knob.

And, perhaps out of habit, turned her head toward Chip's house.

Her gaze landed on Chip, also at his door, keys in hand, casting his eyes downward and doing his best to avoid hers.

Chapter 20

CHIP

He had forgiven her.

Their prank war had gotten out of hand, and she'd almost ruined his chances with the only bank in town willing to hear him out. But since the busy banker had grudgingly rescheduled only because he knew Chip's father—and didn't like him—Chip wasn't going to let her ruin them for good. Not with forty-eight hours to go before the bid.

This was game time.

Focus time.

And nothing would make him miss this meeting.

He was giving her everything she had asked for all along.

Polite distance.

For the past week Russell stayed inside mostly, and when he went outdoors Chip supervised.

He finally got around to putting up new curtains.

Chip gave a polite nod and greeting when they ran into each other mornings and evenings. This morning she wished him luck on the bank meeting when he'd answered her question about his day. He nodded and wished her luck at another day of practice at the warehouse before her audition.

At noon Chip slipped the tie through the hole and tightened the knot at his throat as he watched himself in the mirror. The creases in his suit trousers were so perfect someone could have used them as a ruler on an architectural drawing. His button-up was so white it hurt his eyes. He checked his watch.

One hour until the meeting.

He wasn't going to get there ten minutes early. No. He was going to be there forty-five minutes early and sit there happily, one crisp trouser leg over the other, until the man opened the door.

Chip patted his suit jacket, trouser pockets, and briefcase as he stepped outside his door.

Phone.

Keys.

Financial documents. Résumé. Estimates. Pages upon pages of estimates.

Here we go.

As he pulled into the parking lot of the Bank of Abingdon, his phone buzzed inside his trousers. He hesitated before pulling it out to answer.

But the clock on his dashboard said he had fifty-two minutes of waiting left. He was there. Although he'd told his subs to do their best to hold all calls until 3:00 p.m., there was no telling what emergency had cropped up. Heck, if one of the subs *was* calling him after he'd been so clear, the odds were real and high that whatever was happening was dire and getting costlier by the minute.

He pulled the phone out of his pocket and saw a number he didn't recognize.

That ruled out his mother, his brothers, and all of his dependable subs.

Francis maybe?

Chip pressed Accept and put the phone to his ear. "What's up?"

But it wasn't Francis. Or Eric. Or any one of the three guys who cycled through phones and phone numbers the way they cycled through fast-food meals.

"Chip, is that you?" The woman's voice broke.

Chip paused before turning off the truck's ignition. "Mrs. Leake? Yes, it's me. What's going on?"

Her voice was unsteady. It cracked as she spoke. "I'm so sorry to bother you like this. It's just"—she paused, sniffled—"we've been trying to reach Bree for an hour. Her phone goes straight to voicemail like it's turned off and—and she needs to know about Anna."

Chip held his breath. He cast his eyes down Main Street. "Does she . . ." He fought to find the words. "Is she . . ."

"She's in the PICU now," she managed. "I'm in the lobby. They aren't letting us in. We're all here. Everyone—"

Chip's jaw flexed.

He glanced in the rearview mirror at the bank's doors.

Then back down Main Street where, a few short turns away, the Barter warehouse stood.

He closed his eyes. Exhaled.

His keys dug into his hands as he put them back in the ignition. "I think I know where she is. Don't worry, Mrs. Leake. I'm gonna find her."

Chapter 21

BREE

"Remember, it's *flap-heel-toe-heel, flap-heel-toe-heel,* and then *Maxie Ford pull back.*"

Bree nodded at Birdie's words and without slowing adjusted the clicking step to fit the sequence. In unison they stamped, shuffled, jumped, clicked the tips of their shoes in the air in the breath of a millisecond, and landed, tapping their right foot behind the left on the floor.

"Again," Birdie said. "From the Maxie Ford."

Sweat rolled down the back of Bree's neck. Though the warehouse was 65 degrees, every inch of her black leggings and white leotard was soaked. Her thighs burned, calves burned, body burned, but at this point the sensation somehow just fueled her to keep going. Birdie had said it was her goal to brainwash Bree's body over the course of their limited practice time. Well, she succeeded.

"You're scraping the toes in the air, not clicking. Do it again."

Bree obeyed.

Birdie stood there watching Bree with her hands on her hips, her own ponytail damp. She nodded. "Good. Again."

Bree jumped into the air and clicked her tap shoes in smooth *tap-tap-tap* precision.

She did it a fifth time, a sixth, a seventh. At the eighth Birdie turned toward the CD player. "Good. Let's do it with the music."

Both of them had pulled hard, full days, especially since Kayleigh's Off-Broadway friend had sauntered onto the scene. It didn't take but a few hours for gossip to confirm their suspicions, and while some of their peers threw in the towel then and there, Birdie never stopped working. After Bree's conversation with Chip over chili, she didn't either.

What had he said?

"Is anything worthwhile ever easy?"

Well, here she was, eating, sleeping, and breathing tap dancing, cramming years' worth of lessons into a matter of days, hoping it worked. Just enough to be a chorus girl.

Not a lead.

Just a chorus girl.

That was all she needed.

Violins and drums blasted cheerily through the speakers as only 1950s musical numbers could, and Bree jumped into formation with a lively smile as she placed her hands on her hips. She watched herself in the broad mirror and straightened her posture as she exhaled, waiting for the beat.

Four. Five. Six. Seven. And—

On the seven-and-a-half beat, as she was preparing to lift her right toe, her eyes shifted to a movement in the mirror. To the reflection of the door opening. And the man who entered.

Her arms lowered slowly.

She turned.

Of all the people in the world—Chip? He stopped just inside the warehouse. Looked at her.

But it wasn't his presence that concerned her most.

Or that he knew where she was.

It was his expression: the hard eyes, creased forehead, not even a snicker of a trick on his lips.

He strode toward her.

Just as she strode toward him.

His eyes didn't so much as flicker toward Birdie, toward anything else, as he moved.

"Come with me."

Before her mind had processed what he was saying, her body was moving toward him, with him.

"Um, guys?" Birdie called out, but they were already out the door.

He opened the door of his truck for her.

She got inside.

Bree felt her blood pressure rising while he slipped into the driver's seat and put the car in reverse. He was back on Main Street, but driving away from their homes, when she finally spoke.

"What aren't you telling me, Chip?" Her voice was low.

He shook his head. "Let me just get on the interstate first."

Bree pursed her lips but said nothing. His truck took the on-ramp and shook with the wear of twenty-five years of hard use as it crept up to sixty miles an hour. Seventy.

She watched as Little Downtown Donuts & Dogs flew by. The Highland Ski Center. The Cracker Barrel in the distance.

Finally, with the Bristol sign flashing by, he looked her in the eye.

"Your mother called. About Anna."

Bree's stomach hit the floor with those five words, and suddenly she was finding it hard to breathe. Chip told Bree everything her mother had told him, all the information he knew.

"I don't"—Bree found herself fumbling, pressing her hands against her cold and wet leotard, her leggings—"have my phone. It's at the warehouse."

Chip tossed her his own.

The outside world was a blur for the next thirty-two minutes as her mother spoke to her over the phone, relaying every single bit of information the family had gleaned from the doctors' hourly updates. Retelling every single torturous moment since Anna's downward turn that morning. Anna's parents were the only ones allowed in the room. The rest of the family was in the waiting area. Both of Anna's younger sisters were at home with Bree's cousin, everyone too afraid to let them see what was going on.

By the time Bree hung up she was hunched over, her hand covering her wet eyes.

She lowered the phone to the seat, her immediate surroundings coming back into focus.

She sat back.

The truck hummed.

And then, blinking, she realized exactly where she was.

"What are you doing, Chip?"

She looked down at the seat she was sitting in, the cracked vinyl. The smell of old tobacco. Then the man beside her, the crisp white button-up. The polished shoes. One hand wrapped firmly around the steering wheel as he stared straight ahead at the road.

"I'm taking you to Knoxville."

"But—but your meeting. I could've driven myself—"

"I'm taking you to Knoxville," he repeated. "And you could use a friend."

Fresh tears pricked Bree's eyes as she turned to face the road again, his words more unfamiliar, unexpected, and welcome than she'd ever known words could be. She pressed her lips together as she looked out her window, blinking furiously.

A moment later, she felt his warm hand encapsulating hers.

It stayed there for the next two hours.

Chapter 22

BREE

Two days later the phone alarm chimed softly and Bree's eyes flitted open. The first thing that came into view was Chip's window. The crystal-clear view through his window.

He had taken down the heavy blue curtains he put up last week and taped a sign in their place.

WANNA MAKE A DEAL?

Bree's head popped up from the pillow.

She had stayed in Knoxville Tuesday and Wednesday, taking turns with the family praying, hoping, dreading, sleeping in the waiting area, and living for news from Anna's doctor. They whispered to each other in chairs and beside vending machines and in halls. For forty hours every word was dire. Heart-breaking and chest-exploding and have-insane-urges-to-punch-the-walls dire. But then the news changed.

From *respiratory failure* to *rest.* From *infection* to *recovery.* Finally, the doctor's lips started to twitch toward a smile.

Things weren't over for Anna. They were far from over. But she was, at least for now, out of those particularly dark woods.

Bree hadn't seen Chip since he'd made a quiet exit from the waiting room an hour after dropping her off. But she'd thought about him. A lot. Enough to remember something Cass had said she should do.

Bree pushed the covers off her legs and slid off the bed toward the dresser. Her tangled braid fell down her shoulder as she picked up the legal pad. She paused, nibbling the end of her Sharpie while she thought about Chip's question, then scribbled her reply.

DEPENDS. ARE DOG FENCES INVOLVED?

Bree jerked her head toward the bedside table clock to check the time.

8:00 a.m.

Audition day!

She had one hour.

She taped the paper in the window, grabbed her robe hanging off the closet door, and made for the bathroom.

Energy ripped through her as she turned the cold, then hot, water knobs. She bounced on her toes while she waited for it to start steaming.

Today was the day.

She was ready.

Oh, geez. Was she ready?

Her stomach seized up as she stepped inside and felt the pinpricks of hot water on her skin.

Who was she kidding? Was she ready to stand in line next to Kayleigh and Selena and Birdie and a dozen other girls whose mothers had *My daughter tap-dances better than yours* bumper stickers since they were three?

For that matter, Stephen and the rest of the cast already knew just how long, and short, her résumé was. She had no doubt he was going to sit in those chairs at the Barter today predisposed to believe she was an easy cut.

"Bree Leake?" Stephen would say, surprised to see her name on the list. He'd lean over to the other judges. "Go ahead and strike her name out now. Can someone get me more coffee?"

Bree gripped the bar of soap so tight it slipped out of her grasp and landed hard on her big toe.

She was doing it again. Beating herself up before the fight had even begun.

"Stop," she mumbled aloud. "You are capable. You made it into the cast once. You can do this again."

"That's right!" Evie said on the other side of the curtain, and Bree jumped. "You are a fierce tap-dancing warrior."

Bree smiled slightly as she picked up the soap.

"You will take no prisoners today."

"Okeydokey," Bree said, lifting her chin and calling over the curtain.

"The stage will be full of those slain by the might of your steely heels."

"Allllrighty—"

"The blood of—"

Bree pushed the curtain open halfway. "Thank you, Evie. I'm tremendously inspired."

Ten minutes later Bree toweled her dripping hair as she slipped back into her room, tightening her robe around her waist. She checked Chip's window before ravaging her drawers to find the proper audition attire. She returned to the bathroom.

Two minutes later she wandered back in to find a better pair of tights. Ticked her eyes to the window. No new sign.

Walked out.

Came back for the hair dryer. Checked the window.

Walked out.

Came back on the premise of wanting her phone to keep an eye on the time, realized she was holding it, checked the window. Walked out.

With hair half blow-dried she rushed to the bedroom and peeked inside, just to see if—

And there it was.

Her stomach flipped to see the new note.

MEET ME AFTER YOUR AUDITION AND MY
BID, NO MATTER HOW IT GOES?

Bree pursed her lips to keep the smile at bay.

WHERE?

She threw the old sheet on the ground and taped the new one to the window. After thirty minutes of checking and rechecking, a final spritz of hair spray, and a smoothing of her bun, she dashed into the room one more time to grab her duffel bag and tap shoes.

She slowed as she stepped closer to the window.

Bree's eyes danced around his room to see if he was still there, then moved back to the sign and let herself fully grin.

WHERE ELSE? HOW ABOUT WHERE WE FIRST MET

She checked her phone. She had about six minutes to get down to the Barter, but she wasn't about to miss this reply. Hastily she scribbled on the sheet of paper, ripped it off the pad, and pushed it to the window.

DEAL

She had never been so nervous in her life.

At the bottom of the stairs, Evie gruffly shoved a plate of donuts at Bree.

"Here. Take these to Stephen." Bree looked down at the plate and Evie avoided Bree's eyes. "Everyone knows he gets grumpy at these auditions. He'll need more than a double shot of Zazzy'Z espresso for breakfast."

Bree hesitated, then pushed the plate back. "I'm not going to bribe him with donuts, Evie. Even if it would probably work with your magical elixir."

"Who said anything about bribing?" Evie replied. "This is just a little reminder that you live with me, and if I lose my roommate because she can't afford rent, I'll be unhappy, and if I'm unhappy I don't cook, and—"

"And if you don't cook, no donuts or sequins. I get it." Bree smiled down at her, still clad in her lipstick-pink bathrobe. "I'm touched."

"I'm not doing it for you," Evie added, pushing them into Bree's hands once more. "These are primal instincts. Survival. No female roommate is as large and intimidating as you—"

"What a compliment. Thank you."

"I don't have a stake in this audition of yours at all aside from that."

"Sure. Obviously." Bree opened the door and called over her shoulder as she stepped onto the porch. "Shall I keep you apprised on how it goes?"

"Yes," Evie replied and shut the door.

Bree turned down the steps, her thick hair up in a tight bun, the sun beaming on the dark green sweater covering the thin leotard. Her tights itched under the wool leg warmers, and just as she was reaching down to lift one drooping side, he caught her eye.

Slowly, she dropped her hand.

They went down the steps and met at their cars at the same moment.

Now Bree stood across from him, the man she hadn't seen since he'd driven her to Anna two days ago, holding her hand the whole way. Neither of them had addressed the moment.

Bree tried to think of something to say but couldn't find the words.

One of his hands held the keys to his truck, while the other gripped a leather messenger bag. On his feet were the type of scuffless shoes that were shined as the wearers sat in old chairs. In his eyes was a story, an itch to share.

"Got a most curious call a few hours ago," Chip said, standing at the hood of his truck.

Bree shifted her weight and felt a light coming into her eyes. "Is that so?"

"Yeah." Chip took a step toward her. Rested a hand on the hood. "Oddest thing. Seems your old pal Theo got wind of my financial straits and has an investor wanting to sink some money into a new project. She called this morning."

Bree shifted the duffel bag on her shoulder. "Oh?"

"The coincidence was uncanny."

"Mmm," Bree murmured, nodding. "Indeed it is."

He put a hand on his heart. "You can imagine how I felt telling her how perfectly timed her phone call was."

"Oh, I'm trying." Bree held her deadpan face.

"That Theo is a good man," Chip said, carefully watching her eyes. A question, a curiosity flickered in his own.

Bree paused. Tilted her head. The slightest smile flitted across her face. "Yes. He's wonderful."

He frowned. "Really?"

"Of course." Bree pressed her lips together to fight the smile. "Charitable. Polished. Charming. Like your girlfriend, I imagine."

"Ex," he said gently.

"Ah." Bree nodded, her smile finally beating her will to look detached. "Ex. I see." She let the silence linger for two beats. "Well," she said at last with a shrug. "Perhaps we should get the two of them connected somehow."

Chip's brow rose. "That would be good." He started nodding, a bit too vigorously. "That would be really good. The two of them would be perfect for each other."

"A match made in heaven."

"An angelic duo."

"We could do their toasts at their wedding."

"Oh, we'd have to."

They both held each other's eyes for one long moment.

"Well, I should get going," Chip said, though his eyes weren't checking his watch for the time.

"Yeah. Me too." Bree held his eyes while popping open her car door. "Good luck, Chip. May you get everything you dream of."

He blinked, and his smile lingered on her eyes, her lips. "You too."

Chapter 23

CHIP

He hadn't wanted to get in his truck and drive to the Barter.

Not with the way she had stood there on the other side of the line, her hair in that thick, high bun, her cheeks highlighted by the rising sun. Her eyes had been like flashing emeralds, beckoning him closer even as he said he had to go.

He didn't want to go.

He wanted to drop his bag right then and stride over and—

"Mr. McBride. You're just in time."

Mr. Richardson held open the Barter door as though he were an usher for an evening play. "I was just about to close the doors."

Chip blinked away images of green sweaters and dancing eyes.

"Thank you, sir," he said, ducking inside.

Chip felt the slap on his back as Mr. Richardson spoke. "I was hoping you'd make it."

"I wouldn't miss it for the world."

As he followed him past the theatre lobby, he spotted several five-gallon paint buckets and his smile faltered. "Starting to go ahead on some work?"

"Oh no," Mr. Richardson replied, turning at the hallway. "No, I've just been thinking about colors lately. And some new ideas have come to mind."

"Different from the sunset ceiling?"

"Oh, absolutely not. Well, perhaps. If this new idea works."

"But if the bid—" Chip began to say.

"I wouldn't worry about it," Mr. Richardson said and directed him past several closed doors. "Nothing but a slight change of vision. I have no choice, after all. I'm but a slave to my inspirations." He tapped his temple with a wink. "I'm sure an artist like yourself knows this only too well."

He gave a hearty laugh. Chip mustered a small one.

"Right in here," he said, motioning to the one open door. Its brass sign read *Conference Room* in bold letters.

Chip took a breath.

There was an oblong table in the center of the room. Sturdy. Walnut. And filling up the seats surrounding it were seven men he'd come to recognize over the years as representatives of competitive construction companies. Most important among them: his brother Pete and his father.

Chip had been to enough bid meetings in his life to know the way it was. The competing companies took their seats, and whenever the bidding facilitator was absent, the competition made small talk about the quality of the Styrofoam coffee or how the Abingdon High football team had done the previous Friday. Sometimes, rarely, someone ventured to ask how someone's son was doing on his Eagle Scout project, or whether someone's daughter had picked a major in college, but mostly the group pretended they barely knew each other. And at all costs, they avoided talking about the numbers on the papers in their hands.

"This tastes like Folgers to me."

"Impossible. I take my coffee from Zazzy'Z every morning. I'd wager my wife this is Cowboy Up."

"Well, I'd take that wager, Bill, except you and I both know—"

A stiff silence fell as the men looked up at the new arrivals. Subtly, every expression turned from open, to surprised, to a poor attempt at unsurprised. Every expression, that is, but his father's.

Chip dipped his head in greeting. "Hello, everyone."

"Hello," they returned. All, again, but his father.

Chip took a look to the two remaining seats. One next to Mr. Anderson of Anderson Builds. The other beside Pete, who was suddenly busy checking his bid-sheet numbers. Chip moved to the other side of the room and sat down beside Mr. Anderson.

His father bent to speak into Pete's ear.

Chip knew what it meant to walk into this room. He was no longer the competition of his father and brothers in theory, but in reality. Hitherto he had worked the odd job. Bathroom renovation here, eighteen-hundred-square-foot-house flip there. Nothing over a $100,000 credit line, and certainly nothing within the $500,000 range that would put him on his family's radar.

Until now.

"So, let's get down to it, shall we?" Mr. Richardson said, clapping his hands together. "Mr. Baxter here has stepped up to review your prerequisites for the bid, so if you could please slide your envelopes to him now."

Obediently each man gathered the first of two envelopes in

his hands and passed it along the row to him. When Mr. Baxter collected them all, he stood and left the room.

"Now," Mr. Richardson continued as the door quietly closed. "I'd like to move forward, assuming you each have your subs' insurance policies and information in line. After all, we're all chums here, aren't we?" He smiled in an easy way. "Nobody here has snuck in the back door." His smile turned into a light chuckle, and he removed his fedora and set it on the table.

"So, how about we get to it? Go ahead and pass me the envelopes."

Without hesitating, Chip slid his down the line. This was not the time for thinking or hesitation. He had stayed up far too many evenings the past several weeks, pushing every cinderblock in his path out of the way for this moment. Moving every heavy stone.

He was under-resourced in every way. Manpower. Money. Time. Staff. But he'd found a way around every hurdle. Moving subs around. Finding subs who could work within the price range. Finding different subs when it became clear they weren't licensed and insured. Juggling the sub schedules and needs to fit within the Barter's tight deadline for renovation. Making sure the subs didn't overlap when carpet needed to be ripped up just as walls needed to come down. Trying to find a bid number that was low enough to beat his competitors—most with the insider commercial discounts he couldn't yet reach—yet not low enough to destroy his profit margins—and him.

It was all hard. It was all a puzzle. It had all, at times, pushed him into dead ends.

And yet here, today, he had done it.

"Line item, line item, line item," Mr. Richardson read, his eyes scanning the sheet in his hand. "Ah. And here we are. The total estimate for Anderson Builds is running at $2,734,860."

As Mr. Richardson set the paper on the table in front of him, Chip glanced at several faces. Of course, they were all attempting to gauge everyone's opinion of the bid. It was high. Quite a bit higher than Chip's, but then, Anderson Builds estimated so high on these things everyone often wondered aloud why he even ventured.

One look at each man's expression gave Chip a few clues about what to expect from the following envelopes. Gilbane Contracting was out of the running; Chip could see it in his defeated expression. Huber was already walking out the door. ACL Construction and Hobbs held their poker faces. But his father and Pete, well, they were doing something he hadn't seen before. Pete looked cross as he whispered to his father, and from the few hand motions, Chip guessed Pete was trying to convince him to take back the envelope.

But that didn't make sense.

They couldn't achieve anything by taking it back. They couldn't write newer, lower numbers to try to secure their bid. That was why the bids were done this way, in person, announced aloud. This method ensured no shady dealings were going on behind closed doors, no undercutting, no wasted hours on complex bids.

Regardless, whatever Pete's frustrated expression and terse whispers meant, his father remained stoic and silent, his gaze fixed ahead. Pete might as well be trying to convince a concrete statue.

"And now for ACL Construction. Let's see." Mr. Richardson removed his glasses and squinted at the page. "The total comes to $2,399,000."

Raised brows went around the room as he caught the surprised expressions of the others. Two thirty-nine was good. Terribly good. So close Chip felt the ax sweep past him, the rush of wind as it took off the hairs from his forearms.

Close.

But not close enough.

The bids were read for the remaining contractors except Redpoint and McBride and Sons, and all came in too high. Finally, Chip saw Mr. Richardson pick up his envelope. He watched as Mr. Richardson opened the letter and scanned to the bottom.

A smile crept across the man's face before he opened his mouth. "And Redpoint Construction has come in with an estimate of $2,350,679."

That's right. Down to the last nine dollars. He had whittled and whittled that number down to the final dollar, and when he thought he couldn't lower it by fifty cents, he went line item by line item for a place to drop it again.

Mr. Hobbs whistled and sat back in his chair.

It was done. Chip's bid had been read. It blew the others out of the water. Every contractor but his father and brother stared at him, ready to declare it.

He'd won.

"Of course, we do have one final bid here," Mr. Richardson said, reaching for the crisp white envelope. For the briefest moment he gave Chip a look that said *for the sake of procedure*.

One glance at Pete confirmed what it would say inside. From head to toe his body was taut, his flexed forearms crossed over each other as he sat like a thirty-eight-year-old CrossFit toddler in the middle of a silent tantrum. Pete had known Chip would be competitive. Pete had known they should've done a lower bid. And now, they would lose it. To his little brother.

"Oh." Mr. Richardson cleared his throat. "McBride and Sons have put in a bid"—he paused for the briefest glance to Chip—"at $2,199,999. It seems . . . they have won."

For several seconds, everyone stared at them.

Finally, Mr. Anderson broke the silence.

"You're joking, Art," Mr. Anderson said. He waved a hand at the envelope. "You've got to be joking."

"Unfortunately, we're not," Pete said crisply as he stared ahead, his veins on the verge of explosion.

"You can't do this job that low," Mr. Anderson said, staring at Chip's father. His brows were creasing more by the moment, as though his mind was turning the numbers. "You can't. Nobody can in this business. How . . ."

But his words trailed away. The questions *How did you do it?* and *What's your secret?* brewed in the mind of every man at that table. How on earth had McBride and Sons managed to lowball a bid more than $150,000 below his? *His?* Which was so low he had barely accounted for his own salary? McBride and Sons had an overhead one hundred times greater than Redpoint's. He had lowered his profit margin to a scrape-the-bottom-of-the-barrel percentage and given up his dream of moving to an office anytime soon. The Barter was going to be the build-his-reputation renovation, the job with his sign proudly staked on Main Street for months declaring, "Redpoint Construction: We Build Your Dreams." This was going to be the job to get all jobs.

His name would have been synonymous with the Barter's.

Chip's father pushed himself to standing and extended his hand. "Mr. Richardson. We are looking forward to working with you."

It took but a moment for Mr. Richardson to switch his gaze

from Chip to his father. "And I as well. Do you know," he said, clapping the man's back and turning toward the door. "I just went to visit the Celebrity Stage in Phoenix last weekend, and I had the most marvelous idea about a revolving stage."

Chip watched, crestfallen, as his father strolled out of the conference room, guided by the hand of Mr. Richardson.

"I hope you're happy."

Chip turned to see Pete standing, pushing uneven stacks of papers into his briefcase with jerky movements. Pieces of paper stuck out all over, but Pete snapped his briefcase shut anyway.

"Me?" Chip said. "What reason on earth would I have to be happy about this, Pete? Tell me. My first big job just flew out of my hands. To you. To Dad."

"Yes, and you're the reason we have this nightmare of a job to contend with at all. Honestly, Chip. You thought you could manage this job for $2.3 million? You'd have sunk the first month."

"Wait," Chip replied, putting a hand up. "Now just wait a second. You don't want this job?"

"How could we want this job? Who in their right mind would want this job for 2.1? We're going to lose so much money we'll be a hundred in the hole by the time it's over with. And with all that man's change orders? He'll have us bouncing from one foot to the other with all his crackpot, twenty-four-hour ideas."

Chip felt like he was hearing his brother's words from the opposite side of a tunnel. He was hearing everything, but the words were coming slowly. His brother was actually upset that they got the job. His brother hadn't been trying to take back that envelope to lower the bid, but to pull out. To lose. To lose because his father, for some insane reason, wanted to underbid.

"But why?" Chip began.

Pete frowned. Stared into Chip's eyes. "Why do you think?"

Without another word, Chip pushed past his brother and out of the conference room. He strode down the plush carpet hallway, following the voices as he went through the lobby and turned into the auditorium. Beside the empty stage in the dimly lit room they stood, his father listening as an enthusiastic Mr. Richardson talked with his hands.

"May I have a word?" Chip said.

Mr. Richardson, who was in the middle of circling his hand in the air, stopped.

Chip's father hesitated, then spoke. "Mr. Richardson. If you don't mind."

"Take your time, take your time," said Mr. Richardson, who was now gazing off toward the stage with one finger on his chin like someone in the midst of his biggest breakthrough yet. "Of course . . . ," he was mumbling to himself as they stepped to the back of the room.

When Chip's father finally stopped and turned around, Chip spoke. "I want you to pull out."

"No." His father shook his head. "You know I can't do that."

"Of course you can. The earnest money you'll lose will be a drop in the bucket—"

"McBride and Sons does not pull out of jobs they give their word on. It's a matter of integrity."

"No, it's a matter of stupidity."

Chip's brash words gave him pause, and his father settled his gaze on him. When he spoke, his delivery was slow and methodical. "Son, I have done a lot of stupid things in my line of work. And my life. This is not one of them."

Before Chip could open his mouth to speak, he continued. "I

am aware of the costs—fiscally and emotionally—for this project, and I have accepted them. What I do not accept, however, is seeing my son"—he paused momentarily—"who is capable of *so much*, lose everything in one foolhardy move."

"Foolhardy. It *isn't* foolhardy—"

"This job would've sunk you. You're bonded at this level, Chip. So what are you going to do if this man doesn't work with your change-order requests for a project that's going overbudget out the gate? If you walk away, that red mark will be on your profile forever. No one would ever insure you or loan you money again. So what would you do instead? Lose a hundred grand, two hundred grand, three hundred, whatever it takes to get this project over with. And then tell me, son, how will you *ever* move on from there?"

Chip stared at his father, momentarily speechless.

He knew the job was tight. Extremely tight. And before this meeting, he'd been willing to take the chance. But now, seeing the man fifteen rows ahead staring at the ceiling with new inspiration, seeing the gallons of paint in the café, feeling the sinking confirmation of what was at stake . . .

Chip shook his head. "I can't let you do this. Not on account of me."

Chip's father spoke again. "Perhaps you'll learn this one day, but sometimes, it is a father's job to take the blow for his child. His enthusiastic, strong-willed, ambitious child who may or may not get his feet tangled up in his dreams on occasion."

"Yes, but I'm not a child."

His father's lips turned up slightly, as though Chip had no idea, no earthly idea, what he was saying. His eyes—the same hue and shape as his son's—softened. His voice came low but strong.

"You are *always* my child. Now if you'll excuse me." He took a step around Chip, clapping a hand on his shoulder as he went.

Chip watched him go, each step sealing his fate.

"Oh, and Chip?" As his dad passed the third row of seats, he paused, turned on his heel. "Your mother has requested you bring your cornbread for supper Sunday. Will we be seeing you?"

His father didn't want Redpoint Construction to fail and Chip to come running back with his tail between his legs. His father wasn't trying to pull the rug out from under the competition. In fact, his father didn't even see him as the competition.

No, he was just his son.

Not the disappointing son. Not the last son. Not the disobedient and unyielding son.

Just . . . his child.

It came down to that.

His child.

For whom he would sacrifice himself if needed.

Chip felt his chest tighten. Resisted the urge to tug on the tie suddenly constricting his throat. "I'll be there."

His father nodded and resumed his confident walk to his chosen future.

♡ ♡ ♡

Chip walked out of the Barter into the chilly, sunlit air. It was a funny thing to feel free after losing something he'd worked so hard for.

He felt as though he had unknowingly been trying to survive underwater for weeks, months, maybe years. As he pushed open those heavy doors, he emerged from the water and, for the first time in ages, could breathe. Real, big oxygen power filled his lungs, giving him life. He looked around and smiled.

The truth was, he could succeed bit by bit. Moment by moment. Inch by inch. He did, as his father said, have a problem letting his emotions guide his actions sometimes, blinding him to potential consequences. He had just wanted so badly to be successful; he had just wanted so much to prove himself. Now, somehow, even that drive was flittering away as though it were ash cleared by the breeze.

His cloudy thoughts dissipated. Chip stepped across the pedestrian walkway in the midst of the midday traffic, his feet as light as the bronze fairies' dancing in the fountain ahead of him.

Because today, he knew the one thing he wanted, and it was time, at last, to do something about it.

Chapter 24

BREE

It was time.

Bree's legs felt like electric currents as she leaned against the wall of the dressing room where she'd been standing approximately two hours, biting her fingernails down to the nub.

Some had auditioned and gone on to other things—like Kayleigh, who walked offstage after a riveting performance, kissed her hand then waved toward Stephen like she was Regina George in *Mean Girls*, and said she was off to pick up her Kroger ClickList.

Bree was among those who stayed.

Found a spot to pace backstage.

And waited.

At last, Stephen stood at the wall outside the dressing room door, stapling the cast list to the bulletin board.

"C'mon," Birdie said, grabbing Bree by the arm and yanking her off the wall.

Bree let herself be dragged for several feet.

"Nope." Birdie halted suddenly. Dropped Bree's arm to cross her own. "I don't think I can do this."

Birdie started shrinking before Bree's eyes. Her arms wrapped tighter across her pink leotard waist with each second, as though she were a python trying to constrict herself.

Bree rolled her eyes and sighed. Grabbed Birdie by the shoulders. "Fine. But next time tell me what role you want to have going on here. We can't both play the pathetically insecure actress hiding in the back of the dressing room. Let's go."

Birdie, however, pressed her teeth against her bottom lip so hard it started to turn white. She shook her head. "Nope. I can't."

"Sure you can."

Birdie shook her head.

"Sure."

Birdie, whose face was growing as pale as her tights, shook once more.

So Bree started pushing Birdie down the length of the room like a football player driving a training sled across the field. Which, given Birdie had never taken her tap shoes off and weighed about ninety-seven pounds, made for a fairly simple push.

By the time they were at the bulletin board a crowd had formed. People jostled for a view. Craned necks. Snapped pictures of the cast list and then turned, typing vigorously on their phones.

Bree moved forward, a full head above everyone else.

She could tell Birdie didn't yet have a clear view of the list. She could tell by the way Birdie slid her hand into Bree's and squeezed.

But Bree had seen it.

Five seconds later, when Birdie screamed and jumped straight into Bree's arms, Bree knew Birdie had seen it too.

"We did it!" Birdie squealed, squeezing and hopping and, for such petite arms, crushing the breath right out of Bree's ribcage. "We did it."

Birdie pulled back, her face radiant. "Congratulations, *Zelda Zanders and chorus girl.*"

Bree grinned. "And congratulations to you, *Lina Lamont*. I've never met a more deserving actress playing the undeserving actress."

Evan tapped on Birdie's shoulder, his own face radiant.

While the room hummed, Bree turned and took in the world around her.

The hanging rack of bejeweled costumes glinting in the corner of the dressing room. The dressing-room tables beneath aureate bulbs strewn with mascaras, eyelash cases, lipsticks, curling irons, cans of hair spray. The buzz of conversations, many already turning to topics of practice the following morning, of plans to celebrate with food at Chick-N-Little.

The Barter—theatre as a whole—wasn't a career she had ever thought she'd choose. But still, there was something peaceful, something relieving, something nice about the knowledge that this was going to be her occupational home.

Her place.

Her people.

For now, yes. But maybe, possibly, for good.

Most of the group was now halfway down the hall.

Birdie stopped when it was obvious Bree hadn't followed. "You coming, Bree?"

Bree's eyes flitted toward the opposite hall, toward another exit.

Where, just outside the door, he would be waiting.

"I've got plans actually," Bree said, smiling as she turned her gaze back on Birdie. "I'll see you tomorrow."

Birdie's eyes danced as she pointed at Bree. "Because we'll be here. Tomorrow."

Bree watched Birdie turn back to the group, her bounce so weightless she appeared to be walking on clouds. Probably because she was.

Just as Bree was.

She turned around.

Faced the door.

And took a breath as she started walking toward it.

She noticed the irony as the adrenaline started to well within her, just as it had the first night she had marched down that same hall for that same door. The ball of nerves in her stomach pushed her onward.

Get there. Hurry up. What if he's gone?

Now there was a thought. What if his meeting was over long ago? What if he'd finished up and had sat there, wondering when on earth she was going to get done. Got bored. Started doubting this crazy scheme. Started doubting everything.

Bree felt her steps quickening, getting closer to the door.

She wrapped her fingers around the metal handle and pushed the door open.

Light flooded the hall as she took a step onto the metal platform. A slow one this time. Cautious.

She took another.

Bent down.

A bouquet of flowers stood wedged into a fresh roll of duct tape and the slits of the platform. A simple, folded piece of notebook paper was taped to the bouquet's plastic wrapper.

She opened it.

MEET ME HOME

Home.

Bree's head snapped up. She looked around.

Pressed the bouquet to her chest with one hand and grabbed the rail with the other.

Quickly she descended the steps and moved to her car.

Home.

This time it wasn't Chip but Bree who had the lead foot as her old Subaru sped across Plumb Alley, slammed to a stop at each sign and turn, and ascended the hill toward Stonewall Heights Drive. The bouquet of flowers shook on the passenger seat beside her; when she turned into Stonewall Heights they flew off the seat altogether.

She pressed her lips together and forced herself to ease up on the pedal as Mrs. Lewis yanked on her dog leash while she stood on the sidewalk, watching Bree's car rumble by.

Bree caught Mrs. Lewis's upturned lips, however, as she passed.

What was Chip up to?

Whatever it was, Mrs. Lewis knew.

And as her view rose above the parallel-parked vehicles and shrubbery, she knew too.

Bree pulled the car into the driveway and pushed the gearshift into park.

Russell, with his giant head resting on the porch steps, jerked up at the sight of Bree's car. Bree yanked the glove compartment open, grabbed the Frisbee, and threw open her door.

Because there Chip stood, holding a shovel, no longer the sleek, gray-suited man of the morning but the rugged, holey T-shirt man she'd loved to hate so much and now, somehow, just loved.

Sweat dripped freely from his forehead, as though he'd been too focused on shoveling to stop and push it aside. Fresh dirt was smeared across one cheek.

And almost all the way across the driveway was a new stretch of uprooted dirt, just twelve inches away from the original. A new Invisible Fence line. A real one.

He saw her and frowned.

"Aw, Bree," he said, straightening. "Evie told me she thought you'd be another couple of hours at least—"

But Chip never got to finish the rest of his sentence. Because Bree crossed the line, threw the Frisbee at the oncoming dog, and marched straight into him.

With one hand pressed to his dirt-streaked cheek, Bree caught his lips with hers.

She heard the shovel drop first.

A moment later his hands wrapped around her shoulders and pulled her in with the same power and determination she'd witnessed time and time again as he dug or drilled or hammered.

But his lips were gentle, disciplined. Slow, as if he'd wanted to do this for a long time. Methodical, as if he wanted to explore the lips, cheeks, temples he'd never been quite able to reach.

He wanted her too. Until that moment, until she felt every soft kiss delivered like a whispered affirmation, the grip of his calloused hands like a soft pledge, she hadn't been certain.

Her breath grew shaky, unstable, just as the weight of Russell's flank wedged between them.

Chip pulled back, and when he did, there was a timidity in his eyes as if to say, *Well then, I suppose I've shown all my cards now.*

She leaned over Russell and kissed Chip again once, hard, to show him she could show all her cards too.

Russell nudged her again, and just as her knees started to buckle she recovered. They both looked down to see him, panting through open jaws, trying to press the Frisbee into her hand.

She reached for it and the dog sat, panting, his brown eyes so doe-like, so eager, you'd think she had offered him a Slim Jim.

"Well, whaddya know, Chip? The Frisbee trick works."

She threw the Frisbee, and the dog bounded after it.

When she returned her gaze, she realized Chip was still watching her. With his face inches from hers a smile crept up his lips. A private smile, a challenging smile. His eyes crinkled as he spoke. "Bree Leake. Would you ever doubt me?"

In all her life—with Nana's home behind her, the maroon-and-yellow flags waving merrily at the Barter not so far away, the friends and the neighbors and this man looking at her as if with no intention of ever looking away, and yes, even the dog racing toward her across the yard, drool flying from his rippling jowls—she had never felt more content.

Epilogue

Two Years Later

The sun shone on the sun-kissed yard as Russell chased a chicken and Chip stepped off the porch to greet the last of the cars pulling in.

Inflated blue balloons were tied to the yellow mailbox. Parked cars and vans covered the street as far as the eye could see, abandoned to the long afternoon. A faint beeping of an oven timer came from an open window.

"Is that a . . . ?" Pete's wife said, her words faltering as she seemed to decide whether to get out of the car. She held a large rectangular box wrapped in baby-blue paper dotted with illustrations of teddy bears and bottles.

Chip walked toward them. "Pot-bellied pig? Yes, getting fattened up for Christmas, I'm afraid."

He smiled, watching her scramble to move away from the black-haired, 150-pound pot-bellied pig sticking its nose in the air of the neighbor's yard. His yard. Or rather, his yard until a year ago, when he'd said "I do" to the woman of his life and Evie said, "You sell me this house or I'll never feed you a donut again."

He'd immediately handed her the keys.

He nodded to the pig. "Don't worry. He's got an Invisible Fence."

The pig turned, its purple collar glinting before it made for the backyard.

Chip smiled and shrugged. "Neighbors. What are you gonna do?"

"I heard that," Evie said, pushing the screen door open. His godtwins—two of his six godchildren to be exact—ran out. "Have you heard the oven?"

"It just started beeping," Chip said, moving aside while Evie—and Gerald, their friendly neighborhood UPS man—walked by.

"Guys, don't run until you're outside," Cassie called, her voice followed shortly by her youngest, Timmy, on one hip. Once outside she set him down, and he—with toddler curls as wild and blond as his brother's—flew down the stairs to join the fun.

"Oh, Evie," Birdie trilled, raising her empty glass from her perch on the lawn chair beside Mrs. Lewis. "We're gonna need a refill."

"Get up and help then!" Evie called back.

"Honey, we would," Birdie said, grinning wickedly. "Honestly, we would. But the baby shower is thrown by the *best friend*, and as you have reminded us one thousand times in the past three months, Bree picked you to throw her shower. Ergo, *be her best friend*. So . . . chop-chop," Birdie said, settling back in her seat.

Evie grunted. But even from this angle, Chip could see her cheeks grow pink with pride.

In the middle of the yard, Theo stood in the center of a group of children.

"Now this is the football. And this," Theo said, bending over a blue bucket and lifting a strip of fabric high into the air, "is the mechanism that straps to your waist. The fundamental goal, as I understand it, is to pull this flag from the offensive player holding said football . . ."

Chip's goddaughter Deidre raised her hand.

Theo paused. "Yes?"

"Or we can just knock each other over."

"Oh no," Theo replied, giving a small chuckle. "This is not *Lord of the Flies*. We do this civilly. Not to mention some of your parents have substandard health insurance plans and haven't reached their yearly deductibles."

"Wait for me!" a girl called from inside.

Chip, holding the screen, stepped out of the way just as Anna raced through it. The afternoon light reflected off her cheeks. The baby-blue bandana she had chosen for the day was firmly in place, but just underneath were shoots of brown hair peeking out. She was but a few months from feeling comfortable enough to throw her bandanas away. She peeled off the stairs after them, laughter rising with a strength they had all waited, hoped, prayed for so long to see.

"Are they starting the game already?" Bree's voice came from the other side of the screen now, too, led by her six-month bump.

She grinned as she caught sight of Pete and his wife and spread her arms out for a hug.

As the little house on a nondescript little street beside the Appalachian Mountains settled into the afternoon, bees danced around children as they played their games outside, and laughter leaked from every crack in every window. And word from the neighbors that day was that the house glowed with insuppressible joy.

Like a glimpse into the next world.

♡ ♡ ♡

ACKNOWLEDGMENTS

Where else could I start, but with everyone at Thomas Nelson? From the amazing efforts of the sales team to gorgeous designs of my cover designer, I am appreciative of you all *every single day.* Little did I know when my very first contract came into my inbox two short years ago just how much you guys would mean to me—as esteemed colleagues and as friends. I *love* living this publishing dream out with you all, with special gratitude to: Jocelyn Bailey, Kerri Potts, Kimberly Carlton, Amanda Bostic, Becky Monds, Paul Fisher, Matt Bray, Savannah Summers, Laura Wheeler, Jodi Hughes, Marcee Wardell, Margaret Kercher, and Nicole Andress. And to everyone in sales who gets this book to readers via Target, Walmart, Books-A-Million, libraries, Barnes & Noble, and independent stores, thank you!! You made my dreams come true with *The Dating Charade*, and I'm so terribly grateful for all your continuing hard work on behalf of my books.

Jocelyn, you are my rock, and I'd say I apologize for leaning on you so much, except that implies things will change and . . .

yeah that won't happen. Kerri, um yeah. Same for you, dear. You're stuck with me and TikTok madness chats will continue to ensue. Erin Healy, I *loved* working through line edits with you! Thank you for being so kindhearted and soothing as you masterfully edited this book. Kim, you didn't even work on this book, but I don't care! You are the friend and soul encourager who helps me wade these publishing waters, so you definitely make it on the page too. To the incredible cover designer of this book, Halie Cotton, thank you! And to everyone else, I *always* love being welcomed with your smiles and hugs and thoughtful guidance. I have never desired to work in an office building, *except whenever I go to Thomas Nelson* and daydream about working among *you*. Hence why my next book is about an editor at a publishing house . . .

To Kimberly Whalen, I am so grateful for your amazing industry knowledge and guidance and communication! Thank you for giving 100 percent in all you do, and I only hope to give 100 percent back!

To Abbi Hart (@adventuresofaliterarynature), Amber Vandivort (@ambersrfdream), and Grace E (@readingbee.444) for reading this book in a flurry during Christmas to give me feedback. Thank you!! To Christine Berg, for always listening, reading, and giving me thoughtful feedback!

To the ACFW community, fellow Thomas Nelson authors, Betsy Haddox, Bethany Turner, Megan Gonzalez, and especially my Tea & Empathy gals (Rachel Linden, Rachel McMillan, Janyre Tromp, Lauren Denton, Katherine Reay, Patti Henry, Sue Meissner, Ashley Nicole, Siri Mitchell, Shanna Hatfield, Adele LaCombe, Catherine West, Elizabeth Younts, Susie Finkbeiner, Jessica Kate, Heather Gilbert, Kelli Stuart, Janine Rosche, Julie

Cantrell, Jolina Petersheim, Allison Pittman, Beth Vogt, Lynne Gentry, Lindsay Brackett, and Kristy Woodson Harvey), you all have been an absolute joy in my life. I *love* growing with you!

To Jim Hart, thank you for believing in me and my books! I will be forever grateful to you for that chance and your kind support.

To my patient husband, for all those nights you put the kids to bed so I could work, for all the times you read my drafts, and the thousands (millions?) of hours you've listened to me talk through my books. I love you!

To the barista in Zazzy's coffee shop and the Barter actress who wandered in one day and gave me tips—ah! I wish I had your names to thank you! To Courtney Walsh, for letting me sidle up beside her and ask her for theater-life lingo.

To the Barter Theatre, the Martha Washington Inn, Zazzy's, the Tavern, 128 Pecan, Bone Fire Smokehouse, King Museum, and the incredible town of Abingdon I've been privileged to enjoy as a Bristolian all these years, thank you for being the most Hallmark-worthy town in all creation. You are a world of inspiration, and I can't wait to show readers our wonderful town through this book and my next novella, *Pining for You*!

To the Barter especially, I have been to more plays and musicals at the theatre than I can count over the last fifteen years, and the tradition continues with my children. Thank *you* for being the world's best live performance theatre! You say, "If you like us, talk about us. And if you don't, just keep your mouth shut." Well, here I am, telling the world about you!

To those bookstagrammers and bloggers who have shared my books in the most gorgeous of ways. To Barnes & Noble in Johnson City for being the first bookstore to support me and welcome me so warmly into the published life! I was just a fledgling with my debut, *The Dating Charade*, and your encouragement meant the world.

To my Creator, for rest. This book was about finding peace after the inescapable sense of restlessness we all face in this life, and truly as St. Augustine states, "Our hearts are restless until they find their rest in You."

And thanks to every *single* reader who encourages on social media, replies to my newsletter emails, shares my books, writes reviews, tells your book clubs, and just makes me feel like I'm part of a cozy community. I appreciate everything you do more than I can say.

DISCUSSION QUESTIONS

1. Neighbors can be a blessing in your life or a curse. What is your life like with your particular neighbors? What are some things they do that you appreciate or cannot stand?
2. If you had a neighbor move next door to you who drove you to sanity's ledge, what humorous thing would you *want* to do to get that person out of your life?
3. What do you do to be a good neighbor? What are three things you could do in the coming month to become a better one?
4. Chip and Bree both let their emotions get the best of them. Have you ever made a rash decision in a moment of anger that you later regretted? What is one coping method that has benefitted you in maintaining self-control in those heated moments?
5. Which character's weakness do you identify with most? Why? Which character's strength do you identify with most? Why?

6. Bree Leake has jumped from job to job, relationship to relationship, and house to house throughout her life. Why is that? Why hadn't she settled down?
7. "If I find in myself desires which nothing in this world can satisfy, the only logical conclusion is that I was meant for another world." What does this quote by C. S. Lewis mean? Can you relate to it? How?
8. Despite the fact that Chip argued with him, Chip's father won the bid and lost a lot of money in order to protect his son. Have you ever experienced this kind of sacrifice in your life—someone taking the negative consequences for something in your place?
9. Chip loses the bid, but walks outside feeling like he has won, and that he can breathe for the first time. Why is that?
10. What does Evie learn throughout her time living with Bree that changes her? How?
11. Who is your favorite character and why?
12. The quaint town they live in is Abingdon, Virginia, population of 8,000. What would you love about living in a town this size? What would you dislike? And if given the choice between a city or a small town, which would you choose?

Please enjoy this excerpt from

The Dating Charade!

"Melissa Ferguson is a sparkling new voice in contemporary rom-com."

—Lauren Denton, bestselling author of *The Hideaway*

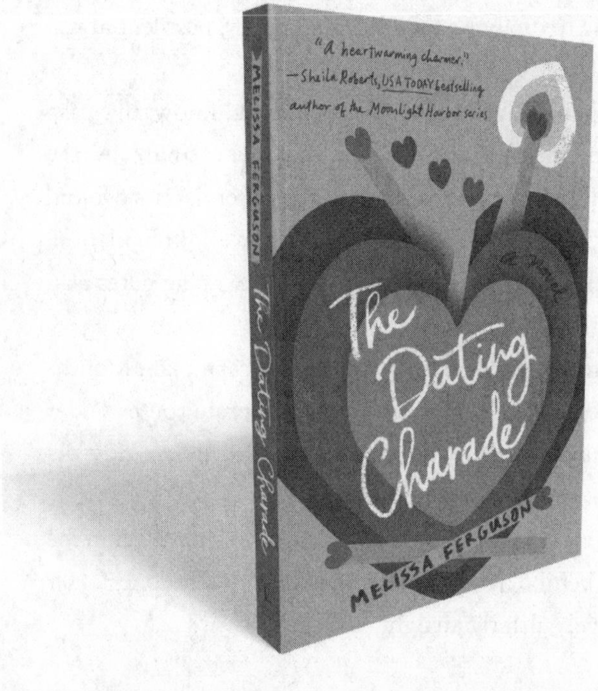

7

CASSIE

If one was going to dip one's toes into the murky, pestilential waters of online dating, an escape plan was critical.

Fake emergencies worked on occasion. You know, the gasp as you take a "phone call" and dash out the door to an imaginary emergency with an imaginary friend. But in general, Cassie found the method too cliché and utterly devoid of, well, imagination. Besides, whenever she needed to make a hasty exit, her dates usually saw through such tricks.

It'd taken months to create the perfect escape plan. Months of trial and error, of late nights scribbling elaborate routes under lamplight, of miniscule alterations schemed up with her most devious of friends.

But here, watching the stingrays circling the scuba diver in the aquarium glass behind her date, she knew she'd finally done it. Her plan was positively, utterly airtight.

"Married, you ask?" He cocked his head to one side as though the question actually required mental searching. His thin lips pressed together, resembling the fish floating behind his head.

"Yes. Are you married?" Cassie's eyes ticked to the culprit: the ring finger on his left hand. The tan line was minimal, almost non-existent. His nails were clean, and in Cassie's mind nothing good ever came from a man with immaculate hands. And yet even if her eyes had wronged her on those matters, there was no getting around the slight indention where a band would be and the slightest puff of the skin between ring area and knuckle.

Two minutes. After a year of online dating, she'd developed the ability to spot a rat in under two minutes. That deserved some sort of recognition.

His hand swiftly dropped from the glass just as hers lifted to discreetly tap it twice.

Escape plan in motion.

"Technically . . . yes. But it's more complicated than you think." He laughed good-naturedly as he scratched the back of his head with his pristine hand.

She didn't smile in return.

His smile slipped down with his arm. "Surely you didn't expect me to drop something like this in the first five minutes, Cassandra—"

"Cassie."

"I was going to tell you. But I just couldn't live with myself if I scared you off right away. Not someone—" He paused momentously, two fingers drawn to his lips. "—like you."

Ah, there it was. The date had moved into stage 2: overly sentimental compliments wrapped in false humility.

Cassie shifted her jacket to her other arm. Right. Here it came. "Because of our energy."

"Yes." He bobbed his head like the baby Groot sitting on her desk at work. "It's kinetic. The way I've been able to open up to you these past few weeks . . ."

Six days. Via e-mail. On topics as deep and moving as the Yorkshire terrier in his profile picture.

Cassie pinched her face into a quiet, patient smile, letting the man go on with his excuses.

She knew she appeared complacent standing beside the floor-to-ceiling glass of Ripley's Aquarium of the Smokies, her gaze on him and yet attentive to her periphery. Echoes of excitement bounced around them as a massive blacktip reef shark slid across the wall. Children in dripping overcoats and galoshes stood on toes and pointed. Since the start of Thanksgiving break, the aquarium had been more crowded than ever.

But crowded was good. Crowded was ideal. The aquarium's ample noontime distractions were key factors in why she always chose her best friend's workplace to meet, greet, and ultimately sprint as fast as she could away from men. A restaurant? Facing your foe at a candlelit table for two? Fleeing from there mid-date would be the real challenge.

She slid her eyes to the glass, relieved to see Bree, her best friend, her quintessential partner in crime, kicking her fins their way. Parting a group of yellowtail fish, Bree halted directly behind her date.

His back touched the glass as he faced Cassie completely. "Why don't we get out of here and find someplace quiet to talk? I know of a great little lunch place that just opened up on Newman—"

The sudden bang on the glass jolted him, halting his monologue. Startled, he turned around to find the scuba diver, all six foot two of her, shaking a gloved fist at him.

She banged again. Every face in the room turned from the glowing ultramarine tank to him.

"Do you know her?" Cassie raised an eyebrow as she took a step back.

"I've—I've never seen her before in my life." He squinted, clearly trying to see beyond the long floating braid, mask, mouth-piece, and BCD vest to the woman underneath.

Bree banged a third time.

Then, at last, she began the incomprehensible—and, it should be noted, utterly meaningless—show of charades. To the innocent onlooker, it looked positively seething.

"You sure? Old girlfriend, perhaps? Did your wife take up diving?"

"No, I . . ." His eyes were glued to the glass, his neck reddening to match his thin polyester collar.

But Cassie was already melting into the crowd of onlookers, sharks, and spotted eagle rays. Her eyes never left his now babbling form as she moved backward like a chessboard knight, slipping around parents and kids and disappearing before he'd even realize she'd gone. At the private, staff-only door, she gave Bree a salute and slipped through it.

Married.

Both her smile and energy melted as she shut the door and leaned against it. For a brief moment she let the slime of the date slip off her, imagining it oozing down her mulberry velvet skirt and knee-high boots to the water drain in the middle of the floor.

Married.

To be honest, she'd really hoped for good things with this one. He was educated, good looking. His pictures avoided posing with toilets in the background. His interests followed the same strain as hers: running, cooking, festive gatherings with friends. He even claimed to volunteer with the residential kids at Wears Valley Ranch. She'd been particularly interested in talking with him about that one.

But what had happened? Where was she now? Back in her trusty panic room beside a rack of wetsuits, cleaning tanks, and a bucket of squeegees.

Cassie let herself indulge in one more minute of pity partying before kicking off the wall and heading for the exit door. Gold and persimmon maple leaves danced around her boots as she stepped around the backside of the building to her car. She dropped her purse into the passenger seat and, with the engine humming, sorted through her choices for the suddenly free hour. It didn't take long before she shifted her car into Reverse.

Back to work it was.

Eight minutes and twenty-three seconds later, she pulled into her parking spot with its rusted sign: *Crazy Boss Parks Here: All Other Cars Will Be Sold on the Black Market.* (Sure, she probably shouldn't have kept the sign the Haven girls gave her a handful of years ago—encouraging delinquent behavior and all that. Still, it made her smile.)

Two large pots of orange mums sat on either side of the otherwise dull entrance to Girls Haven. It was a typical government building: all sharp brick corners and long-paned windows. The cobwebs adorning said windows were about as permanent as the emotionless beige paint on the inside walls—and not for Cassie's lack of trying. She'd vacuumed the webs from her office window at least five hundred times in the seven years she'd been director at the center for disadvantaged girls. As punishment for unruly moments, girls had been guided to her office window with a vacuum and bleach bottle more times than she could count. And yet somehow the webs always grew back overnight, wafting in the breeze as if laughing each morning at her return.

"What're you doing back already, Miss C?" Star's Chucks rhythmically slapped the brick wall she sat on, her feet swinging as she watched Cassie ascend the concrete steps. "Don't tell me. You got another flake."

"Oh, quite the contrary," Cassie replied, reaching the top step. "I'd say he was *quite* keen. Maybe by our third date he would've had all three of us out for dinner—him, me, *and* his wife."

"Hey, at least you would've made it to a third date." Star laughed, then dropped off the wall. Pausing, she looked Cassie up and down, then rested her fist resolutely on her hip with all the sass a fourteen-year-old could give. "You know what, Miss C? You're too picky."

Cassie gave a blunt laugh. "Is that so?"

"And I think it's about time you let us girls have a shot at finding you a man." The wind picked up, making the beads at the end of her dreadlocked ponytail clatter together. "Because let's admit it: you're cute, but you're not getting any younger."

"Cute but not getting any younger. How did you know *exactly* what I needed to hear today?" Cassie smiled, her eyes catching a glimpse of the rows of fire trucks parked across the street.

At least once a month someone asked if she was married. Had kids. Once she was asked if she had grandkids. She was just thirty-three. But anyone age twenty-five or older was the same to these girls—lumped into a giant bag labeled "ancient."

"Nice 'do." Cassie took in Star's new locks. A silvery blue string weaved through it, all the way down to the bare, bony shoulders Star was sporting in thirty-degree weather. "You do it last night?"

"Yeah."

Cassie looked closer, and her smile faded as her antenna rose.

Star stepped back, slipping the craftily spun lock through her fingers.

It looked good. Too good. "You do it yourself?"

Star's eyes darted to Cassie's boots, then the mums, before finally resting on the basketball hoop on the aged concrete pad beside the building. "No."

Cassie crossed her arms. Waited.

Seven years on the job at Girls Haven, and she was a master of the teenage standoff. People from nonprofits around the nation sought her advice and expertise on the teenage standoff. She practically led conference workshops on the teenage standoff.

Finally, as though the words had been extracted by pliers, Star spoke. "Ershanna did it."

Cassie's lips pursed. The times Star let anyone experiment with her hair were few and far between. Whenever she showed up with something worth keeping, you could bet a dime it was because Ershanna had taken her in. And the only time the nineteen-year-old, barely-an-adult-herself neighbor took Star and her sisters in was because something bad had happened at home.

"Why didn't you call me?" It was difficult to execute a perfectly even, calm tone.

"Because it wasn't a big deal." Star leaned against the brick, her eyes on the parents toting their kids across the Dollar General parking lot. A taut banner hung between two fire engines: *Touch a Truck, 12–2 p.m.* "Nothing worth calling about."

"Then *why* were you at Ershanna's? Because we both know it wasn't to do homework."

Star wrapped her arms tightly around her chest.

Cassie shrugged, tucking her arms around her own chest, protecting her fingers as they pressed between the layers of thickly quilted down. "Fine. I can wait out here all day. And, Crazy Girl in a Tank Top, let's remember I'm the one who dressed for winter."

Star shifted her weight from one hip to another. Seemed to fight a shiver with another frostbitten breeze. "Antony just came back. I didn't want to get into it, so—" She shrugged. "I left."

At that, both Cassie's breath and fight fled. The last gift Star and her sisters should be getting for the holidays was a crusty, sporadically violent, drug-abusive stepdad back in their living room. Cassie would know; she'd been around for the sorry details the last time he landed in jail. "Last I checked, he wasn't allowed to be in the same three-hundred-foot radius as you. Or your sisters."

Star laughed without smiling. "Yeah, well, last I checked, he wasn't much into playing by the rules."

"Let me make some calls. You can stay with me tonight—"

"No, don't do that," Star said quickly. "He said he's moving on this week. We're staying with Ershanna until he goes." Star paused, then pointed a finger at her. "I'm calling confidentiality on this, Miss C. You can't tell. You'd only make it worse."

"I think we should—"

Star glared.

"But—"

Star glared harder.

Cassie clenched her jaw. *"Fine."*

Star nodded and put her finger back into her jeans pocket as though holstering it. Then she involuntarily quaked in the cold.

Cassie put an arm around the girl's shoulder. "But I *do* want to hear that he's gone by Sunday, all right? I'm going to be blowing up your phone the next few days until you confirm that."

"Yeah. I know. I already blocked your number." Star gave a mild smile beneath Cassie's downy wing, and together they spun toward the double doors.

A blast of hot air greeted them from the radiator. The entrance hall was empty, only a few voices coming from the game room. It wasn't surprising. Girls Haven always emptied out during the holidays. Those who showed up did so because they either had no other option or were loyal to the Haven. Star, the special case, came for both.

Together they walked down the hall. It smelled of bleach and microwaved popcorn. To be fair, it *always* smelled of bleach and microwaved popcorn.

"So? What'd'ya say?" At the last second Star slipped past Cassie into her office and dropped into Cassie's rolling chair. She spun it in a circle before putting her hands on the keyboard.

Cassie slung her purse onto the hook behind the door. "What do I say to what? You being in my seat? Move."

A gleeful scream echoed down the hall, and a second later a girl grabbed the door frame like a life raft before two others popped up behind her. Whatever game they'd been playing was swiftly abandoned, the girls lured in by the sight and sound of fresh gossip.

"What are ya doin'?" A suspicious tone lilted Bailey's voice as she pushed her hair from her eyes and strolled in.

"We're setting Miss C up on hotornot.com," Star replied.

Cassie raised her voice. "It's *not* hotornot.com," she said, nudging Star out of her chair.

Still, in a matter of seconds the girls crouched around Cassie and the computer, breathing the same twelve inches of air despite the two hundred square feet of unoccupied, perfectly good office space. Through the window, flakes started to dust the road as a song played from one of the girl's phones. Cassie couldn't hear the words but recognized the unsavory tune enough to double tap an icon on her desktop. Sinatra's "You Make Me Feel So Young" filled the room.

All four girls moaned.

Cam spoke, the song from her phone still playing somewhere within her cheetah-print jeggings. "This song definitely *doesn't* make me feel so young. I feel a hundred and five listening to this cra—"

"Crazy awesome mix, Miss C," Star said. She threw two thumbs up. "It's downright inspirational."

Cassie rolled her eyes. Clearly Star was more interested in spending the next hour searching for suitors than listening to another of Cassie's soapboxes on self-respect and teen pregnancy.

"Knock-knock." Bree's words matched the rapping on the open door. Her fire-red hair fell to her waist in a wet braid, the weave so thick one could've trusted it to rappel down a burning building. She held up two gas-station coffees. "I came as fast as I could. Left a trail of gear all the way to my car." She handed the coffee to Cam, who handed it to Bailey, who bypassed Star and gave it directly to Cassie.

Bree pushed a couple of stacks of papers aside and took a seat on Cassie's desk.

Cassie huffed and waved a hand around the room. "All right, guys. There are, like, five other chairs here if you haven't noticed."

Nobody moved.

"So, what happened with the guy?" Bree said. "Besides, of course, trying to get me fired after you left."

Cassie's brows shot up, both shoulders and knees pinched

together from being compressed between the group and wall. "He talked with Louis?"

Bree gave a flippant wave. "Oh, you know how he is. Louis fiddled with his whistle while your guy rambled on. But then your guy turned on me and started to get in *my* face about it, and you should've seen Louis. Went all Hulk on the guy. I ended up pulling him back and calming *him* down." She smiled as if at a fond memory. "Good ol' Louis."

Cassie grimaced. Bree's supervisor, Louis, was *not* the kind of man who'd spent his prime years scuba diving in Bermuda and off the coast of Peru, in much more adventurous places than Ripley's Aquarium. He was *not* the type who'd purposefully shaved his head to achieve a Bruce Willis look. No, Louis, poor Louis, was a kindly middle-aged man ten years Bree's senior. He was fond of whistles—some would say oddly so. He liked the twelve African black-footed penguins that made their residence there. Rumor had it he sang to them with squid-and-fish cake on their birthdays. Last, but certainly not least, Louis was head over off-brand Keds for the woman with enough spice to flavor a ten-gallon pot of chili.

Bree.

Louis's happiness was a crucial piece of the perfect escape plan.

"Don't worry, Cass. I took him to the café to cool off. He practically passed out when I let him pay for my chili cheese fries." Bree picked up one of the many misplaced fidget spinners from Cassie's desk and began spinning.

Cassie stared at her cup for one long moment, then looked to Bree, the girls, the computer.

It was time to call it.

"Well, on the bright side, I don't think we have to worry about this happening again. I think I just had my last blind date."

Bree halted the spinning spinner. "That bad?"

"Somewhere between the guy who shoplifted the stuffed dolphin and the one who ate through a pack of gum in five minutes and stuck every piece on the walls—"

Bree's eyes widened. "No, Cass. Not Gum Man."

"He was married." Cassie set her cup down on the only available inch of table space in front of her. "The charming youth volunteer who stated loyalty was the biggest characteristic he was looking for . . . was married." She shrugged. "So, I'm done. I think we can all agree I gave online dating more than a decent shot."

Star and the others looked to Bree, who gave them a resolute, don't-worry-I-got-this nod. "Let me see for myself. I'm hearing you, Cass, but let's take a look before we try to cut the one cord that's been sending men your way—mad as a March hare or otherwise."

Cassie pushed the keyboard her way. "Be my guest. Username is 'Cass0312.'"

Bree started typing.

"Password is 'mrjeeves.' No caps."

Bree's fingers typed the letters and then froze. She removed one hand from the keyboard and pinched the bridge of her nose. "Cass. Please don't tell me you created a password out of your cat. Please tell me I misheard you."

But sure enough, the pop-up disappeared, and a dozen male faces filled the screen. Cassie pushed herself up and slid over the desk, mulberry skirt and all. If she was going to be humiliated, she might as well get a little distance. While the girls scrolled, she moved to the window, taking her coffee cup with her. Across the street a fireman in full gear stood with his back to one of the trucks, talking to a group of kids.

"This guy seems nice."

Cassie flicked her head back to see Star pointing to a message titled "READY FOR LOVE WITH SOMEONE LIKE YOU."

"It's spam."

Star read aloud anyway:

HEY LADY,

READ ABOUT YOU LAST NIGHT. CAN'T STOP THNKNG ABOUT YOU. WANDERING IF THERE KOULD BE SOMETHING SPECIAL ABOUT US, SPARKS TURNING TO FIRE. MSGE ME BACK. CAN'T WAIT.

Cassie returned her attention to the fireman, now holding up his ax in demonstration. "Told you."

Star pointed to the screen. "What about that one? He likes cats too."

"Yes," Bree began in an instructive voice, "but let us all remember there is a line between having a cat and wearing a cat on your head in your profile picture. Not a big line." Bree threw Cassie a hard look. "But still, a line. And the goal here is to keep our girl from wandering entirely over to the other side."

Five more minutes with no leads, and the girls began to sink back in their chairs.

"You can say it: there's no hope." Cassie took a sip of her lukewarm coffee. Across the street, the fireman was now lifting a toddler into the driver's side of the fire truck, the child looking as though he was on the best rollercoaster of his life.

At least she'd have Bree to depend on the rest of her life. Bree, the free-spirited tropical fish without a care in the world. Bree never worried when she didn't have a boyfriend. In fact, whenever she did have one, she tended to forget him.

Cassie flicked a new cobweb off the windowsill.

"What is this?" Bree pointed to the line halfway down her profile. "What do you mean you *don't* want kids?"

Ah. Bree had found it.

Star unscrewed the cap of the large jar of pretzels on Cassie's desk and dug a hand in. "You don't like kids? Miss C, hate to break it to you, but you got the wrong job."

"No, of course I want kids. I just can't have them. Physically, I mean." Cassie smiled, her tone upbeat though she kept her eyes on the world outside. "A few years ago, I was in an accident. As it turns out, sometimes you make things worse when you try to fix them."

She trained her eyes on the firefighter settling another kid into the driver's seat, trying hard not to think about the scar tissue presently sitting like a bowling ball in her uterus or the lines across her stomach from the surgeries she'd endured in attempts to repair it.

A loud honk erupted from the fire truck, and the fireman laughed while pulling the toddler's hand away from an overhead cord. Cassie allowed herself a whisper of a smile.

"By that she means she should've sued the socks off the doctor. Then she could've bought herself a husband and we wouldn't be having this conversation." Bree paused, giving the memory the moment of silence it deserved. After all, she, too, had been there amid everything Cassie lost those years ago. She'd watched Cassie learn the hard way that not all scars were physical.

Suddenly, Bree stood and dropped her hold on the mouse and,

along with it, the moment. She waved an accusing hand at the computer. "Well, that's your problem, Cass. You're attracting jerks because you put yourself in the jerk category. All the nice guys are on the other side. You need to get out of the 'I love traveling, gourmet food, and myself' world and move into the 'Athletic man seeking companion to whisper sweet nothings to as he coaches beloved children's little league.' Now, of course you know *I* don't want to be tied down to little life suckers, baking pies in floral aprons, but *you*, now . . ."

Several of the girls shot her a dirty look. Bree pressed her hand to her chest and amended herself. "*Unless* they came out fourteen and potty-trained, of course. But babe, aprons and kids are *all* you. All you have to do is change your preference in your bio."

"Were it that simple, I would jump on the opportunity. But I had to check one way or the other: do or don't want children. And I have no intention of leading someone into the wrong impression on a first date. Wanting kids is a big deal. Monumental."

"And you *do* want kids."

"And 'by adoption' wasn't one of the options, was it?" Cassie shot Bree a meaningful look, the kind that warned her friend she was putting her hand too close to the fire. The kind that said, *"Yes, but from personal experience, you and I both know that I know exactly what it feels like to be dropped—brutally—right when the man you thought was your soul mate finds out you can't have biological kids. I won't dare go that route again."*

"You know who I need?" Cassie turned her head again and this time pointed to the window. The firefighter was now lifting what must've been the fifteenth toddler into the driver's seat. "That guy. Right there."

They all watched him put a helmet on the little girl. The girl giggled as the protective gear wobbled on her petite head.

"*That* kind of guy wouldn't be caught dead on a dating site. That guy, I just know, is making someone the luckiest girl in the world."

ABOUT THE AUTHOR

Taylor Meo Photography

Melissa Ferguson lives in Bristol, Tennessee, where she enjoys chasing her children and writing romantic comedies full of humor and heart. Her favorite hobby is taking friends and acquaintances and turning them into characters in her books without their knowledge. She is confident you should read all her novels, starting with this one. Connect with her (and prepare for the possibility of becoming her next character) at:

Instagram: @melissafergusonwrites
TikTok: @melissafergusonlife
Website: www.melissaferguson.com
Facebook: @MelissaLeighFerguson